No Good Mitchell

by
RILEY HART & DEVON McCORMACK

Cover Design by Black Jazz Designs
Cover Photo by Wander Aguiar
Beta read by Leslie Copeland
Edited by Keren Reed Editing
Proofread by Judy's Proofreading and Lyrical Lines

CHAPTER ONE

Cohen

"MOTHERFUCKING GEORGIA. SMALL-ASS, rural towns," I grumbled, looking around and trying to figure out where in the hell we were. It was dark outside, pitch fucking black. I saw closed buildings, quiet roads, the shadows of trees, and not much else. No people, no signs pointing me in the right direction.

"Simmer down," said my best friend, roommate, and current pain in my ass, Isaac, from the passenger seat. I was likely a pain in his as well because I was grumpy and ready to get where I was going.

"We don't even have cell-phone service. How in the hell is there a town in the United States that doesn't have a cell-phone signal?" We'd made it to Buckridge, that much I knew because we'd seen a

1

Welcome to Buckridge! Population: 5! sign when we'd pulled into town—if you could call it a town, and obviously, it had more than five people in it, but that's what it felt like.

I didn't even want to get started on the name. There were a whole lot of jokes I could make about that, but I bit my tongue. I was *tired*.

Not to mention, clearly lost. I had no idea how to get to Mitchell Creek Distillery, which was on the Mitchell Creek property, which was suddenly mine. A parting gift from the dear ole dad I knew nothing about other than he'd had zilch to do with me my whole life. Small snippets of stories Mom had told me about him teased my subconscious—about her loving him, Dad loving me, and him doing the right thing— whatever that might have been—but I was only five when I lost her, the memories so old, I didn't know if they were even true. I probably made them up because as a kid, I'd needed them to be true. But what it came down to was, he hadn't been around, and he hadn't come for me when she died.

Isaac pulled me from my thoughts, saying, "I'm sure the town has cell service, we just don't, but we'll get it, and then our GPS will work. If not, we just ask someone where Mitchell Creek is. It can't be that hard to find—and hey, did you know there are *two* popular distilleries in this town? Or rather, they were both really popular, but then yours closed down two years before your dad died. Isn't that kinda weird?"

No, no, I hadn't known that, and at the moment, I didn't much care. I knew I was being a dick, but I was on edge. It wasn't every day you woke up in the premise of a rom-com—the whole small-town-legacy thing you didn't know about. Not that there would be pretty gay boys for me to fall in love with, or that I'd be interested. That was how those stories always went, but yeah, I was fairly certain the gay population would consist of me and Isaac. Plus, I didn't even know how long we would stay.

"Who do you suppose we ask for directions?" Teasingly, I slowed to a stop and rolled my window down. "Excuse me? Mr. Bear? Can you tell me where the distillery I have no idea what to do with is?"

"*Oooh!* Is it a sexy bear?" Isaac joked. He knew I didn't mean the gay, human kind. "Wait. Are there real bears here?"

I turned to look at him. "I don't know. Aren't there bears in every rural town? Isn't that like a thing?"

Rural towns weren't something I was familiar with, but it sounded like bears would be a thing. Great. Now I was going to worry about being eaten by a bear.

"I'd rather gay, human bears," Isaac replied, and we both chuckled.

"Me and you both." I eased my foot onto the gas pedal of my Lexus.

We'd taken this road trip from San Francisco to Georgia after being contacted by my biological dad's— that felt weird to think—by *Harris Mitchell*'s lawyer and told I was now the owner of a closed-down distillery, a house, and land. It was all very cloak-and-dagger. I still didn't know what the fuck was going on or why it wasn't open. Losing money? Bad investments? I knew it had come as a shock to patrons when they'd closed. That much I read online. It had been very popular whiskey. All I knew was, suddenly it was mine, and it hadn't been all that hard to find me if he'd ever wanted to.

What the fuck was I doing there? I shouldn't have come. If my adoptive mom and Isaac hadn't talked me into it, I probably wouldn't have.

We drove down Main Street from beginning to end. Right as we were coming out on the other side of town, I heard the *thump* of music.

"Oooh! Civilization!" Isaac bounced playfully in his seat.

We kept going, and then off to the right was a…well, a fucking barn was what it looked like. They must have remodeled it and turned it into a bar or something.

A shit ton of cars were parked out front—probably everyone from town was there. Fucking *country* music blasted through the air. People hung around outside, and the large barn doors were open, showing a full house inside as well.

I pulled over and killed the engine.

"Think this is where we come to die?" Isaac asked. "That's how the movies go. We pull up somewhere, meet a psycho killer, only we don't know he's a psycho killer targeting us."

"Why us?" I played along.

"We're new faces. Towns like this don't like new people. I saw this true-crime story once where—"

"Oh my God. No. Don't. I don't want to hear small-town horror stories right now. Come on. Let's get directions and get out of here."

I climbed out of the car. I felt way too overdressed

even though I was only wearing a light-blue polo and a pair of dark jeans.

"We should have bought cowboy boots," Isaac said, and I rolled my eyes. "Let's get a drink first. We wanna fit in. This is going to be our new home, after all."

Maybe...I still wasn't sure what I planned on doing with the place. Why would I want some consolation prize from my dad, who obviously hadn't wanted me? I had a life in San Francisco, even if I was out of a job now because an asshole ex-friend had used Isaac and me to get his business running, then ditched us. I could always go back to work for my adoptive father's financial institute, but I wanted to avoid that. That's why Isaac and I were playing around with the idea of an investment firm, but that first job for my ex-friend hadn't worked out so well.

Isaac and I were both really good at what we did. I had a bachelor's in business, and Isaac had one in marketing, and it just clicked for us. We knew our shit and worked well together, so it made sense when Teddy—the aforementioned ex-friend—approached us to get his startup off the ground. Isaac and I helped him do that, had basically done the work ourselves.

Once he had what he needed from us, we'd been expendable.

So yeah, I had time on my hands, but eventually I'd want to get back to California. I'd given myself a month because, well, because I needed a break anyway, and that would give me time to figure out what in the hell to do with Mitchell Creek Distillery and the property.

"One drink," I agreed. I sure as fuck could use it.

"Hi, hi, hello," Isaac said to every person we passed. "Howdy," he added to the last guy before we walked inside.

Howdy? I was sure he'd never said that word in his life. The guy—who *was* a bear but likely a straight one—looked at Isaac like he was crazy. I couldn't blame him. "Excuse my friend. We're just getting him socialized."

"Fucker." Isaac chuckled.

Inside, the place was packed. There were two bars, one on each side of the barn, a dance floor, tables, chairs, and… "Are those haystacks?"

"Yes, those are indeed haystacks," Isaac replied. "We're not in San Francisco anymore."

We sure as fuck weren't.

We made our way to the bar, and Isaac threw out a few more *howdies* at people. It felt like every eye was on us. There was no question in my mind that we stood out in the crowd—or at least they didn't recognize us, so they knew we were newbies.

The woman behind the bar had rainbow-colored hair, which I figured had to be a coincidence. She gave us a big smile when we approached, having just finished making a drink for someone else.

"Howdy, ma'am," Isaac said. I was going to fucking kill him. Still, I bit down on the inside of my cheek so I didn't laugh.

"Hey…what are two city boys like you doing out here?"

See? I knew they could smell fresh meat.

"How do you know we're city boys?" Isaac asked her.

"I'm psychic."

"*Ooh!* Can you tell me my future? Am I going to meet a Georgian Bear—not the animal kind."

She laughed, obviously having gotten his joke, so maybe the rainbow hair wasn't a fluke.

"I'm not getting a reading off you," she told him, then turned to me. "You, on the other hand, I'm getting all sorts of stuff from."

I frowned. It was impossible to tell if she was serious or not. "No, thanks. I like to be surprised."

She crossed her arms. "You're no fun." She looked about thirty and had a kind smile. "I'm Lauren, by the way."

"Cohen Mitchell, and this is Isaac—"

"I knew it!" she cut me off. "The second you walked in, I wondered if you were the long-lost Mitchell boy! There were rumors that there was a Mitchell boy, but we never knew for sure until your daddy passed, God rest his soul, and Byron—that's your daddy's lawyer and best friend—said you'd be comin'. My mama used to know your mama, ya know? Though they didn't get along. Apparently your mama tricked Harris Mitchell into falling in love with her, got pregnant with his baby at eighteen, and hightailed it out of town with some of his money. I don't believe that, though; it's just one of the stories going around."

My brain was spinning. *One* of the stories? How many were there? And why in the fuck would someone tell me something like that about my mom?

I said, "Harris Mitchell was a bastard who—"

"We'll have two whiskeys!" Isaac cut me off. "Can we have some Mitchell Creek?"

I had no idea why he asked for that, considering he knew the distillery'd been closed, but knowing Isaac, he had a reason. I wouldn't be surprised if he was suddenly playing detective.

"We don't have any because the distillery is shut down. I assume that'll change now that y'all are here. Like I said, I don't believe the story about your mama. The Mitchells have their own history, like most in this town. I'm sure your mama's great. Plus, ya know, Harris Mitchell never got married again. I bet he still loved Pam, and...well, shit, that does make it sound like she ran off on him. Scratch that."

I hated this town already. Were these people crazy?

"How about I give you guys some O'Ralley Reserve Bourbon? Oh no, you probably don't want that, being rivals and all. Your families' history goes way back."

I opened my mouth to ask Lauren what rivalry and what history, but then snapped it closed. I wasn't sure I wanted the answer, and if I did get it, I didn't know if I wanted Lauren to be the one to give it to me. I shot Isaac a warning look not to ask, and turned back to her. "Can we just have a beer?"

"Sure thing. What do you want?"

"Surprise us."

Lauren filled two mugs with some kind of dark draft and handed them over. I went to pull my card out, but she waved it off. "My treat, it being your first night in town and all. Perfect night for it, really. It's the Annual Buckridge Queerfest."

Wait... "Queerfest?"

"In rural Georgia?" Isaac added.

"I thought city folks weren't supposed to be judgmental. Are you assuming we're not gay-friendly because we're a small town in the South?"

Well, we had been, but I wasn't going to tell her that. "No, no. It just came as a surprise, is all."

"Are y'all boyfriends? You look like boyfriends."

"No, we're not."

"Hey, are *you* assuming we're gay now? I mean, we're gay as fuck, but still," Isaac said. "Just because we have better style than anyone here doesn't mean we're queer. That's presumptuous of you."

"Good point," she replied, then added, "You don't seem as angry as him. Y'all have this good-cop-bad-cop vibe going."

My brain was spinning. I couldn't slow it down to get my footing. I didn't know how to take this all in.

Lauren turned to get someone else a beer, and I asked Isaac, "Is this place for real?"

"Unless we're having the same dream. I believe in that. I bet Lauren does too since she's psychic. I wonder what her sign is."

Isaac was into that shit, but I wasn't. He also had wannabe detective fantasies, so I was sure he'd be doing some investigating into the rivalry thing. I, on the other hand, was still trying to find out how we'd left Earth and landed on some planet where we were at a queer country hoedown, and where there were stories about my mom and family history I'd had no idea about but sure as shit planned to google if they had Internet out here.

Someone bumped into me, and I looked over to see…well, to be honest, one of the most gorgeous men I'd ever seen. He was probably in his late twenties, and he was tall, with brown hair, with strands of a dark red mixed in. His eyes reminded me of milk chocolate. Sparse freckles danced across his nose and cheekbones—oh, and nice broad shoulders and a small dimple beneath the right side of his mouth. It was clear he'd run into me by mistake. I took a second to appreciate the view, and if I was reading it right, he was doing the same. Maybe Buckridge wouldn't be so bad after all.

"Who are you meeting, Brody?" a woman said to Mr. Sex On Legs.

He pointed at me. "Him. He's my date." He gave me wide, pleading eyes. "I've been looking all over for you," he told me, pulling me toward him and covering my lips with his. I was still for a second, and then all my nerve endings started firing off, telling me it didn't matter if I knew who in the hell this was—a gorgeous man was kissing me.

I grabbed his waist and pulled him closer, slipping my tongue into his mouth and tasting beer. We both seemed to freeze for a moment, and then we were at it again. It wasn't the first time I'd kissed a stranger in a bar, but it was the first time that happened in Georgia. And he was...fuck, he was *good*. I nibbled his lip, and he gave me a hungry little moan, his hands tightening on my waist. I threaded my fingers through his hair because if he was going to kiss me like he wanted to fuck me, I sure as shit planned to do the same. My dick perked up. I was suddenly really liking Buckridge, but before I knew it, he—Brody, she'd called him—was pulling away.

We both gasped a little and stared at each other, the air snapping and popping between us.

"But he's a... You're not... He's a guy?" She frowned, shook her head, and left.

Brody seemed to snap out of it first, winked, eyed me up and down, and said in this husky, rugged voice, "Thanks, man. I owe you one," before walking away.

Lauren's eyes were wide and on us. Her mouth had dropped open.

"What?" I asked, and she shook her head. Oh, *now* she didn't want to gossip?

I'd had about enough of this place for one night. I pulled my wallet out and handed her my card to pay. She still refused the payment, so I took it back. "Can we get directions to the Mitchell Creek Distillery?"

She nodded, then laughed.

I had a feeling she was laughing at me.

CHAPTER TWO

Brody

GROANED, STEADILY returning to consciousness. My eyelids felt so heavy, I could barely lift them. If that wasn't bad enough, there was that fucking headache. "Ah," I moaned as I opened my eyes and—

Shit.

Everything was black as night.

"Holy fuck! Holy Jesus!"

"Brodes, my hat's on your face!" I heard from nearby.

Thank fuck, I thought, unconvinced I was in the clear until I managed to remember where my limbs were and got the hat off.

Light streamed in through the window at the back of the horse stable.

Yup. There I was, stark-ass-nekkid…and a little

damp, it seemed.

Walker lay a few yards away, by the stalls, near my mare, Elliecomb.

"Jesus Christ, Walker. Why the hell did you take off my clothes?"

"Take off your clothes? You were the one ripping them off, saying it was too damn hot outside. I had to pull you out of the pond and carry you here." He glanced around uneasily, as though deeply troubled by something. "Can you hear me breathing, Brody? My breathing…and my heart. They're so loud."

As I sat up, I could feel the hay sticking to my back and pricking my ass cheeks. I did my best to remember what I could of last night's outing.

"Okay, there was drinking at the barn…and then Karissa…and then more drinking…and Karissa…"

"Don't forget Karissa's prick new boyfriend she cheated on you with."

As if I needed the reminder.

"Then I vaguely recall Brett Parker handing us a brownie," I added.

"Okay, you got almost everything, minus the part where you made out with a guy."

I certainly hadn't forgotten that bit. That kiss

shocked the hell out of me, as much as it must've that guy.

"Fuck." I thought about all the feelings that returned when Karissa wanted to "talk"—and about fucking what? The summer she spent telling me she was taking extra shifts teaching horseback-riding while apparently doing all sorts of riding with her new man? I recalled doing what I could to get rid of her, finding the nearest guy, hoping he wouldn't deck me for the move, then pulling away and seeing the prettiest fucking face.

And those fucking lips.

I'd never kissed a guy before, and it took me completely by surprise that I didn't hate it...not even close.

"That was a disaster," Walker said. "My straight brother got more action at my first time going to the Barn to look for a guy."

I rolled my eyes. "I'm sure he would have preferred the pretty, gay O'Ralley."

"Who you calling pretty gay?"

"Pretty and gay, Walker."

"Gee, thanks." For the first time since I'd woken up, he looked at me. "Oh, rise and shine over there, Brody."

I quickly covered my cock with his hat.

"Reminds me," he continued, "that I'm prettier, gayer, *and* bigger."

"Shut the fuck up. It's plenty big."

"Still doesn't make what I said untrue." Walker winked, and I couldn't help laughing.

Fuck him if he wasn't right, not that any of the O'Ralley men had any problems in that department.

"My heart. It's beating so fucking loud," Walker said. "This is my punishment. This is what I deserve."

"No one's punishing you for being gay."

"No! For being selfish. I split that brownie and gave you half, but you said you wanted me to save yours. But I didn't save it. I ate it. I'm so sorry." He cringed like he was about to cry, which I would have enjoyed far more if I didn't feel like a goddamn raccoon was banging around in my skull.

The stable door opened. "Found ya!"

"I'm not decent!" I called out.

"I can see that," Mel said, running her fingers through the freshly dyed blonde bangs in her light-brown hair. "This is very familiar, by the way. Reminds me of high-school days."

"*Our* high-school days. You were in middle school

and too young to see these things."

"I was raised with the Internet. I'm that generation that's seen everything way too soon. Now, Lee and Dwain have been working all morning on breakfast, so get your asses up and over to the house, or I'll tell Big Daddy about the rumors you'll both be having to deal with at some point."

Rumors?

My thoughts went right to my tongue being down that guy's throat. I hadn't meant to make it that believable, but when a mouth felt that good…

What the fuck was I thinking? I didn't do men.

"Okay, heading out," Melissa went on. "Brody, these led me to you guys. I figured you might need them." She tossed my jeans and boxers from the night before onto the floor. "Also, your wallet's floating in the pond. You're welcome." She headed out, closing the door behind her.

Wet clothes were better than no clothes, so after sliding them on, I helped Walker to his feet and guided us back to the house. Dwain and Lee were on the back patio, setting the table for breakfast.

"How's your heart and breathing going?" I asked Walker, still feeling the powerful headache I could only hope would be soothed with some hydration and painkillers.

"Good. I can do this. I can't believe you made out with a guy last night…or that the naked man I got to wake up with was you. That was supposed to be my big gay night. What do you think Melissa meant by *rumors*? You think someone saw us out and told Big Daddy that I'm… I'm…"

"It's a little premature to jump to conclusions, especially as we get closer and closer to him being able to hear us. So unless you want to sing your way out of the closet, you should go ahead and work on not talking right now, okay?"

With the local paper in his lap, Big Daddy gave us a friendly wave, and we settled into the chairs opposite him. "We were over at the stables," I said, "working on—"

"I don't need a lie," Big Daddy said. "You weren't helping those horses any more than your sister babysat skunks in college."

Mel chuckled as Dwain and Lee approached and set the coffee and creamer on the table, then took their places opposite each other.

Six chairs taken, leaving one empty.

One for Big Daddy.

Another for Walker, the eldest.

Then one for me.

Then Dwain and Lee—my other two brothers—or the O'Ralley runts, as they were known around town, even though both had outgrown Walker and myself.

And another for Mel, the baby.

But that one lonely chair would always remind us of who was missing—no, who was *taken*—from our family.

After taking a silent moment to remember a bright smile and delighted laugh, I noticed Dwain narrow his eyes, his jaw tightening as he looked at me. It was the way he'd get sometimes when we were kids and he wanted a fight.

"So word has it you both had a good night at the ho-mo-sexual event at the Barn last night," Big Daddy said.

Mel bit her bottom lip, clearly trying to keep herself from correcting him about not needing to use the word *homosexual* or drag it out so goddamn long.

Walker eyed me uneasily.

"Yes, we had a really good time," I said.

Big Daddy nodded. "That's good. I'm glad that in

these hard times, when orders have been down and distributors have been on edge, when we've had the worst quarter in five years, you two were able to get out and cut loose a bit."

I knew Big Daddy well enough to know this was going somewhere, though I couldn't imagine where the fuck that could be.

"Brody, are you proud of being an O'Ralley? Do you respect the blood, the sweat, the tears…our ancestors' crimes during prohibition…all that went into building this business and keep it running for nearly a century?"

"I'm very confused about where this is going, Big Daddy. Did we suddenly turn into the mob?"

"Can you shut your smart mouth for five seconds?" Dwain asked, still eyeing me like he was about to knife me.

"Dwain, you keep looking at me like that, and I'm liable to—"

"Liable to what? Kiss me?" The way he said it left no doubt about what he meant.

Or what he knew.

"What are you on about, Dwain?"

"You were at the Barn last night, and I know what

you were doing there."

"How the hell do you know anything about what was happening at the Barn?"

"Because Karissa messaged Lynda, and Lynda messaged Brian, who FaceTimed Bentley before telling Angela, who I was with—"

"And what were you doing with Angela?"

His face turned bright red, his fists tightening on either side of the table. "This is not about me."

Big Daddy closed his paper, a declaration of war in our family.

"Are you about to disown me because I made out with some guy at a bar?"

"The hell kind of father do you think I am? I don't care if you're a ho-mo-sexual any more than I care that Melissa's a pan."

Mel cringed again.

"Dad, I'm not gay," I told him, feeling a little less confident about those words since that kiss.

Big Daddy pushed to his feet. "Do you have any idea who that guy you made out with was?"

"I barely remember his face," I lied, since I could remember plenty about it for having only seen it a moment. Didn't come across a face like that often.

"That face was the face of Cohen Mitchell," Big Daddy said. "Let that sink in."

As soon as I heard the last name, I knew what this conversation had been about.

"Oooohhhh…"

"Fuck," Walker muttered beside me as I became even more acutely aware of the throbbing headache tormenting me.

"So you can imagine how your father feels about his son parading around with the family's sworn enemies since prohibition…and since no one from the law is around, safe to say, before prohibition."

The family feud.

The goddamn Mitchells versus the O'Ralleys. How in the hell could I have known that the random guy I found to lock lips with was, unwittingly, part of the convoluted feud I'd heard about all my life, right up until the Mitchells' distillery closed down two years prior.

"Big Daddy, I didn't even realize there were still any Mitchells left. I thought it was a rumor."

He paused a moment, reflecting on my comment. "So this wasn't some grand statement you were trying to make to shame our family name?"

"Not at all. I ran into Karissa last night, and she wanted to talk. I grabbed someone, a total stranger, and kissed him, hoping to shake her. It worked. That was the end of it, short of kissing a Mitchell, who looked so out of place, I doubt he's even planning on being in this town very long. That's the entire story."

"You didn't find him on social media?" Dwain asked. "Bring him out here to cause trouble?"

"Dwain, that's nearly as dumb as the rest of this conversation. I do not know this guy. I had nothing to do with why he's here. And I doubt I'll ever see him around here again."

Big Daddy seemed to be soaking in everything I'd said.

As much as I wanted to soothe him, I really didn't see a fucking reason why it would have been any of their business if I did want to parade around town with a Mitchell. This was not a hundred years ago, and I had no beef with some guy I'd never met before.

"I believe you, Brody," Big Daddy said, which earned a scoff from Dwain. "I have to admit, with business going the way it has been, knowing a Mitchell's in town feels like a bad omen. That family never did nothing to help us stay in business, would have reveled in our defeat, and part of me feels like this guy might have come at the right time for that."

What had begun as such anger with me for what Big Daddy had believed was a stunt was followed by a familiar sorrow I'd seen in him as we had greater and greater issues keeping the distillery open. I saw the hardworking father I'd come to know all these years, the man trying to keep the business going and provide for his family.

"I'm sorry for raising my voice," Big Daddy said, sitting back down and retrieving his paper, but Dwain's expression seemed less forgiving. "I'd like to think you wouldn't do anything intentionally to shame this family and our history...our legacy. I know it doesn't mean as much to you kids, but history and our name is all we have to hold on to. Without our past, what do we have? What can we hold on to?"

I knew he meant Big Momma.

And I also saw, plain as day, that the whole fucked-up situation was a perfect example of the dysfunctional mess we'd become since her death. In some ways, it had brought us closer together, but even though we would have killed without question for each other, there was something else that lingered—a certain distance that kept us so very far apart.

"So let this be a reminder," Big Daddy went on. "You sit at this table, you stand against all Mitchells. There is no middle ground on this. So long as this Mitchell is in this town, we, as all O'Ralleys have done since 1931—well, 1935, if the law asks—stand against him and his wicked blood."

"Amen, Big Daddy," Dwain and Lee said together.

Walker and Mel didn't respond, but it didn't seem that their responses mattered as much as mine, because Big Daddy's eyes were right on me.

"Fine," I muttered.

Big Daddy would see how ridiculous this all was once Cohen finished appraising the place or taking out whatever he needed to take back to wherever he was from.

But it was going to be a real shame not to get to taste his mouth again.

CHAPTER THREE

Cohen

'D BEEN UP most of the damn night.

Isaac was sleeping in one of the bedrooms, while I sat awake with my laptop—and fucking Internet, thank you very much. Byron Palms, Harris Mitchell's lawyer, had assured me he'd kept utilities on and had housekeeping in once a week, keeping things clean since Harris's death.

The only room that hadn't been touched was the office, which only Byron and I had a key to, and it was where I'd spent the night doing two things: going through Harris's files and business information on Mitchell Creek Distillery, and researching the fuck out of the Mitchells and the O'Ralleys.

"Did you sleep at all?" I looked up to see Isaac standing in the doorway, wearing a pair of red boxer trunks. He yawned and scratched his head, his blond hair sticking up all over the place.

"Dozed for a little while, but not much. None of this makes any sense."

Isaac padded over and plopped down on the brown leather sofa I'd wiped off last night. "Hit me. I've always wanted to solve a mystery."

I rolled my eyes playfully. "Simmer down, Shaggy."

"Does that make you my Scooby?"

"And fuck off," I teased back. "Seriously, though. I didn't get a lot of information when Byron originally contacted me. We met up. He showed me paperwork leaving me the distillery and land. That shit's in the car. I'll pull it out today. I didn't go through it with a fine-tooth comb, to be honest."

Isaac nodded. "Go on."

"The thing is, according to these files, Mitchell Creek was doing very well. He has everything on paper, literally. There's no computer that I can find. I'll contact Byron about that today. So Harris has balances and numbers for the few years before he closed, and he was in the black. I see his estate also gave the employees who lost their jobs when he closed a good severance package. I guess I don't understand why he closed. Or why he didn't sell. Did he simply not want to be in the whiskey business anymore? Where the hell is the money—not that I want it. And where are the files that go further back than the years before he closed?"

"I bet there's a journal. There's always a journal. Did you look for false bottoms in the drawers?" Isaac winked, and I chuckled.

"We'll be sure to search the house, Shaggy."

"This is exciting!" Isaac rubbed his hands together.

"Probably not. I'm sure Byron will sort it all out. He wanted to meet again when we got into town anyway." I couldn't get over how well the distillery had been doing. I was a numbers guy. Business was my thing, whether I was working with my father or helping someone else with their company. I didn't mean to pat myself on the back, but I was good. I'd saved businesses before. Mitchell Creek hadn't needed saving, though. Harris had just closed the doors, paid his employees very well, and from what I could tell, spent his last two years living a simple life at Mitchell Creek.

And still not looking for me. I shoved that from the

forefront of my thoughts, telling myself I didn't care. I had an adoptive mom and dad who'd chosen me. Yeah, it was a little awkward at times. They came from money on both sides, and then my dad made even more of it himself. The only thing we ever bonded over was business. He taught me more than college did, but I also knew he didn't really love me. Not the way a father is supposed to love a son. He liked me, but I didn't think he saw me as his kid, and I knew he only adopted me because Mom had wanted a child.

And I knew Mom loved me. She tried her best, but it was still always…distant. She wasn't real affectionate, and she'd been as busy while I was growing up as Dad had been. It wasn't the type of family most people had, I didn't figure, but then I always felt like shit thinking that way. They had taken me in, given me a home. I'd never lacked for anything.

"What about the Hatfield-and-McCoy thing?" Isaac asked, pulling me from my thoughts. "I can't believe you have a real family feud and you didn't even know. I'm so jelly. I want a secret past and a family feud," he said, making me laugh again.

"You're such an idiot."

"Which is why we're friends. Are you the Hatfields

31

or the McCoys?"

I sighed. That was something else I couldn't piece together, and it was making me crazy. I had no idea why there was a feud, or if Lauren had been exaggerating. "I've seen stuff online about it. They were in competition, obviously—both distilleries specialized in whiskey and opened up around the end of prohibition."

"The start date is probably a lie. I'm sure back in the day they were doing illegal shit."

"Probably," I agreed. "I found some articles about public disagreements, numerous think pieces on the feud, ten different reasons for how it started, but I don't know which are true, if any. I don't know if it was just a business thing or what. Some are sensationalized—love stories and all that shit. I plan on asking Byron." At thirty-three years old, I was suddenly feeling adrift, wishing I could ask my biological mom all these questions swirling in my head. Why hadn't she ever told me anything about Mitchell Creek? Why wasn't Harris on my birth certificate, and why hadn't he come for me?

I added, "The only thing that's incredibly clear is that whatever the reason, the Mitchells definitely hated the O'Ralleys, and each generation has for almost a hundred years."

"I think this might be the coolest thing that's ever happened to us."

I cocked a brow at him. "Us, huh?"

"Yes. I'm your best friend, your almost-brother, whom you dragged across the country with you. I'd say we're a team." He was right, of course. Isaac and I were always a team, a package deal. I was the only family Isaac had, and I loved him like he was blood. "And I hate to break this up, but I'm about to go all gayzilla on your ass if we don't get some coffee, STAT."

"There is none." I'd almost lost my shit when I realized that. Since Byron kept everything on, I'd assumed there would be food, or at least coffee.

"Blasphemy!" Isaac shoved to his feet. "I'll get dressed. We'll hit up Starbucks and then find breakfast."

"I doubt there's a Starbucks."

His blue eyes widened. "What in the hell is wrong with this town?"

"See? That's what I tried to say last night." Though I was starting to feel like I was more determined to stick around than I originally planned. I was really curious about the whole past with the distilleries and the feud. Plus, learning to run a distillery could be a cool project and—No. What in the hell was I thinking, opening a business in Buckridge?

"You're doing that thing where you have entire conversations with yourself in your head. Yes, you're going to decide you want to open this place back up to prove something to yourself and probably your bio-dad. If we're being honest, I'll probably help you. It's not like I have anything in San Francisco that matters if you're not there. Now can we go get coffee?"

Sometimes it sucked how well Isaac knew me. "Fuck off. That's not what I'd been thinking." Even though it obviously was. "And I don't need to prove anything to him. Plus, I can't. He's dead. Even if he wasn't, I wouldn't want to prove anything to him."

"Great. Sounds good. Keep lying to yourself. Coffee." With that, Isaac walked out of the room and back upstairs. I really hated my best friend.

I followed him up and went to the other spare room, where I'd left my bag last night. I wasn't sleeping in the master. That felt...weird, sleeping in the room of my father who'd wanted nothing to do with me until he died.

I grabbed my shit and made sure to take a really long shower, rubbing one out while I was there, because just like Isaac knew how to annoy the shit out of me, I knew how to annoy the shit out of him.

I pulled on a pair of nice jeans, a button-up, short-sleeved shirt, brushed my teeth, ran my hand through my hair a few times, and I was ready to go.

I didn't see Isaac as I went through the downstairs. It was an older house—dark wood, hardwood floors, lots and lots of brown. There was even a fucking deer head on the wall in the living room, which would sure as shit have to go.

I would definitely need to give this place some color, well, if I was staying, which I wasn't.

I looked out the window to see Isaac leaning against the car. He had his Aviators on, arms crossed, and wore a polo with beige shorts. Because we didn't stand out—at all.

He tapped his foot when I went out. "You suck. I'm hungry, and I need caffeine. You took forever on purpose."

"Then I guess you better be nice to me now, huh?"

He flipped me off. "How many acres is this place again?" he asked as we climbed into the car.

"Twenty-five or some shit. It's crazy. Who needs that much land?"

Though it really was gorgeous. The house sat back at the end of a long, tree-lined driveway. Once you got to the house, it was like everything opened up and you weren't boxed in with trees anymore, just wide-open space, lots of green and rolling hills. If you followed the drive past the house, the distillery was out that way, though I wasn't sure how far as I hadn't been out there yet. It had been too late last night.

Isaac said, "Let's find somewhere really greasy for breakfast. Like those diners in the movies with small towns. We'll get a waitress named Bea, and she'll wear a little hat and a matching apron. The coffee will be shit, but the grease will be *awesome*."

I didn't know anyone who could eat as much as Isaac and never gain a pound, the fucker. "You sure have a whole lot of stereotypes in your head."

"Like you don't?" he countered.

Okay, maybe I did.

I put the directions for Main Street into my phone. Both of ours suddenly had a signal on the drive back to Mitchell Creek last night. I was beginning to think there was something plotting against me or something that had made me end up at the weird queer hoedown.

Not that I was complaining after that kiss, but everything else had been fucked up.

We found a little diner that was exactly what Isaac was looking for. It was an odd shade of pink and white. What even was that?

There was a bell on the door, and the second we walked in, I was pretty sure time froze. Everyone stopped moving and talking. This one dude legit had his fork halfway to his mouth as he looked at us, and a piece of silverware from someone else clanked to their plate. It smelled like grease and country, but there were no hats on the waitresses. The apron thing was happening. "Should we make a run for it?" I whispered.

"Hell no, this is *awesome*. Just don't let me get beat up." He took a step, then another. "Howdy, y'all."

Jesus fucking Christ, if he didn't stop with the howdies, I was going to kill him.

An older woman approached, wearing pink and white like the building; her nametag read Kay instead of Bea. "Isaac and Cohen Mitchell, I assume."

Um...what the fuck? Were we in the *Twilight Zone*?

Isaac took a step back. "I think maybe running was the correct option."

"Oh, hush. Lauren told me about y'all. Even if she hadn't, it's all over Buckridge already. 'Specially that part about a Mitchell kissing an O'Ralley. I bet Big Daddy killed Brody when he found out."

Huh? "Big who?" The hot guy with the great mouth had a father people called Big Daddy? And he was an O'Ralley?

"You'll see." Kay winked. "Follow me."

Everyone stared at us while Kay led us to a table. We sat, and she put menus in front of us as Isaac slipped his Aviators on top of his head. "What's good here?"

She ignored his question. "Ya know, y'all are gonna keep standin' out if you dress like that. Not that you wouldn't anyway." She turned to me. "'Specially you being a Mitchell and all. Half of us thought there were no Mitchells left. I mean, we all knew about your mama and her secret-not-so-secret relationship with Harris, but when she up and disappeared, rumors went around that maybe your granddaddy had her offed, so we never knew for sure. Not that he was that kinda person, of course." She winked. Fucking winked again. Did that mean he *was* that kind of guy?

I opened my mouth, but nothing came out. She

was the second person I met who had a different story about my mom and my dad—this one including the possible murder of my mom by my grandparent, apparently; I wondered if he'd been involved in something illegal, given her wink. "Is there something wrong with you—"

"Coffee!" Isaac said loudly, cutting me off. "We need coffee, STAT! Or ASAP, like right now. Please and thank you, Kay. That's a lovely name, by the way. You remind me of my aunt Bea."

Aunt Bea, my ass. He sure as shit didn't have an aunt Bea.

"I'll be back in a jiff with your coffee," Kay said before walking away.

"Enjoy your breakfast," I told Isaac, "because after this, we're going to the grocery store to get food. I never plan on leaving the house again."

"How will that work when you reopen your distillery and live here forever?" Isaac offered.

I opened my mouth to say I wasn't, when I noticed the guy behind him looking at us and listening. Nope. I wasn't giving them any more gossip. Let them all wonder what I was doing here—not that I had any idea myself.

CHAPTER FOUR

Brody

BEHIND THE STEERING wheel of his truck, Dwain jammed out to some pop song, his shoulder bumping into mine as I sat in the middle seat, wedged between him and Walker. There was something delightfully amusing about seeing my Goliath-brother singing along with whatever female pop artist he had blasting through the speakers. But despite how entertaining it would have normally been, I was still suffering from a splitting headache and had to turn the volume down.

"The fuck, Brodes?" His demeanor shifted from excitement about the song to rage in an instant. He snarled, "This is my favorite Hailee Steinfeld song."

As he turned the volume back up, he glared at me the way he had at breakfast, which I was still pissed at him about. He didn't need to get Big Daddy all worked up over that stupid kiss, which admittedly wasn't stupid at all…and I was thinking way too much about it, considering it should have been wiped out with the rest of my memory of the night before. I reminded myself that the event had surely been exaggerated in my head because of the alcohol. No way was this Cohen Mitchell as attractive as I was now imagining.

I was being ridiculous about the whole night, just like Dwain had been ridiculous to make such a fucking big deal over nothing. Although, despite being annoyed with him, neither Walker nor myself had been in any position to operate heavy machinery, so we'd asked him to give us a ride for our weekly Feed & Seed trip and now were on our way to the grocery store for painkillers and Pedialyte to soothe Walker's and my pain.

When we arrived at Murray's, Dwain parked in the front lot and waited in the car while Walker and I ran in to pick up supplies.

"How ya feelin', buddy?" I asked Walker as he inspected the Advil ingredients to ensure we got the highest strength, something we both desperately needed.

"Not as bad as a few hours ago. Still, must feel better than getting reamed by Big Daddy. Who knew you went and made out with the family archnemesis?"

I sighed. "Right?"

"Speaking of which, do we need to talk about anything...with that kiss...? I mean, you were here for me, so if you do have any feelings for guys, I hope you know I have your back no matter what."

"Okay, I don't not have feelings about *that kiss*. I know that much, but let's say I'm sorting it out, just apparently not—under any circumstances—with the Mitchell guy. But thank you for that, man."

"Anytime, bro. I'll be here when you need me."

I loved all my siblings, but I'd always been closest to Walker. We'd had each other's backs since we were kids. And it was nice that despite everything our family had been through, that hadn't changed.

Walker's gaze wandered, and then he cringed. "Oh fuck."

"What? Are you okay? Is it the heartbeat? The breathing?"

"No, just...speaking of that Mitchell guy... Two o'clock."

I glanced at his two. Mitchell and his friend were chatting up Murray's daughter in a nearby aisle, her gaze on Walker and me like she was waiting for us to notice our official town outsiders.

Fuck.

"Ugh," Cohen's friend said, sounding exasperated. "And you don't know where else carries unsweetened vanilla almond milk?"

"Um…no. We have soy," she replied, looking back to Walker and me.

It'd been hard to tell the shade of Cohen's hair in the lighting the night before—waves of a medium brown that hung over the left side of his forehead.

Oh, where did that *come from?*

I didn't have time to give myself much hell for what was clearly my mind playing tricks on me because of the hot kiss, since his friend noticed Murray's daughter eyeing us and nudged Cohen. I looked away quickly, pretending to be too absorbed in inspecting Walker's work to spot them.

I wasn't even sure why I was making a big deal of it. I didn't give a shit about a nearly hundred-year-old feud, but at least in part, I wasn't eager to be caught by the guy I'd used as my escape plan when Karissa had confronted me at the Barn.

As they continued discussing almond-milk alternatives, I whispered to Walker, "We're gonna pretend not to see them. Just get the fuck out of here and not cause a scene, okay?"

"You don't have to tell me twice."

Easier said than done, since we couldn't exactly evade them for very long in our small local store, and as luck would have it, as soon as Walker and I approached the cash register, Cohen and his friend were right behind us in line with a full basket.

Murray stood behind the register, glancing between us nervously, like he was expecting Walker and me to start swinging punches.

"Morning, Murray," I forced out. "How are you doing today?"

"Doin' all right. You?"

I did my best to make small talk with him, but I couldn't fight my desire to get a good look at Cohen once again, if only to prove to myself I'd greatly exaggerated his appearance in my mind. Before I knew it, my eyes were set on bright-green irises, which sparkled under the lights Walker found so bothersome at the moment. Cohen wore an uncertain expression before a friendly smile tugged at his lips, shifting his high, cut cheekbones ever so slightly. There was a light dusting of stubble along his jaw.

That face looked even better in broad daylight.

He looked in his early thirties, and his lean physique managed to nicely fill out the polo he wore, biceps and triceps pushing at the sleeves. They weren't the kind of muscles a guy got by working the land, but sculpted like he put in some time at the gym. Well worth it, as far as I could tell.

It was no surprise that I hadn't thought twice about kissing him, because if I was going to kiss a man, it should be one as hot as Cohen.

Hate 'em or not, there was something to these Mitchell genes, which was probably why I couldn't help but return that beautiful smile.

"You guys sure are tall," his friend piped up, extending a hand to me. "I'm Isaac."

I barreled right through my not-so-brilliant plan and said, "Hi. Brody. This is my brother—"

"Walker," he jumped in with.

"This is a sight," Murray said. "Didn't imagine I'd be present for the first run-in between the Mitchell boy and the O'Ralleys."

"It's not our first run-in," I noted, and that made Cohen's smile broaden, and damn, why did that excite me?

"Well, I guess if we're sworn enemies or whatever, we should at least be formally introduced," Cohen said. "I'm—"

"Cohen Mitchell. Yeah."

I felt the need to explain last night, but this definitely wasn't the moment, and before either of us had a chance to say more, the bell on Murray's door chimed.

A knot twisted in my gut.

"Well, whatda we have here?" Dwain's voice practically echoed through the whole damn store as he approached the register.

"Oh my God. Do they have steroids on tap in this town?" Isaac said, his eyes widening with concern as Dwain started through the narrow aisle, which admittedly made him look much bigger than he already was.

I took a step toward the aisle opposite the register, blocking him from getting near Cohen and Isaac, if only to keep him from freaking them out.

"Dwain, get back in the truck and turn on some

crappy pop music. We're almost done."

"We're not done with anything here yet, Mitchell boy."

It felt insane to see my brother expressing this hostile attitude toward a total fucking stranger over some dumb family feud. This wasn't fucking 1935...or '31...or whenever the hell all this shit started up. Surely, a Mitchell who hadn't even spent his life in Buckridge wouldn't know enough about any goddamn feud, nor have to get roped into it just because of the tenuous connection to the Mitchells Big Daddy grew up around.

Dwain went on, "Walker, Brody, whatdaya think? Maybe we should take these city kids out into the woods, strip them down, hogtie them, and let them know what we do to rivals."

"I'm willing to adapt parts of this plan," Walker said, winking at Isaac, who gave him a strange look, clearly not detecting my brother's interest, since Walker was pretty much always that awkward about hitting on guys.

"Holy shit," Isaac whispered to Cohen. "They're gonna torture us like those inbred guys in *Wrong Turn*."

"Who the fuck are you calling inbred?" Dwain shouted.

"No, no. That's not what I meant," Isaac spit out. "I meant the torture part. They just happened to be inbred, and it was the first descriptor I thought of for the movie...and..."

"It's probably safest if you stop talking now," Cohen told him. "Also, you should probably work on your whispering skills."

Isaac pressed his lips together.

"My name's Cohen. Dwain, right?"

He extended his hand to my brother. Dwain eyed his hand, leaving him hanging, so I took it. "Nice to officially meet you, as we were saying before being so rudely interrupted."

I looked to Murray, surprised he hadn't already kicked us all out, when I noticed him holding his phone up.

"Are you recording this?" I asked, slightly mortified. "Just finish ringing us up."

He lowered his phone and told Walker the total, and I had to urge Walker to hurry up and pay, since he seemed rather absorbed in checking out Isaac.

"How long do you guys plan on being in town?" I

asked Cohen, eyeing his basket.

There was more than a few days' worth of stuff in there, which didn't leave me much hope that Big Daddy's fears would be easily soothed.

"Playing that by ear," Cohen replied. "Just grabbing enough stuff to get me through next week."

"Don't make small talk with the enemy," Dwain muttered.

"Dwain, get back to the truck. We're almost done."

"Oh, did you guys want some privacy so you could make out again?"

Cohen eyed me, his smirk expanding. "I mean, there are certainly worse things I could see myself spending my time doing."

Fuck, my cheeks were hot like fire.

What the hell? I. Do. Not. Blush.

No, that was not me at all.

But God, my face must've been red as a tomato under the store lights.

I figured Cohen might have just been trying to grate on Dwain's nerves, which had clearly worked by the way he was huffing and puffing beside me.

I decided it was best to ignore Cohen's comment

and deal with the issue at hand.

"Dwain," I said, giving him a look that apparently expressed enough of my rage and willingness to kick his fucking ass if he persisted. He backed down.

"Fine," he said through his teeth. "Five minutes."

He stormed out just as our receipt started printing. *Thank fuck.*

"Sorry about my brother. And about what happened last night."

But I wasn't sorry about that last thing, not even a little bit, especially now that I saw how wrong I'd been—he was *gorgeous.* If I were gay, the things I'd do to Cohen...

Wait. What the hell would I do to him exactly?

I'd only ever dated—hell, been in love with—women.

"I guess we'll see you around town," Cohen said.

"Yeah. We will," I told him, wondering what that meant about his stay.

Walker and I took our bags back to the truck, and as soon as I climbed in, I got an earful from Dwain. I let him rag on me about it, then said, "Just don't mention it to Big Daddy. There's no reason to get him worked up."

"Then don't keep fraternizing with the enemy," he barked.

"I'm just saying, Big Daddy has enough on his mind with the distillery right now. We don't need to get his thoughts caught up in a bunch of town gossip."

"Fine."

"His friend Isaac seemed nice," Walker said, and I turned to him, noticing again his interest—something Dwain was as oblivious to as Lee and Big Daddy.

"The one who called us *inbreds*?" Dwain asked.

"Dwain, Walker and I've always thought you looked a little too much like Aunt Mona...and you know how she loves to ply some moonshine in Big Daddy."

He scoffed, shaking his head. "Here. Lemme help your hangover," he said, amping the volume of his pop song.

As the talking subsided and Dwain took us farther and farther away from Murray's, I just couldn't get that Mitchell guy outta my head.

CHAPTER FIVE

Cohen

S ERIOUSLY, WHAT THE fuck was up with that family and their genes? They were all tall, muscular, glistening with this rugged glow, and hot. Well, at least Brody and Walker. Dwain was sexy too, but if I never saw him again, it would be too fucking soon.

After our run-in with the O'Ralleys, we came back to the house, put the groceries away, and I called my mom.

She was the main reason I'd been willing to come to Buckridge. We had a strange relationship—or so it seemed to me—where she encouraged my curiosity about my past, and coming here was part of that. All I knew was that my biological mom had been great, my world, and then she'd died in a car accident. I went into foster care until I was adopted. After that I'd always had such conflicting emotions: wanting to discover more about my mom's past warred with the guilt I felt about it, because my adoptive family had given me the world, in their own slightly reserved way. Then the mixed emotions about them keeping my last name Mitchell, and loving them but not always feeling like I fit, and getting lost in it all.

After the call, we'd headed straight back to the office. We'd been in here for hours, trying to make sense of everything, while I pretended the O'Ralleys didn't exist and Isaac continued to bring them up every few minutes. I'd also put a call in to Byron and was waiting to hear from him.

"What did Lydia have to say?" Isaac asked as we sat in the office, surrounded by paperwork.

"Nothing really, which I expected." I'd been hoping something might've been said to my mom over the years, buried in adoption paperwork or something, that could make sense of all this. "She's got nothing."

"You ask her about the feud?"

"No." There was really no point.

I looked at the paper in my hand. There had to be some shit missing. He gave totals, but there were no bank-account numbers. I still couldn't find any information except for the few years before he closed.

My thoughts went from that to the family feud, then settled on the tall, gorgeous, broad-shouldered man with those freckles that were cute as fuck. The guy I was supposed to hate without even knowing anything about him other than he could really fucking kiss. He seemed to be the most sane O'Ralley...and the sexiest, though Walker wasn't bad either. Maybe if I could get Brody alone, I could get some information out of him...

"Think I can fuck Walker?" Isaac asked, jerking me out of my thoughts.

"What the hell?" Though I shouldn't have been surprised.

"Um, because you wouldn't do the other one? I saw you. I know you. You want him. Don't lie to me."

"He's my sworn enemy!" I countered, and Isaac rolled his eyes. "This is some crazy-ass shit. I didn't think stuff like this was real. I'm still not convinced we're not part of some government experiment or something."

"Blah, blah, blah. Who cares? Do you think I can fuck Walker? I mean, obviously Brody swings our way a bit, since he shoved his tongue down your throat and couldn't keep his eyes off you, but I think Walker might too. It was hard to tell, but I wonder if he was trying to flirt with me, only he's really bad at it? I don't know. It was adorable in this rugged sort of way. Like he would work the land, then come in, all sweaty and demanding, throw me over the counter, and fuck me hard."

I couldn't help laughing, then immediately started thinking about tossing Brody over a counter somewhere and fucking him. I mean, it wasn't *my* feud. What did I care? "Sounds like you have this all figured out."

"I do. I have an active imagination. Want me to set you up with a Brody fantasy too? I think you guys will both battle for dominance. It's so fucking hot when that happens."

My head started throbbing—both of them, to be honest—but I concentrated on the one on my shoulders, and rubbed my temples. "This isn't what we're supposed to be here for. This shit is stressing me out." More than I would likely admit. As much as I didn't want to be involved in anything that had to do with a father who'd thrown me away, I wasn't sure I had it in me to walk away. I'd spent my life telling myself I didn't care about him, but now that I was here, it was screwing with my head.

Isaac sighed. "I know, baby." He reached over and squeezed my thigh in support. "I'd pretend I didn't know what's going on inside that head of yours, but we both know that would be a lie. Your dad, whatever his reasoning was for everything he did…that doesn't say anything bad about *you*. Maybe he had a reason for doing the things he did—not being involved in your life and all that. Maybe he didn't. Still, that's his shit, not yours. I love you. Go take a break. I'll be in charge of all this stuff. I'll organize the paperwork, and we'll start getting it transferred to electronic files and all."

There was a reason Isaac and I had been friends for so long. We teased each other relentlessly and drove each other crazy sometimes, but we knew each other better than anyone else did. We were always there for each other and shared the same work ethic, wanting to do something with our lives on our own. "Thank you." I lifted his hand and kissed it, then pushed to my feet. I grabbed the keys off the desk. "I'm gonna go check out the distillery."

"I'll be here, drowning in paperwork and thinking

about sleeping with your sworn enemy." He winked, and I chuckled and walked out.

It was hot as balls outside, the Southern humidity nearly choking me. Seriously, how in the fuck did anyone live here? I already felt like I needed another shower.

I'd just stepped off the porch when a pair of long jean-covered legs walked around the corner of the house. The sun was behind him, shining off his reddish-brown hair, and yeah, wasn't going to pretend I didn't want this guy.

"Oh, hey," he said when he noticed me. "I come in peace. And bearing gifts." Brody held up a jug of unsweetened vanilla almond milk. "You gotta go to A Step Ahead. It's on the opposite side of town as Murray's. Lauren's mama owns it, and she's into all that healthy, New Agey stuff."

"Almond milk is New Age?" I asked with a cocked brow, and he gave me this sexy little half smirk.

"To the folks in this town? Yeah. It's right up there with astrology and dream catchers. Just so ya know, it's probably already all over town that Cohen Mitchell went into Murray's lookin' for this stuff, and then Brody O'Ralley went to A Step Ahead to buy it. Big

Daddy'll know by dinner."

Which meant he would get shit for bringing it to me. I didn't think that was why Brody told me, but it was the truth.

"But I guess I owe ya since I kissed you and all—well, that and Dwain."

"Your brother could use some social skills, but you sure as shit don't owe me for the kiss." I hadn't planned to say it, but the words had sneaked out, and the pink now dotting his cheeks made it worth it. So I was flirting with my family's enemy.

"That was, um... I—"

"I'm not here, I swear!" Isaac cut Brody off. He jogged toward me, pulled the milk out of my hands, and took off for inside again.

"He's an interesting fella," Brody said, and it shouldn't have been so cute the way he said it. At all.

"You don't know the half of it," I replied, then nodded toward the back of the house. "Wanna head out to the distillery with me?" He'd brought milk over and all. It was the least I could do.

"A Mitchell inviting an O'Ralley into his inner sanctum. Be still my heart." He winked, and oh yeah, I definitely wanted to bone him.

"Don't really consider myself a Mitchell—not in that sense, I mean. Obviously, it's my last name, but I don't feel a tie to all this."

Brody frowned. "Yeah, I didn't really know for sure if there were any Mitchells left. There was a rumor Harris had a kid, but you never know what's true."

Which I sure as shit didn't want to talk about. "How'd you get here?" I asked instead.

"Parked down the driveway, of course. If your daddy were still around, stepping foot on Mitchell property was likely to get me a bullet in the ass. I was planning on leaving the milk on your porch."

"Jesus fucking Christ," I said as we continued to walk. "Are you shitting me? This whole feud thing is real?"

"Crazy, right? Try growin' up with it."

Nope. I had zero interest in that.

"Our properties butt up against each other, but there's a fence in between. Wasn't cheap, and it's not even like we can see each other's houses with all the land, but they had to have something to separate us. There's one on each side with about a foot in between just 'cuz the O'Ralleys and Mitchells couldn't share a fence."

I stumbled, and Brody's hand shot out and wrapped around my bicep. There was a zing of, fuck, I didn't know, *something* between us before he pulled his arm back. "This is some crazy shit. Hell, I didn't even know I had any part of Mitchell Creek, and now it's left to me, along with a family feud I know nothing about, and it's a little fucking nuts, if you ask me."

"Oh shit. You didn't know?" Brody asked.

I shook my head.

"So you planning on stayin'?"

"No comment."

We were in front of the distillery now, and he stopped and grinned. "I see how you're playing this. Trying to give me as little information as possible." Brody crossed his arms, and I didn't look at the way his T-shirt stretched across his broad chest and muscular arms...or maybe I did. "Don't worry. I promise I won't tell anyone over at the *Buckridge Bugle*."

"Please tell me you just made that up."

"No, but I really wish I had."

I couldn't help laughing, which based on his satisfied expression, made me think that was exactly what he'd hoped for.

"Okay, so what's the feud about?"

"No comment."

"Fucking O'Ralleys," I replied, half serious, half playful. I didn't know what it was about Brody, but I already liked him.

"Fucking Mitchells," he countered.

Then we stood there, watching each other, neither of us willing to back down, and damned if it wasn't kind of fun.

CHAPTER SIX

Brody

'D MET PLENTY of green-eyed folks in my life, but there was something different about Cohen's. They were strangely lighter in the center and darkened toward the edges. Although, just as soon as I thought I was obsessed with his eyes, there was that face...that sexy-as-sin stubble.

And his attitude.

Even the way he said *fucking O'Ralleys* was like his goal was to drive my already-twitching dick crazy.

Something about Cohen simultaneously grated on my nerves and made me want to revisit those lips— which I was thinking about way too much for a straight guy.

Keep your goddamn cool, Brodes, I told myself before saying, "So this is your inner sanctum?"

Jesus fucking Christ, why couldn't I stop saying *inner sanctum*? The whole inexperienced, bumbling shit was Walker's thing, not mine.

Cohen turned back to me, those green eyes catching my attention once again as he winced like he wasn't sure what to make of my comment either.

I glanced around his space. "Fuck, I'm already jealous."

"Jealous?"

"Yeah, some of your equipment is more up-to-date than ours. Can't persuade Big Daddy to update shit, so we keep fixing old stills and boilers. I call them ancient. He calls them classics. But I guess the best question I could start with is, what do you know about distilleries? I don't want to waste your time."

"I like a Jack and Coke…"

I started to laugh, but his serious expression didn't let up.

"Oh, damn. Okay. The official tour it is."

I could tell he was already overwhelmed, and I figured it didn't just have to do with the distillery.

"How about we start with the tasting room? Looks like it was locked up pretty tight, no broken windows, so hopefully no one's looted anything."

I led him through the main warehouse, to a door I assumed went to the tasting room.

Bingo.

Through two windows on the opposite side of the room, the afternoon light flooded into the space. Still decorated with a rustic look, deer antlers hanging on the wall behind the bar, alongside old family photos and various awards and certificates the Mitchells had received for their product.

I opened the hinged part of the bar that let me behind it as Cohen walked around to a nearby stool, where he sat down and made himself comfy.

"You're making yourself pretty at home here."

"Same setup as ours, looks like. Not surprising, considering our ancestors started in business together. If it ain't broke and all… Besides, you visit enough distilleries, you learn they're all basically set up the same."

I rifled through the cabinets and storage spaces.

"So…while you're making yourself at home in my inner sanctum, the other night…"

My cheeks caught fire at the mention. I was fucking glad I wasn't looking at him right then.

"Oh, that…"

I was relieved when I found a locked cabinet. An excellent excuse to change the subject.

I turned to him. "Hey, mind if I borrow those keys you grabbed to get us in here?"

He fetched the keys and handed them to me, and I opened the cabinet.

"Oh, that is fucking beautiful," I said, admiring the stash left behind.

As I sorted through the bottles, I decided I could be honest with Cohen about last night without describing how intensely hot the experience had been for me.

"So…there's this woman I've been seeing for the past two years, off and on…then off again…then on again. Then…well, you get the drift. I think I've been off and on my horse fewer times than we were—sorry. That sounds a bit too much like I do bad things with my horse."

"And here I assumed it was an awkward euphemism for barebacking," he teased with a wink.

"Any rate, Karissa's her name. And I was smitten, but evidently, every time I thought we were on again, she was off again…or getting off again…with a few other guys, one in particular…Jeffery-Dean. Without getting into it too much, she's seen me out a few times, and tried to make up one excuse or another for her bad behavior, and at that party—"

"I was your way out of an uncomfortable conversation."

The way he worded it made me really consider the consequences of my actions. I took a breath, stepping away from the cabinet and back to the bar. "I'd had a lot to drink, but I can't even pretend it was all that since I remember it all perfectly clear. There was a moment when I thought, not only would it get her off my tail for a night, but kissing a guy would really throw her enough to leave me the hell alone. And…yeah, well, there it is, Cohen. I'm really sorry if you feel like I was using you."

"That seems like the definition of using a person."

"Yeah, and I am very sorry. I know drinking is no excuse, or being in a bind. I should have asked you or…"

Damn, I was really hoping he'd interrupt me, but he just kept those goddamn beautiful green eyes fixed on me as though he needed more than that, so I did my best.

"I could have pulled you aside…and I don't know

a way out of this awkward conversation."

"Funny that you don't enjoy awkward, since I'm enjoying it so much right now," he said with an expanding grin.

Seemed like everything he said drove me crazy, and I couldn't tell if it turned me on or pissed me off, but it was exciting all the same.

"If it makes you feel any better," he said, "if I hadn't wanted it, you would have found out right away."

"Guess you're right. I remember one guy trying to drunk-kiss Megan Fehr, and she exercised her Second Amendment rights until he was racing across the river in his underpants."

He laughed. "Sounds like that taught him to try and kiss a stranger."

"Stranger? They were dating. They're getting married next June."

Cohen leaned back and laughed, putting his hand to his face in what might have been the most adorable way I'd ever seen.

"But you didn't resist it...me kissing you," I remarked, thinking back to his comment.

"No, I didn't."

"So you liked it?"

"I didn't say that. Did you like it?"

"I'm straight."

"That doesn't answer my question, does it? Or explain why some straight guy is running around kissing random men?"

He didn't seem to be letting me get out of this one easily. "I think I will definitely need a drink before we get into this."

"Stalling is what it sounds like," he noted.

"Can't it be both?"

He grinned as I returned to the cabinet, fishing through the bottles, looking for one in particular.

"I don't have a problem with gay guys, if that's what you think," I added.

"I've suspended my judgment until you say something wildly homophobic."

"My brother Walker's gay, and I love him to death. He's always liked guys. Been like that since he was eight years old. While I wanted to hold hands with Nancy Finnegan, he wanted to do that with Benji Moore. But while I got to hold hands with every Nancy in my life, he could only allow himself to daydream...had to keep it all in. Makes me sad and pisses me off at the same time."

"Why does it piss you off?"

"It isn't right. He shouldn't have felt like he had to keep that in...or from me. I know it wasn't about me personally, but of all my brothers, I'm closest with Walker, and it made me sad that he wasn't able to talk to me about that. Like I'd done something or said something that made him feel uncomfortable."

"It's a little more complicated than that."

"I imagine. Just... Oh, here we go!" I said as I discovered what I'd been looking for. I displayed the bottle to a less-than-impressed Mitchell.

"Am I supposed to know what it is?"

"This is your family namesake right here. Mitchell's Buckridge Deluxe Scotch."

I handed it to him, and he stared at it blankly as I fetched two shot glasses from a cabinet. I wiped them down with a rag and set them on the bar before Cohen.

"Those can't be clean," he said.

"I'm sure they're as clean as they were back when your pa was serving people in this place. Here, let's see what kind of a lightweight you are."

He handed it over, and I poured us shots. We each

took a glass and raised them. "To your heritage," I said, clinking my glass with his before we downed them.

"Damn," he said, clearly impressed with the taste. There was more Mitchell to him than he realized.

"God, I won't admit it's better, but it's at least as good as the O'Ralleys' Buckridge Deluxe Scotch."

"Wait. You guys have the same thing?"

"Ah, someone's finally wising up to the feud between our families. Gimme a sec…"

I greedily poured another round, enjoying the warmth against my throat as I downed the next shot. A little hair of the dog wasn't going to kill me.

I turned back to the photos hung on the wall and found one of Cohen's pa when he looked like he was in his twenties.

I couldn't help noting their similar appearances. His father was in a button-up and tie in the photo, but between the cheekbones and strong jaw, even the shade of brown hair, if someone had told me it was a photo of a younger Cohen, I would've had a hard time knowing any different. I pulled the picture down and handed it to Cohen.

"Let me set the stage. Early twenties. Prohibition.

Our great-grandparents were the best of buds and a bunch of deadbeats whose parents were waiting for them to get wives and kids. But not our great-granddads. No. They wanted to have a good time, enjoy life with their buddies…which involved a lot of parties, where they could get their hands on the much-coveted moonshine of that time. Now, being as charismatic and cool as my side of the family must have been—"

"I know a dig when I hear one," he joked.

"Okay, maybe as cool and charismatic as both our sides were, they wanted to be the ones throwing the parties. They started on our great-great-mamaw's property, because she thought it sounded like a great way for Randall to find a wife. So they got to making their own moonshine with their buddies, having these small parties. Well, first they were small, but apparently they knew how to make some liquor, and soon everyone was coming to these parties. They started to make a killing. Keep in mind this was illegal, so they could charge high prices for their time."

"Oh, I'm sure."

"And both of them dreaded the idea of having to do any labor that didn't end with them getting to throw a big party, so they kept it up. And getting bigger and bigger all the time. They basically turned into chemists as they became obsessed with expanding the products. They wanted people to come from across the Mason-Dixon line to get a taste of their alcohol. And they did. But they also managed to pick up some colorful clients along the way…"

"I feel like this is going somewhere shady real fast."

"Technically, it's been shady for a bit, but yeah. Now, there was a woman named Dorothy Mills, who owned the most popular house in town, if you get my meaning."

"She was a lady of the night…?" he deduced.

"I think she'd be offended that you called her a lady, but yes."

I clinked my glass to his and said, "To Dorothy. You'll see why in a moment."

He smiled, and I downed my shot and went on. "There were some brothels in town, but Dorothy ran her own house, worked alone and often. She arranged for Randall and Arthur—that's your great-grandpa—to bring their product in three times a week, compensated them with plenty, and they'd go on their way. Well, so each of them *thought*, but Randall got involved with Dorothy and was planning on marrying her. Kept it secret until he decided to propose. Then he told Arthur, who, it turned out, had a similar arrangement with her. And these guys, as you can imagine, had it out. Best of friends turned on one another and agreed to a duel for Dorothy's hand. We're talking pistols-at-dawn kind of duel."

"What?"

"Oh yeah. Now, the properties we're on, back in the day, they shared. Bought several miles from where their parents lived to start their own distillery as they were expanding. But both had houses a ways from one another, so they planned to have the duel at the creek in between. Invited all their buddies, had a few drinks, and then met up at dawn for the big duel—"

"I'm assuming they chickened out since later they both had kids."

"Nope. Great-granddaddy Randall got shot...right in the shoulder, fortunately for me today. But you can imagine it left a real sore spot on his shoulder...and heart."

"So my ancestor married the town prostitute?"

"You'd think, but Dorothy didn't much care for violence, so when she heard about the duel, she wouldn't have either of them."

Cohen burst into laughter. "You have got to be kidding me."

"Not at all. She was done with them as lovers, but she was very interested in continuing business as usual, so Arthur Mitchell decided to leave the shared business and start his own. However, their most popular product at the time was...the Mitchell-O'Ralley Buckridge Deluxe Scotch."

"Oh no."

"Oh yes. Also, Dorothy's clients' favorite, and she agreed, during their split, to buy from each of them, but neither could agree on who had come up with their secret recipe. Now no one knows. Great-granddaddy claimed they wrote it down and it was in his handwriting, but he could never show anyone the paper, so looks like we'll never know. But it's made for plenty of gossip through the generations. And also competition like no one's ever seen before."

"Scandalous," Cohen joked.

"And that's just the bits from the past. Apparently, Big Daddy was sweet on your mom when they were younger. And rumor has it that, in the meantime, she was busy being sweet on your dad."

"Are you serious?" Cohen asked, his mouth agape as he clearly heard the news for the first time.

"Yup. But don't ask me none of the details. Big Daddy don't talk about it, and all the reasons she ran off are so varied, you're probably the only one who has a chance of knowing what really happened that far back."

"Feels like I'm learning more every day," he said. "I know even less than you thought."

He seemed to be struggling to absorb everything I'd just shared, which I more than understood, so I offered a compliment in hopes of distracting him from the shitbag of history he'd just gotten a stiff taste of. "I like the way you pour a shot."

That green-eyed gaze looked right into me as he offered his killer smile once again, assuring me the distraction had worked to ease him up a bit.

"Must be some bad combination of you and liquor that does something to me," I confessed.

"Is it a *bad* combination?"

"Depends. How bad do you want to kiss me again?"

I was sure my eyes were about as wide as his. What was I fucking saying? I wasn't *that* drunk yet.

Cohen Mitchell just did something to me, though, sparked some sort of misfire of my genetic hatred toward his family.

"I wouldn't think a straight O'Ralley would be interested in kissing his Mitchell nemesis."

I leaned down, resting my elbows on the bar, looking him right in his beautiful mug. "Well, you got one confused O'Ralley thinking a little too much about those Mitchell lips."

Cohen eyed my mouth, then assessed my expression, like he was trying to figure out if I was joking. Hell, I was still trying to figure out what the fuck I was feeling—what, in a way, felt like he was making me feel.

"But you're not gay?" He eyed me curiously.

"Well...at least not as straight as I'd believed I was."

He chuckled. "That's something I'm willing to drink to."

He started to pour some more whiskey into our glasses when I noticed the bottle was already half-empty.

"I can do one more, but then I got to get back to work."

"Just one more," he assured me. "Wouldn't want to tempt you any more than I already have."

We took the glasses in our hands, our gazes lingering a little too long before I said, "To temptations and rivalries."

He snickered, his eyes practically glistening with a reflection of sunlight coming from behind the bar.

"To temptations and rivalries."

CHAPTER SEVEN

Cohen

I DIDN'T LEAVE the distillery with Brody. Honestly, I was still reeling over what he told me. The Mitchells and O'Ralleys had started out as friends? Had gone into business together? Had been illegally running alcohol through the South with a lady of the night, who'd then come between them? Christ, I'd traveled across the country and onto the set of a Hollywood movie.

It was crazy to think these things happened in real life. Nearly a hundred years of feud between our two families over a woman and a recipe? And, well, maybe something between my mom and Big Daddy too. Life was stranger than fiction sometimes. But then, I thought about someone stealing my business secrets— thought about the betrayal I felt when Teddy asked

Isaac and me to help him get off the ground, only to take all the credit for himself and hang us out to dry—and I understood it better. Christ, I really fucking hoped my great-grandfather hadn't done that. I wasn't sure we would ever know, one way or another.

I walked around the tasting room, examined the photos on the walls. In one of them, captioned *The Mitchells*, three men were standing together, arms wrapped around each other: my biological dad—Harris—with who I assumed were my grandpa—Bobby—and great-grandpa—Arthur. The latter two had smiles stretched across their faces, ear to ear.

But my father…my father didn't. Maybe he just didn't smile in photos? Maybe he'd had a bad day? Whatever the reason for his obvious melancholy, it was no skin off my back. It wasn't as if he'd ever cared about me. *Then why did he leave me Mitchell Creek? Why didn't he contact me before he died?*

I shook those thoughts from my head. I had a family that loved me, even if they weren't blood. Harris Mitchell didn't matter.

I continued my self-guided tour, first through the tasting room and then the rest of the distillery, taking the time to examine the equipment Brody had pointed out to me.

From what I could tell, most of it looked in working condition, not that I knew a damn thing about distilleries. Everything was fairly clean, which I figured had something to do with Byron, who'd been taking care of the place since Harris passed. There were also things that needed to be replaced and fixed, according to Brody. Obviously, though Harris had closed down operations, he'd kept up on most of it. Again, I couldn't stop myself from wondering why.

I couldn't make sense of any of it. This cloud of mystery surrounded my family, Brody's, and the distillery, giving me a fucking headache.

The smart thing would be to take the money and run. To sell Mitchell Creek, maybe to the O'Ralleys to end a ridiculous feud, and take my happy ass back to San Francisco, where I belonged.

My thoughts flashed back to Brody, to the way his lips curled when he spoke, the flush of his skin when he was nervous, and, well…to be honest, I wanted more of him. Wouldn't be so bad if I found a way to make that happen before I left.

Forcing myself out of the warehouse, I locked up and started the walk back to the house.

The property was prettier than I wanted to admit. I looked out in the direction of Brody's place but couldn't see it from here. Did he live in the same house as his father? Did all the brothers live there? What would he look like on his knees with my cock in his mouth? Okay, so that last one made me smile and had nothing to do with anything other than said cock, but it was a fun thought.

I was sweating from the fucking humidity in this state by the time I made it back to the house, still feeling a slight tingle beneath my skin from the shots I'd taken with Brody.

Isaac was back in the office with paperwork and a laptop when I came home—back, when I came back. This wasn't my home.

"How was he?" Isaac waggled his eyebrows.

"What do you mean, how was he? I didn't fuck him."

"Sucks for you." He winked. "Kidding. What did he say?"

Groaning, I sat down in the office chair and re-counted everything Brody had told me about the feud.

"Shut the fuck up!" Isaac's eyes went wide. "You're shittin' me."

"I wish I were."

"Do you think your ancestors *stole* their secret recipe?"

My gut clenched. "How would I know? I really hope not. If so, all this is a lie, isn't it?" And it meant the O'Ralleys really did have a reason to hate us—them, a reason to hate them.

"Wow. This is crazy, Cozies," he mused, using his familiar nickname for me. "We really did find ourselves in a good ole Southern mystery. How are you holding up?" The question was spoken with concern in his voice.

"I...don't know." It was weird. As far as I was concerned, I had two parents back in California. They'd always been open about what they knew about my past, which obviously wasn't much. I'd had a single mom and no father on the birth certificate. She didn't have much history, making them wonder if she'd changed her name. She got into a car accident. Her last words had been about me, about taking care of her son, and then she died.

Now I had a legacy, and a distillery with a feud, and a mystery along with it.

"Things would be a whole lot easier if the only

thing I had to worry about here was whether I was going to fuck Brody O'Ralley or not. Christ, he's fucking hot."

"So hot. I would even watch," Isaac teased. "Being serious, though, it's okay if you want to figure this out; you know that, right? It's okay if you're curious about your history. That doesn't mean you love your adoptive parents—"

"My parents," I corrected.

"Your parents, any less. Lydia knows that."

He was right, of course. Logically, I knew that, and I'd be lying if I didn't admit I wanted to sort through all this shit. I'd also be lying if I didn't admit that part of me wanted to keep this distillery, wanted to open it back up and see what I could do with it. To try and rebuild it on my own and do something different. As much as I loved California, I needed a change too.

"Come on. Byron still hasn't returned my phone call. Let's go see him."

Isaac didn't question me. We got the address and drove to his office, which wasn't hard to find. I doubted anything in this town was, other than Mitchell Creek our first night.

Byron's office was in a small brick building that

looked more like a house than a place of business. A woman who I assumed was a paralegal looked up the second we walked in. "Well, if it isn't Cohen Mitchell and Isaac Connors. I was wondering when I'd get to meet the two of you."

"Wait. How do you know my last name?" Isaac asked.

She grinned. "News travels fast." She was probably sixty or so, with curly red hair and a mischievous grin.

"Yeah, but I never told anyone. Are you guys scoping us out on social media or something?"

"This is a small town, sugar. We know everything about everyone, and if we don't, we find out; if we can't, we make somethin' up anyway."

"I totally belong in a small town," Isaac said.

Huh. Funny, I was thinking it all sounded pretty creepy to me.

"Anyways, I'll tell Byron you're here, though I'm sure he already knows. He can usually hear through the door. I'm Dottie, by the way—Dottie Jensen. I knew your daddy, of course. Well, your whole family. How can you live in Buckridge and not know the Mitchells?"

"Or the O'Ralleys," Isaac added, and I nudged

him.

"Well, yes, them too, but we have to admit, they're a little different from the Mitchells, with the rumors and all."

"What rumors?" I asked.

"Well, I don't know how true it is, but my mama, bless her heart, didn't trust Bobby Mitchell or his daddy as far as she could throw them. I mean, we all loved them because that's what we do here, but I'd be lyin' if I didn't say I questioned their morals, if you know what I mean."

My heart spiked. This was the second time someone made it sound like there was something dirty going on where my family was concerned. "No, I don't, actually."

"Well, those are all stories, and I'm not one to spread rumors," Dottie countered.

I was pretty sure she was exactly the type to spread rumors. Unfortunately, I didn't have a chance to ask. The side door opened, and Byron said, "Mr. Mitchell, Mr. Connors, please come in."

I nodded and signaled for Isaac to go first, following Byron into his office.

"Please, sit down. Sorry I haven't replied to your

message. It's been a busy day."

"No problem," I said, even though it was. "I was going through the paperwork, and I had a few questions. First, there are bank-account balances—"

"Which will go to you after one year. It was one of your father's stipulations. I wasn't supposed to tell you until you arrived."

"Did he always play games like this?" I asked, frustrated.

"This isn't a game, Mr. Mitchell. Your father loved you. He—"

I held up a hand. I didn't want to hear about him loving me. When he looked at me, obviously offended, I said, "I apologize if that came off harsh. I'm just dealing with a lot."

"Well, thank you for that, and I'm sure you are."

We eyed each other for a moment as if unsure what to think. This man had been my dad's best friend. There had to be things he wasn't telling me.

"I have a question for you…" He hesitated. "Do you know what your plans are? With Mitchell Creek? Do you intend to sell? Reopen? Keep it until you decide?"

"Reopen," I said without thought. Well, shit. The

answer had been right there all along. I hadn't wanted to admit it, but I was sure I knew since before I'd arrived. I was curious about my history. I needed a challenge.

Mitchell Creek was just that.

I turned to Isaac. "With his help, hopefully."

"Are you kidding? I'd never let you have all the fun."

His answer didn't surprise me. Isaac and I were family.

I wonder what Brody will think, danced through my head. *That* surprised me. It didn't matter one way or another what that gorgeous man, whose family had feuded with mine, thought. It didn't matter at all.

"Then I have something else for you," Byron said, making me frown. Something he could only give me if I was opening the distillery again? "I'll need you to sign an NDA first. I understand that seeing this might change your mind. Your father stipulated that you had to want Mitchell Creek before I gave it to you. Afterward, you're welcome to stay or walk, but you won't be able to talk about what you read."

What I read? Holy fuck, this really was like a movie. "Okay."

Byron already had the NDA ready and handed it over. "I'll prepare a different one for you, Mr. Connors."

I read it while he prepared Isaac's, I assumed because he was there at the moment and I mentioned him helping with the distillery. It was all standard stuff, so I signed and waited for Isaac to do the same.

"I know it's hard for you to believe, but your father really did love you," Byron said. "He did the best with what he was given, and he tried to make things right. When he fell in love with Pammy White, that changed things for him. He wanted to be the man she deserved."

I froze. Isaac reached over and placed his hand on my knee. My mom's last name had been Miller. Pam Miller. "White?" I asked with a tremble to my voice.

"Shit. I wasn't thinking. I forgot you didn't know that. Your mama changed her last name because she didn't want to be found easily. It'll all make sense to you soon. She gave you your daddy's last name, though, obviously."

This was such a fucking mess. I had no idea what to think or feel.

Isaac took over for me, talking and asking questions. A little while later, I was walking out of his office with my father's journal and the numbers to a bank account in my name. Apparently, he was giving me a small portion of money now, to help get Mitchell Creek off the ground, and then I'd get the bulk of my inheritance after a year.

"You okay?" Isaac asked as we were driving back to the house.

"I don't know," I answered honestly. This was all a lot. Journals, name changes, NDAs, feuds and secrets. I had no idea what I'd gotten myself into.

Isaac knew me better than anyone, so he left me alone as I locked myself in my father's office and read.

The journal was filled with recipes and formulas for whiskey, names of people they worked with, and lots of pertinent information I would need about the distillery. That, however, wasn't what kept me up until the next morning. No, that was the other stuff, the personal things in the letter Harris Mitchell had written me.

Cohen,

I don't imagine I'm your favorite person, and I can understand why. It's probably confusing to you. Hell, it's confusing to me, but the truth boils down to two things. The first and most important is that I love you. I have always loved you. I loved you and your mother with all my heart.

The second is that I'm a coward.

My dad always had a strong hold on me. I never crossed him. Never did what he didn't want me to, unless it had to do with you and your mom. He never approved of our relationship, not liking that she was friendly with the O'Ralleys, but I wouldn't walk away from her. I loved her too much.

We planned to run away together. The Mitchells…well, they have never been on the up-and-up. The truth is, we were involved in illegal activity my whole life, hell, since before I was born. Laundering money and likely more. It started with your great-grandpa, then every Mitchell afterward. When Pammy got pregnant, all I wanted was to give you a better life, but I also understood my daddy. If he knew there was another Mitchell child out there, he would have wanted you here with us, and I wouldn't have had the courage to say no. So, we came up with a plan.

Your mom would leave. I'd give her money, then when things calmed down here, I'd go to you guys. Like I said, I'm a coward. I kept putting it off, using the excuse that my daddy would find us, that he would discover Pam and I had a son. There were rumors of her being pregnant when she left, but I played them off as lies.

When your mom died, I went to California. I knew you were heading to a family who hoped to adopt you, and when I saw them, I told myself you'd be better off without me, and I walked away...

My eyes blurred after that. I closed the book and cried. Then opened it again and continued reading. More of him saying he loved me, of calling himself a coward, saying that as far as he knew, the Mitchells hadn't stolen the recipe from the O'Ralleys. All the things he said I needed to know.

I stayed awake all night.

The next morning, there was a knock on the office door, and Isaac was there with coffee. We sat down, and I told him what I'd read.

"Wow...that's...wow. I don't know what to say."

"Yeah, me neither. I don't think I've processed it all yet." How could I? The truth about my family, about my parents…

"I'm still in if you are."

It was the perfect thing to say. I looked at him and told him, "We do this legit, and we do it our way."

"Wouldn't have it any other way," Isaac agreed. "You're my family. Where else would I be?"

CHAPTER EIGHT

Brody

"IF YOU'RE NOT having a good time, you might need to ask that Mitchell to come on over and suck your dick," Walker teased, glaring at me from the riding lawn mower he was working on fixing.

In a white tank, stained from years of being covered in oil and mud, he took a socket wrench to the side of the riding lawn mower, which had gone down a few weeks earlier. Walker had always been the handyman around the house, fixing everything from the garbage disposal to broken equipment in the distillery whenever it wasn't so bad we had to call in a pro.

"I'm having a perfectly good time, thank you very much. Here I thought I was being sweet by keeping you company."

"You are. Now can you make yourself useful and hand me those sockets?"

He indicated the plastic case on the tool chest against the wall, near his ATV. I fetched it for him, and he fished out the socket he needed. As he affixed it to the ratchet handle, he went on, "Now don't play with me, Brodes. I know you didn't just head over to the Mitchells' the other day to give him a tour of his own place."

"Here you have me wishing I hadn't mentioned it."

"Think you just proved my point. You did tell me, and you sounded like you enjoyed talking to him. I'm fine if you don't want to put a label on what's going on just yet, but you can admit you want to spend more time with the guy. As Big Momma woulda said, you're sweet on him." He grinned, knowing damn well how much I hated that expression.

"I'm going to throw up."

"Oh, is that what he's into? Not judging, just seems pretty damn intimate for this soon in your courtship."

"Shut it."

A knowing grin slipped across his face as he continued loosening a bolt on the mower. "Don't like that I'm getting warm?"

"Not even close."

"Ooh, more like hot?"

"He's a nice guy. Totally cool, considering my family is a bunch of assholes, present company included."

"Hey, just Big Daddy and Dwain." He'd pulled the bolt from the side of the mower and cupped it in his hand with the others. "Walker's pretty awesome."

"He's *aight*," I said playfully, earning an eye roll. "But if Cohen wants to chat some more, he'll text or—"

"Oh, so he has your number?"

"I handed him my phone. It took, like, two seconds for him to key it in. That all-knowing look you have for not knowing shit makes me want to deck you."

"Maybe because you're looking to work off some hot tension with a certain prick Mitchell."

"He's not a prick," pushed past my lips, and judging by the satisfied look on Walker's face, it was exactly what he'd wanted.

"Awfully defensive for a guy you just think is cool." He winked, reveling in having caught me.

"Whatever. I'm not pushing anything. He's right next door. Whether or not Big Daddy and Dwain are okay with it, we're going to be seeing him and Isaac around plenty."

"Oh, that's right. Wonder what that guy's story is. Interesting how close they are. You think they...mess around?"

"What? No." Again, I sounded far too defensive for someone who didn't give a damn about him. But I would have been envious at the thought of anyone getting to explore what I was denying myself.

"Would that piss you off, knowing they did, since you'd be all jealous?"

"Jealous? Of a guy I've known for five minutes? Please. You're ridiculous." Walker glared at me until I confessed, "Wouldn't hate trying it again, is all. You happy?"

"As a clam."

"I feel like I don't tell you enough how corny you are. And here you're acting all smart when, as I'm sure you've noticed, you don't see me, Mel, Dwain, or Lee being the go-to guys for fixing shit."

He chuckled. "Aw, poor bro. Hasn't anyone ever told you the great commandment? *He who fixes the lawn mower doth not mow thine yard."*

I laughed. "That can't be how you say that."

"Eh, something like that. But I think you'll find once I'm finished with this who the real sucker is."

Namely me. "Damn, you smart fuck."

We shared a laugh, then shot the breeze some more before finishing up and heading to the house for dinner. As usual, Big Daddy got to talking about business before saying, "And by the way, what are all these horse pictures doing on our Instagram page?" He eyed me from across the dining-room table.

"People like horses. Gets more likes and shares than anything else we post."

"That's not what we do."

"Do you just want me posting boring pictures of the distillery all day long? I'm doing the best I can, and even then, I don't think the two hundred people we have following us on Instagram will be rattled by the deviation from business as usual."

He didn't seem satisfied with that response. But I reminded myself his critique had less to do with my not-very-impressive skills as our part-time social media PR guru and more to do with our overall lackluster annual performance.

I sighed, Walker and I exchanging looks in that way where we didn't need to do more to express our frustration with Big Daddy. Big Daddy continued our business meeting over dinner before I felt my phone vibrate.

I slipped my cell out of my pocket, surprised to see *No Good Mitchell* pop up on my screen. I couldn't help but chuckle. Hadn't expected him to be such a smartass, but I probably should've.

"Gotta take this real quick," I said, hopping up from my seat.

"Take what?"

"Official social media affairs here, Big Daddy. Gotta call Instagram and get them to take down those offensive horse posts, ya know?"

"It wouldn't kill you to learn to take some constructive critic—"

I was in the adjoining hall before he could finish his sentence, eagerly answering the call—

"You fucking smartass," I said, unable to stifle a grin.

"You need to get over here right now." It wasn't Cohen's voice. It was Isaac's. "Holy shit, it's coming this fucking—"

"What the hell is going on?"

I didn't hear anything on the other end, so I checked my screen only to find we'd been disconnected.

Fuck.

"Everything cool?" Walker asked, stepping into the hall.

"We gotta go visit the enemy. Now."

He didn't ask questions. We excused ourselves, and Big Daddy assumed it was because I was annoyed about the Instagram stuff, so he didn't ask questions either. Walker and I jumped in his truck and headed over to the Mitchell house.

"You sure we don't need to call 911?" he asked, not for the first time.

I'd dismissed it when he'd first made the suggestion, but I decided he needed more to soothe his concern. "They're city boys. If they needed emergency services, that's the first place they would have called. Not looked up my number."

"Fair point."

Although, given Isaac's tone, it didn't keep me from being concerned about the guys. As soon as we pulled up the gravel drive to the house, I noticed just a few lights were on.

I pulled the truck to a halt, and we hopped out, headed up the front porch, and rang the bell.

We waited in silence.

I rang again…then again.

Still nothing.

"Strange," I muttered.

"You think they're over at the distillery?"

"Let's run over there, I guess…" I began before a loud sound, like screaming, came from inside.

Walker and I shared another look, like the one at dinner earlier.

I checked the doorknob. Locked. Suddenly, 911 seemed like a more reasonable suggestion than I'd initially considered.

"Take it down," I said, holding the screen door open. Walker backed up and launched himself at the door, full-force.

"Fucking hell," he said, grabbing his shoulder.

"Okay, together." I propped the screen door open with a planter, and we barreled into the door on a count of three, popping the wood on the doorframe as we forced our entry.

"We're here! No one shoot!" I didn't imagine either of them had guns, but being born and raised in Buckridge, I knew better than to break down a door without clearly alerting the homeowner of my presence.

The screaming sound came again.

"Upstairs," I said, following the sound up the stairwell.

We entered the upstairs hall, and I noticed the ladder descending from the open attic door. I didn't waste time, and when I reached the top, in the dim light of a lone bulb hanging from the middle of the space, I saw Isaac and Cohen, arms stretched to the sides as they stood totally still on adjacent walls.

I eyed them peculiarly before Isaac pointed toward the floor, where a cell-phone light danced around. In its shadow, it took me a moment for my eyes to adjust and see the little guy.

A raccoon.

Walker stepped up beside me as I approached it. "Oh, hey, fella…aren't you a cutie?"

As soon as it spotted us, it dropped the phone and hissed.

"Don't make it angry," Cohen said. "I think he was looking for food or something when I found him."

"Aw, he's just scared," Walker said, moving to the middle of the room. "They scare easily, so you have to get him in a corner, and then…" He had this cocky expression on his face as he rushed the coon…who charged him.

"Holy fucking shit!" he called, backing up to the wall beside Isaac. "Fuck, fuck, fuck."

I couldn't blame him, since that thing looked like it was about to tear him the fuck apart.

I got a quick idea, so I pulled my keys out of my pocket. Removing my mini-flashlight, I turned it on and flashed it about, catching the critter's attention. I headed to a nearby window and popped it open.

"Come on, cutie," I said as it climbed a few boxes to get closer to my light.

I stepped back as it got close, then chucked the flashlight out the window. It hurried after it, giving me time to pull the window closed.

"Aw, our hero," Isaac said.

I could tell by Walker's tight jaw and squared shoulders that he was annoyed about me getting credited as hero of the night.

"All that fuss was over a raccoon?" I asked.

"No, not just a raccoon," Cohen said, slightly defensive. "That thing… You should have seen the way it was howling at us. I didn't realize raccoons even made sounds, let alone like fucking banshees."

"It could have had rabies," Isaac said. "I could have gotten rabies, and then I would have had to bite Cohen."

"You think rabies turns you into a zombie?" I teased.

"That thing was crawling all over me, and I could have sworn it bit me." Isaac kept checking for a spot.

"Where?" I challenged.

"I don't have a bite mark, but it *could* have bitten me."

I couldn't help laughing. "So everyone's fine?" As soon as I said that, I noticed red on Cohen's arm.

He followed my look. "Oh, fuck. I think that must've been from when that thing jumped out of the box I was holding. There were some loose boards in there. Looks like one got me."

"Come on. Let's get you patched up."

Walker helped Isaac clean up the mess from the coon scare while Cohen and I headed to the kitchen. I found an old first-aid kit under the sink and got to helping him bandage it up as he relayed the rest of his great raccoon tale to me.

"I was going through boxes to find…hell, I don't know. Anything about my family. And that's when it jumped out. Isaac had been getting me to take some new app pics for him earlier in the day, so he was loading them when that thing decided to hold us hostage. Once Isaac dropped his phone, it got distracted, and we scared it and it scared us, and it became this standoff."

I couldn't stop chuckling.

"You're getting a real kick out of this, but I saw the way Walker freaked out with that thing too. It's not just city boys that thing can scare."

"Fair point. It definitely looked rattled. Just be glad it wasn't a snake."

"Snake? In the attic?"

"Yeah, welcome to Buckridge, where snakes are…well, everywhere." I finished wrapping the gauze around his arm. "All set. Now I think that calls for another drink."

"Of the rival's stash?"

"Nah. I think I have some of the actual good stuff in Walker's truck. I'll be right back." I hurried to the car, grabbed a bottle, and returned to his kitchen. I was pretty excited about sharing some of my family's namesake with him.

"By the way," I said. "I should probably tell you that I'll have to be back tomorrow to fix your door."

"Fix my door?"

"It was locked, and when we heard screaming…"

"That was the raccoon screaming."

"If you say so. I would have probably believed you more if you'd said Isaac." I winked, and he shook his head before grabbing glasses from a cabinet.

"So you guys just throw your weight around to get what you need around here?" Cohen asked as he set the glasses down.

"Eh…when you grow up with as many siblings as I did, you get used to breaking down doors…and fixing them. Although, that deadbolt might have nearly knocked Walker's shoulder out of its socket."

He enjoyed a laugh but eyed me uncertainly, clearly unsure how serious I was being. It seemed we both had a hard time reading each other. I wondered if that was part of what was so intriguing.

We stood at the counter, where I finished pouring our drinks and handed him one. "Here. Best remedy for your flesh wound."

We clinked glasses and took a drink.

"Mmm." His eyes filled with a certain knowing that reminded me of that look he got when he'd tasted his family's brand.

"Ha. So you admit you like a good premium O'Ralley whiskey?"

He feigned a disgusted expression. "Sorry. I always say *mmm* before I'm about to vomit."

"I saw the look in your eyes when you took a sip."

"Nope. Not gonna get me to cave." He winked, and I wished I could've kept from grinning as hard as I did.

"Well, if you're gonna be an ass, I guess I can fairly ask how long I'm gonna have to deal with this ass?"

He eyed me suspiciously. "Depends on how many demonic raccoons I'm gonna have to deal with."

"Just *normal* raccoons."

"You didn't look that thing in the eyes," he teased before his expression turned serious. "There's something about this place. I don't know what it is, but I got a feeling in my gut that I need to be here and make something of it."

"You want to reopen it? Trying to make your way on our turf?"

"Trying to make my own, really."

"That sounds…heavy."

He took a drink, a big gulp of the whiskey, like he needed it. He leaned back against the counter behind him. "I'd like to do something new. My parents—the ones who adopted me—well, my dad taught me a whole lot about finance and business. He knows his shit. Isaac and I have always been a package deal. I got my bachelor's in business and he in marketing. We worked for some startups and were good at building or saving companies. The last one, though, it was a friend. I brought Isaac on board, of course, and the guy did us dirty. Got rid of us both when he got what he wanted out of us. It'd be nice to have something that's just ours, ya know? See what he and I could do with this place together. I think I might need it."

As he told me about his past, I could see this strange mix of sorrow and hope in his expression. He seemed confused and lost, but not like a guy who would throw in the towel too quickly.

"What we have here is a unique opportunity," I said.

"A what?"

"That's what Big Momma always used to tell us.

When shit got hard or things got out of whack...it was a unique opportunity. In her mind, it was the good Lord's way of making us step out of our comfort zone so that we could do something better, something greater."

He smiled. "That's lovely."

"Yeah, well, losing her was one of our biggest unique opportunities..." It was hard to say that without my voice quaking. "She was the kind who believed everything happens for a reason, though."

"And you?"

"I believe sometimes things just happen, and you pick yourself up and get on with it even when that's the hardest thing to do."

"I agree with that."

"Well, it's gonna be a big challenge. You sure you're up for it?" I pressed.

"I don't have a fucking clue, but I've never been one to let a little worry—or a lot of worry—stop me."

"Hmm...you're hard not to like, *No Good Mitchell*."

That bright smile returned. "You're gonna have to like me since I'm gonna need some expertise from someone who knows the ropes."

I knew he meant it, and I knew I wasn't going to tell him no. "You're gonna get me into trouble with the O'Ralleys."

"Don't you like a little trouble, O'Ralley?"

His voice and expression were filled with desire and interest, something I more than reciprocated, so I replied, "I'm gonna refuse to answer on the grounds of entrapment. But if I'm gonna help you, then you have to help me."

"With…?"

"You're curious about how to run a distillery. I have some things I'd say you know quite a bit about that maybe I need some assistance with…" I moved closer to him, my gaze fixed on his lips, something he must've noticed.

"Um…"

"Business stuff," I spat out quickly, realizing he wasn't getting where I was going with that. Fuck my life. "The O'Ralleys haven't been so savvy on the business front the past few years, and I was thinking with Isaac's and your expertise, you might be able to help the O'Ralleys out; in secret, of course."

"Oh," he said with a chuckle. "Fuck, yeah. I…wow…I thought you were going somewhere very different with the needing assistance with something I had expertise in."

I moved closer to him, until our noses touched. "I figured that was already going to be an even exchange. Sounds like you're gonna be here for a while, so I don't mind taking my time."

"Based on that first kiss, I didn't take you for a guy who liked to go slow."

"I enjoy going slow...until I'm ready to go fast."

I smiled, and he had this wicked expression on his face, like he was all about it. He moved quickly, seizing his opportunity. I relaxed into it, cupping my hand behind his head as he moved toward me, pushing me back against the table. He was about as forceful as his mouth was wet. And so fucking warm.

I took control, shoving him back to the counter, but he rolled toward me, and I found myself back against the table. The frenzy, this tug-of-war for control, electrified me. It was even more intoxicating than the bit of whiskey I had pulsing through me.

As we pulled away from each other, our gazes shifted between our eyes and lips.

"Yeah, I think we have some serious trouble in our futures," I teased, and we shared a laugh.

CHAPTER NINE

Cohen

THE FOLLOWING FEW weeks flew by. I'd been involved in a business before, but nothing close to a distillery. While I was good with numbers and big-picture ideas, I definitely needed Brody's help with the nitty-gritty specifics. I was shocked and pleased that he'd suggested we work together, even though it was kept on the down-low. Seemed Big Daddy really would lose his shit if he found out—and I swear I was never going to get over someone's actual father being called that.

Porn daddy? Yes. Biological big daddies were totally new.

Isaac and I had worked day and night making plans, setting up services, figuring out what the fuck we were doing. When they could, Brody and Walker would sneak away and spend evenings with us at the house or in the distillery. I was learning that while they knew whiskey in a way I wasn't sure I ever would, they struggled with the business and marketing aspects, but any time I tried to bring it up, Walker would interrupt the conversation and steer it back to us. Obviously, *that* O'Ralley brother was a little more cautious in letting us know the ins and outs of their brand.

Not that I could blame them, because apparently, I came from a whole line of criminals—well, my grandfather and great-grandfather, at least. Outside of the prohibition years, I doubted the O'Ralleys could say the same.

I shook my head, not wanting to focus on what I'd learned in the journal. It was much easier if I concentrated on what I could change—getting Mitchell Creek off the ground again, continuing what my father had tried to do, and, you know, *not be a criminal.*

About a week ago, I'd found the key to the locked room tucked away in a box in the attic. When I unlocked it, I'd been surprised that it was just an empty room with a desk, like maybe there had been an office there at some point. Somehow I thought it would be full of answers or proof of dubious behavior.

The truth was much more boring.

I plucked another nail from the counter I was working on in the tasting room and got busy again.

"Cohen! They're delivering the new machine!" Rusty shouted from the other side of the distillery, interrupting my hammering. He was just another way Brody had saved my ass lately. They knew each other, and Rusty used to work for my dad and knew the ins and outs of Mitchell Creek better than anyone. He'd been looking for a job and had been eager to jump in and help us get stuff figured out. He was about ten years or so older than me, and he was good people. I liked him. We sat around and shot the shit every once in a while.

"Be right there," I called back.

"I'll deal with it," Isaac answered. Sometimes it felt like I'd been given a lucky extension of myself in Isaac.

I'd be lying if I didn't admit I was not only out of my league, but dealing with a whole lot of confusing stuff going on in my head. I closed my eyes, saw bits and pieces of journal entries I'd read over and over in my dad's messy handwriting.

Handwriting that looked like mine.

Without, you know, contemplating the fact that I

was closing my eyes and hammering at the same time, I swung the damn thing. It connected, making pain shoot through my thumb. "Motherfucker!" I cried out. It immediately started to throb, and ridiculously, the first thing I thought was, *Oh, great, Brody's never going to let me hear the end of this.*

First, attack of the killer raccoon, and now this. He and Walker already liked to give Isaac and me shit because we were city boys who stuck out like a—*Goddamn it.* He was going to make a sore-thumb joke. I knew it.

I tossed the hammer onto the counter and rubbed a hand over my face. I was tired as hell. I hadn't been sleeping the best. I was off my game, which was totally unfamiliar territory to me.

"Hey," Isaac said as he entered the room. "You look tired."

"I am." It didn't matter that weeks had gone by. The journal was weighing on my mind every hour of every day.

"Why don't we cut out early today? Rusty is leaving. We can spend an evening not thinking about the distillery. Maybe go grab some food and have a movie night?"

The truth was, I didn't know if I had the energy for that, and the thought of heading into town was draining. Every time I was there, I heard a different story about my family or me. "I like the cutting-out-early part, and the eating-and-hanging-out part."

"So all the parts that don't include going into town?" Isaac asked.

"That's about right."

"Deal."

We finished at the distillery, locked up, and headed back to the house. Isaac ordered a pizza and teased me about my thumb before I went to take a shower. Then we ate dinner together, and he asked me what I wanted to watch, but nothing was sounding good.

"I know what you need." Isaac plucked my phone from the arm of the couch and unlocked it.

"Wait. What are you doing?"

His fingers started moving over the screen.

"What are you doing?" I asked again.

"Texting that super-sexy O'Ralley brother you want to bang to come hang out with you."

"What the fuck, Isaac." I leaped toward him, but he moved too quickly, the twinky little thing. I went after him, and he ran around the living room with my cell in his hand. Finally, I caught him, wrapped my arms around his waist, and tugged him to me just as my phone beeped.

"Goddamn you." I jerked my phone out of his hand.

I read the text Isaac sent as me, then Brody's reply.

Hey. Can you come over tonight? Just you. I thought we could...hang out. Bring whiskey!

Um, yeah, sure. I can do that. Let me shower. Be there in about forty-five minutes.

"You fucker!" I told Isaac.

"You can always tell him it was me playing a trick on you."

But I didn't, and I wouldn't. He knew that as well as I did. Brody intrigued me—this guy who said he was straight but kissed me the first night we met. Who brought us almond milk and helped us out even though most of his family would be pissed. The guy who broke down our door to save us from a killer raccoon, then showed up first thing the next morning to fix it.

The guy I kissed in my kitchen yet hadn't had my hands on since.

"So...I'll stay in my room tonight. I'm gonna take a bubble bath, do an exfoliating face mask, and

116

probably watch some porn. Have fun." My annoying best friend waved at me and went for the stairs.

But the truth was, I couldn't really be mad at him. I was having a shitty day, so it wasn't like drinking with a gorgeous man, whom I did, in fact, want to bang, would be a hardship.

I went to the kitchen, grabbed two glasses, and headed out back to the screened-in porch. Like everything else in the house, it had been cleaned while it sat empty, waiting for me to arrive. There was a table, along with a weather-resistant couch and two chairs.

And then…then I waited.

It was definitely less than forty-five minutes later when I heard Brody's truck pull up. I left the porch and walked around the side of the house to signal to him where I was. It was evening, the sun just beginning to set in the distance, all bright reds and oranges, trees dancing in the light breeze. I tried to pay attention to that rather than ogling the sexy man who stepped up beside me.

"So…" Brody started.

"Isaac sent that text."

"Oh."

Shit. Did he sound a little dejected? "But I was okay with it."

"I *am* fun to be around, so it makes sense," Brody teased.

He was a sweet Southern boy from what I could tell, but I wasn't going to tell him that. "You're *aight*," I joked, and he laughed.

"Are we going to stand here all night, or are we going to drink? I notice you're asking for my whiskey even though I know you have some."

Yeah, yeah I did, but as much as I wanted to make Mitchell Creek mine, I felt weird about it since reading my dad's journal.

"What?" Brody asked, obviously reading my expression.

"Nothing. We're gonna drink. Let's go."

He nodded. I opened the screen door and signaled for him to go inside. We each flopped into a chair, facing the back of the property, where the distillery could be seen in the distance.

We watched the sunset, and Brody opened a bottle, poured two glasses. We each swallowed them down in one long gulp. It burned as it slid down my throat, and I shook my head. "Wow. That was rough. What's this one?"

"O'Ralley's Buckridge Deluxe Scotch. It's got a kick to it, that's for sure. Oh, hey, what happened to your finger?"

Damned if I didn't feel my cheeks heat. "Nothing."

"Aw, did my city boy hurt himself?" Brody poured two more glasses.

"*Your?*" I looked at him over the edge of mine, then tilted it back and swallowed again.

He gave me this aw-shucks look, and I couldn't help wondering how someone could look so innocent yet mischievous and full of trouble at the same time. "Is *my* country boy embarrassed?"

"Did you hit your thumb with a hammer or something?" he asked playfully, but the shock must have shown on my face because he practically shouted, "Oh my God! You did! How in the hell?"

"No comment, and drink your fucking whiskey, lightweight. I'm ready for another."

I should have known right then and there that I was in trouble. Hell, I probably did, but I'd been known to ignore warning signs a time or ten before.

So we sat there and drank.

A lot.

Evening turned to night. I flipped the switch to turn the light and ceiling fan on, and we drank some more. We talked about stupid shit—his brothers, fishing, this one time he got caught screwing this girl in her barn, and her daddy (his word not mine) chased him naked across the lawn with a shotgun.

"I thought that shit only happened in the movies," I said, my brain feeling fuzzy and light.

"You're obviously not a country boy if you think that." He gave me this playful half grin, and shit, my dick stirred.

"What'd Big Daddy do?"

Brody winked. "Told me not to get caught next time."

We laughed as he poured us each another glass. This one we nursed more slowly.

"You're a college boy, huh?"

"Yeah, San Francisco State. It's where I met Isaac. You?"

"I went to college for a semester in Atlanta. Figured I'd give it a try, see what that was all about. City living, university life, along with some life stuff, but found it wasn't my thing. I was eager to get back home and to work. Other than that, what I've seen of the world has been work-related. Conventions and meetings with distributors. But nothing's ever inspired me to leave this place. It's home...where my blood and heart is, ya know?"

The truth was, I didn't really. "Maybe? Fuck, I don't know. I'm drunk as shit. I grew up in the Bay Area. I liked it, thought I was happy, but I never felt tied to it like you do to Buckridge. That's probably part of the reason it was so easy for me to come here...I think. I mean, I didn't want to leave my family, the adoptive one. I love them, but I didn't feel a tie to the place, and then I felt guilty about wanting to leave, but I was always curious, ya know? About where I came from—and what in the fuck? Did you slip something in my drink? It's like I can't stop my fucking mouth from moving. I keep telling it to, but it won't listen."

Brody barked out a loud laugh, and before I knew it, I was laughing too, so hard my stomach hurt, and I almost tumbled out of the damn chair.

"Fuck...I'm not drinking that shit again. What the hell did you give me? I think I might die. My heart is beating too fast."

"What is it with people waking up from a less than sober night thinking that about their heart?" he asked.

I didn't reply. There was this quiet voice in the back of my mind telling me I'd be embarrassed about this later, that if I weren't so drunk, I would never say half the stuff I was, but since I was inebriated as shit, I didn't care.

I grabbed Brody's hand and put it to my chest. His body was tight for a moment, then loosened as he looked at me, at my eyes, then my hand holding his to my chest. "Well...it's beating."

"Too fast?"

"What the shit kind of drinking do you city boys do? You can't handle your alcohol."

"Shut up and tell me if I'm dying."

"You're not dying, city boy."

"Oh," I replied softly, though I wasn't letting go of Brody's hand and he didn't move it.

"Should I help you into the house?"

"No. I want to stay out here." Fuck, I *would* be embarrassed tomorrow. Stupid O'Ralley whiskey.

"Here, let's get you to the couch, then."

"I can do it." I tried to move, but then Brody's arms were there, and he was helping me lie down and licking his lips. Damn, I wanted to taste them, wanted to do more with him. "I thought we were supposed to be getting into trouble together? What was that about temptation?"

He sat in the chair closest to me. "Not tonight, that's for sure."

"Have you ever had sex with a guy?" I found myself asking.

He hesitated, then said, "Nah. I knew guys who I thought were attractive, sure. But first girlfriend I had, I felt this spark and thought that was all I needed to know. Didn't really consider it until I ended up lip-locking with a city slicker not too long ago."

I had to admit, his response made me a little nervous. "From everything you've told me, I'm a little confused about how you're handling this. Are you actually cool about this, or are you quietly having some sort of identity crisis?"

"Don't know what the crisis would be," he said with a shrug. "Always known guys who were bi or gay. My brother Walker is, and I love him to death. Doesn't change anything for me, not really. Like most things in life, guess I just gotta play it by ear."

"Well, aren't you something, Brody O'Ralley?" I

chuckled, but I couldn't imagine this totally lax attitude when there was something else he was surely considering. "What about Big Daddy? You think he'd care about your attraction to men?"

"He'd care about my attraction to *you*."

"This fucking feud is such bullshit. It was a hundred fucking years ago."

"Yeah, I know, but it's different for you. He's grown up with it and had his own issues with your daddy."

That made everything slam back into my brain—the journal, what happened. My fucked-up family legacy. "Harris loved my mom," I said softly.

"That's always good."

"And she loved my dad…at least…that's what my dad said."

Brody cocked a brow. "Talk to him lately, huh?"

I chuckled. That voice was back in my head, telling me to shut up, that I wasn't supposed to talk about this, but still I did. "No. I got his journal. It talked about the feud, about my mom breaking up with your dad because she fell in love with mine…and he loved her…he loved me. I didn't think he did. I thought he wanted nothing to do with me, but he sent her away to protect us from his dad. My grandpa used to launder money, ya know?"

"Fuck, shut up. You shouldn't be telling me this." Brody sat up straight.

He was right, of course. I didn't know the law or if anything could be done now, but I assumed if they had proof of illegal activity, I could lose Mitchell Creek, even if it hadn't been me who'd done it. Still… "I trust you. Don't know why, but I do. Anyway, my grandpa—Bobby—didn't want my dad to be with my mom. Dad knew Bobby would want me, so he told Bobby she left him. She went to California and changed her last name. But he was going to go to her, to us. Years went by, and he didn't—was scared, I guess. He thought Bobby would find them, but then she died and I ended up with my adoptive parents, and he thought about his life here, his dad, and did what he thought was best. He said he stayed away to protect me…and by the time Bobby died, he figured it was too late and he didn't deserve me." My eyes were getting heavy, blackness trying to pull me under. "But he loved me…and her…and he got this place legit. Got out of that illegal shit. I'm gonna carry it on for him."

It was all dark now, my eyes too heavy to remain open. I felt calloused fingers brush my cheek, my forehead. "Hush now. You go to sleep, city boy," I heard in the distance. "I'll stay out here with ya."

I did exactly what the voice said and let go.

CHAPTER TEN

Brody

I STOOD AT the stove, stirring sausage links in the skillet.

"I trust you."

He trusted me? That wasn't something I took lightly.

I was an O'Ralley. Trust was reserved for family. We might have our issues, but when the going got tough, we were always there for one another.

Even though his words had surprised me, I had to admit I trusted him too—enough that I was willing to disclose secrets of the O'Ralley empire in the name of helping Cohen.

The sound of someone coming downstairs pulled me out of my thoughts before a familiar voice filled the air, "Oh, Cozies, that smells amazing."

Cozies?

I turned to Isaac, who was wearing a pair of black leggings. As soon as our gazes met, he squinted.

"Huh," he mused. "I must have been tired to think Cohen actually got up early to make me breakfast in bed."

"Yeah, I'm not sure what time your buddy will be getting up. He had a rough night." I snickered, thinking of how tipsy he'd been before passing out. "I already put some coffee on. Making some sausage and then was going to fix some omelettes if you wanted one."

"You're going to poison just *his* omelette, right?" he teased.

"So...you'll take your cyanide on the side?"

He laughed as he fetched a mug from a cabinet and made himself a cup of coffee. As he headed to the fridge, I warned him, "You're running low on almond milk, if you're planning on using it for creamer."

"Only running low since Cohen doesn't take good care of me like this. I've basically been living off Lucky Charms and Shredded Wheat since we got here."

He put some milk in his coffee before heading to the kitchen table and plopping into a chair.

"So...O'Ralley, should I be concerned about your intentions?"

I stirred the links in the skillet. "My intentions?"

"Yes. You aren't planning on just slipping over here and getting some fucks out of my buddy so that you can enact some fucked-up revenge over some early twentieth-century feud, are you?"

"What? No!" I spit out.

"That's too bad. That could have been hot." He winked at me, and I finally got that he was kidding.

The sound of footsteps preceded Cohen, who came around the corner. He'd thrown on some socks and a pair of pajama bottoms. He squinted in the morning light pushing through the window over the sink, and the way his face tensed up, I was waiting for him to hiss like a vampire.

"Morning, *Cozies*," I made sure to say before Isaac.

"What are you doing sharing our friend-secrets with the enemy?" Cohen asked Isaac.

"He's very persuasive. He's making me an omelette."

"Clever bastard," Cohen said, his lips perking up despite his otherwise worn expression. "Did you stay the night?"

"Nah. You started to get a little restless on the couch, so I tucked you into bed before heading home. Got up early because I figured a certain someone might be hungover, and brought over painkillers."

"Why didn't you start with that? Where?"

I laughed, showing him a bag in the corner near the sink. He quickly downed some pills, and after I finished making breakfast, we sat down together. Cohen watched me eat.

"You didn't have breakfast with your family? Isn't that a big deal at your house?"

"Oh, I had it all right. And I'll be eating all this. I recommend you do the same. We have a big day ahead of us."

"Wait. Big day?"

"Yeah. I got the morning off so I could stick around and help out around this mess of a place you call a distillery."

He groaned. "I've already been working so hard." I could tell by his tone and the way he smiled that he was kidding.

"Don't worry. It's nothing serious."

"Well, just so both of you know, I'm taking the day off," Isaac chimed in. "I'll be catching up on *Real*

Housewives of New York."

Cohen and I smiled, finished our meal, and then Cohen headed upstairs to get ready for our day. When he stepped out of the bedroom, he was dressed in a red and blue striped flannel shirt and jeans adorned with a brown belt with a thick buckle. It reminded me of the photo I'd seen of his dad. Cohen had started wearing clothes like that after finding a box with some of Harris's old clothes.

The way the sleeves gripped his arms, the top buttons undone down to his chest…it was enough to act as a cruel tease.

"Let's get to work," he said.

He couldn't have been up for that, considering the night he had, but I kept on with that story. "Come on, cowboy," I told him as we headed out the front door.

He immediately noticed Elliecomb, my Thoroughbred, tied to a post by the front porch. He stopped and turned to me.

"Yeah, so I was thinking you deserved a day off."

"Really? And you thought you would just whisk me away on a horse and have your way with me?"

"That sounds about right." I untied Elliecomb from the post, hopped on, and urged him to get on behind me. I thought he might struggle, but it seemed like he had something to prove in showing me he could do it, and soon he was right behind me, his body tucked close to mine.

"Hold on real tight now," I told him, and he hooked his arms around me. "That's all you've got? I expected more from you, Cozies."

He snickered against the back of my neck before pulling even tighter.

"There we go. That's the way a man needs to be held," I said, turning so that our noses just barely touched, his lips close to mine, reminding me of those moments I'd shared with his wet mouth.

I let myself enjoy those memories briefly, our gazes meeting long enough for me to realize I'd just been sitting there, staring like an idiot, and I needed to get moving. I led Elliecomb through the property, toward a path in the woods. It had been some time since it'd been cleared, so I was cautious as we made our way through. Cohen made a few comments about the mystery spot we were heading to, but I wasn't going to tell.

When we finally brought Elliecomb to a stop, I glanced over my shoulder. "Here we go."

He searched around. "Um...is this where you're planning to kill me and hide the body?"

I laughed. "Just get down, and I'll show you."

He eyed me skeptically but went along with it.

"You got to learn to trust me, *No Good Mitchell*."

"I thought we established that I do trust you."

"Touché."

I hopped down and led Elliecomb to a tree to tie her to. Cohen was still searching around, as if he *was* actually wondering if this was where I was planning to hide his body.

"Come on," I told him, leading him a little farther down the trail, to a tree with bolts sticking out the sides. I indicated the deer stand a couple of yards up, which didn't seem to curb his skepticism, but he followed me up the stakes that had been nailed up the trunk.

"You could have just asked me to climb up there and jump off, if this is how you're planning to get rid of me."

I laughed as we reached the top and crawled onto the planks making up the stand. We had a good bit of space. It'd been made for several people, and there was a blanket, a lantern, and a few other miscellaneous items in the corner.

Cohen caught sight of the creek, his gaze fixed on it before he continued glancing around. "This is a pretty view."

"One of the best views on the property."

"Wait a minute," he said, his expression full of suspicion. "How do you know about this spot? This is Mitchell property."

"Well, best way to never get caught being up to no good at the O'Ralleys was to be in the last place an O'Ralley would ever look for you."

"What kind of no good would you be up to?"

"If you're patient, I'm sure you'll find out."

"A straight answer would be nice for a change."

"Well, I told you I'm having struggles with *straight* these days." He shook his head, but I opted to share. "This is where I'd bring girlfriends, and we'd...play around."

"You'd hook up in here?"

"Well, yes, but usually it was just making out...or a little more. Hindsight, I got the idea when I was out here with a buddy when I was thirteen. We were up here, and he wanted to show me a cool trick he'd learned."

"What kind of trick?"

"The kind you get at thirteen and never stop playing."

Cohen threw his head back, releasing a howl of laughter. He was such a strange mix—there was sadness and pain and then this lightheartedness. It was intriguing as hell.

"I thought you said you'd never messed around with a guy before," he said, his tone playfully accusatory.

"I said I'd never fucked a guy before, which is true."

"Wow. I'm going to be a lot more specific next time I ask you anything," he said, grinning and shaking his head. "So you and this guy would come up here all the time and jerk off together?"

"Not all the time, but most of the time."

"But you never did more than that?"

"No. We didn't think about it much, other than it feeling good. We were good friends. His name was Buddy, and we'd come up here and do that together. Seemed very innocent. He'd ask me to lick his nipples sometimes. And we'd get our mess on each other because we thought it was funny."

Cohen put his hands to his face to stifle his laugh. "Sounds like Buddy was a *very* good buddy."

"Oh yeah. He's happily married now, living in Phoenix with his new family. But we'll always have the deer stand."

"Buddy and a lot of girls, apparently."

"Eh. Only so many options I had in this town, but if deer stands could talk, I'd imagine this one would have plenty to say."

"Sounds like it. Did you guys hunt over here?"

I popped open a pleather strap affixed to my belt and retrieved my binoculars. "This is what we'd do out here."

Cohen laughed. "What?"

"If you're real quiet and a good boy, you'll see why." I peered through the binoculars, scanning the woods.

"This is so weird."

"Shh," I offered softly as I continued searching around.

We sat in silence, and it must have been killing him around the five-minute mark because he finally said, "So you said you licked Buddy's nipples, but I assume he would have licked yours at some point…?"

"Of course he licked mine. Just wasn't my thing like it was his. Now be quiet."

He did his best, but started fidgeting, unable to keep still. I could tell this was driving him insane.

"This is the problem with city boys. No patience."

"That's definitely not one of my strengths."

"Then get better at whispering."

He smiled, shaking his head. I continued searching around until I noticed a herd of deer moving through some bushes a few yards away. I passed him the binoculars, aiming them in that direction and pointing.

He looked through, taking a moment, a sort of calm sweeping over him. "Well, fuck me," he muttered. I could tell by the way he watched them that despite his annoyance at having to be still, he could see why it was worth the wait.

He turned as he followed the herd, his fascination, his sudden silence impressing me.

As he pulled back, he seemed...surprised. "That was really cool."

"And if you keep real quiet, they get even closer. Also fun to watch hawks out here."

He looked at me, this awestruck expression on his

face.

"What?" I asked.

"I never would have thought I'd enjoy something like this. Or know anyone who did. You see shit like this on YouTube or documentaries, but it's different seeing things in the wild. Just…being alive and free."

"You've been here for five minutes. I think it's a little premature to decide if you like something or not."

"No, it's just…a feeling a got. A different sort of fun than I'm used to. I can't imagine some of my friends ever wanting to do something like sitting up in a tree and waiting for deer to walk by."

"You've got that look in your eyes again," I re- marked, which made him wince. "Like you do when you drink whiskey. I don't know…something like this shit is in your blood and you're just now figuring it out."

I was wondering if his city ass would be offended by my remark, but he seemed to be considering it. It reminded me of this thing in me that I was just starting to sort through, and whatever came over me was too strong for me to fight. I moved quickly, my mouth on his, our lips pushed together, offering me that same relief I'd experienced the past two times we'd made out.

We scrambled together as I pushed him back, and he lay across the planks.

Our kisses intensified, my awareness of my surroundings slipping away from me as I focused on his buttons and fly. As soon as we'd freed his cock, he rolled on top of me, and we worked in a similar rush to get my pants down.

Cohen certainly didn't have any confusion about what to do. Before I knew it, he had his mouth around my cock, moving up and down.

So wet.

So warm.

I was painfully hard as he worked me up. This was definitely not anything I'd ever done with Buddy.

I gripped the back of his hair, enjoying every nerve he stimulated with his expert tongue until he pulled off my cock and kissed me again. At some point while he was blowing me, he'd tugged his pants down to his ankles, allowing him to straddle my right leg as he leaned forward, keeping flush with my body.

I didn't feel like we were two grown men. We were just kids, fucking around, learning what our bodies could do. I tasted his tongue, probed his flesh, inhaled his scent. Our cocks pulsed side by side as we thrust against one another.

"Cohen, if we keep this up, I'm gonna…"

He leaned back and licked his palm, positioning his cock on top of mine and stroking them together.

"Don't worry. I'm close too."

He leaned forward more, breathing against my face, looking me in the eyes. I leaned up and offered another kiss, grabbing the back of his head and pulling him close.

I didn't know why it was too much…maybe the kiss…maybe the moment I felt his warm cum spraying across my abs…maybe the way he started biting on my lip, but I came too, white ropes shooting across me as my body spasmed and twisted. I fell onto my back, struggling to endure the hypersensitivity that seized control of my will.

Cohen collapsed on top of me, and I could feel the puddle of cum on us spreading as our lips collided, our noses pushing up against each other's faces as we continued thrusting and groping. Just a fucking mess of lust, caught in whatever fever had made us lose control from the start.

We both found ourselves gasping for air as we finally pulled apart, covered in each other's sweat and cum.

He licked my lips once more and winked. "You and Buddy ever get into that?"

"Definitely not," I said with a chuckle.

"Does this mean I get to carve my name into the stand?"

A roar of laughter escaped my mouth, but I didn't allow myself too much time to keep apart from him.

And as we continued kissing, licking, nibbling…from the back of my mind, my cruel conscience echoed: *Big Daddy. Is. Gonna. Kill me.*

CHAPTER ELEVEN

Cohen

I T WAS SILLY, but I thought I might be a little obsessed with Brody O'Ralley.

He'd taken me to the woods, where we climbed onto a damn platform on a tree and looked at deer before jerking off, and I couldn't stop thinking about it. Sure, it had only been a couple of days, but it had just felt so...different. Like this easy pleasure I hadn't known existed, one that wasn't a rush but sneaked up on you slowly until you suddenly realized how full you were of it. Which didn't make a damn bit of sense, but there you had it.

I'd been embarrassed as hell when I'd woken up that morning. I was a goofy drunk, but always remembered what I did and said. I'd told him about my family, about illegal activity and my parents, which

I'd signed an NDA not to tell anyone.

I didn't regret it. I'd told Brody I trusted him, and I really did. There was something about him, this pure honesty with a bone-deep need to do the right thing that had me twisted up inside in a strange way.

A strange way I hated...and liked.

After our jerk-off session, we'd stayed up there a little longer. He'd pointed out more deer and some hawks. From there, he took me to the creek, exploring some of my land with me, land he seemed to know like the back of his hand.

Then he'd taken me home, kissed me at the door like a good Southern boy, and left.

And yeah, I was obsessing, and it was annoying as fuck.

"Are we gonna go shopping or what?" Isaac asked, and I groaned. We'd both been working on Mitchell Creek stuff all day—Isaac buying domains, thinking about websites and marketing, researching new ways to promote once we were up and running, while I'd been running numbers and setting budgets and adding to my business plans.

"Do we have to?" I was quickly falling in love with the house, with the land, and I enjoyed chatting with

Rusty, but every time I went into town, I felt like I was on the set of some fucked-up movie about a creepy small town. I wasn't sure I'd ever get used to that. Well, except when I saw Lauren. Isaac and I drank a whole lot of no-sugar-added vanilla almond milk, and sometimes Lauren worked at A Step Ahead for her mom. Sure, she'd made me crazy that first night at the Barn, but she was a riot. I had to admit she could make me laugh.

Isaac crossed his arms. "Brody would take me shopping."

"Maybe you should ask him, then." Plus, it wasn't like he couldn't take my car.

"You wish I would ask him so you could see him and go all googly-eyed over him. I was nervous you'd start humping his leg like a dog last time."

I flipped him off. "Fuck you. Methinks someone's jealous because Walker hasn't made a move."

"Pfft." Isaac waved his hand at me. "If I wanted him, I'd have him. I don't want, so I haven't had. We're...friendly. Now let's go to the store, Cozies."

I sighed. "Fine. Whatever."

While I'd come around and tried to fit in more with the locals, Isaac was wearing a salmon-colored button-up shirt I knew cost a pretty penny and a pair of beige shorts. He was who he was, and I loved that about him, even though I liked to give him shit.

We made the quick drive to the store, and the second we stepped inside, I felt like everyone was looking at me.

"We should make me a shirt that says something like, *Yes, I'm the long-lost Mitchell.*"

"Oh, sweetie. It's cute you think it matters. They already know, and they'll be looking and gossiping regardless. That's just how it works."

He was right, of course.

We made it halfway through the produce aisle before I was stopped for the first time. It was an older man who looked to be in his eighties. "You're that Mitchell boy."

I smiled. "Guilty." I immediately regretted my word choice. I still couldn't wrap my brain around the stuff my grandfather had done.

"How do we know you're really a Mitchell? And that your daddy wanted you to take over?"

"Um…because the lawyer, from here, who also happens to be my dad's best friend, tracked me down? And I knew nothing about this place?"

"He's opening back up, Dick," a woman stepped up to say. "You leave this poor boy be. He's been through enough. I heard his mama abandoned him and he lived on the streets most of his childhood."

"So? Wass that gotta do with anything?" said Dick, who was, in fact, a dick.

"He's one of those tragic stories, ya know?" the woman replied.

The two of them continued arguing back and forth about me as if I wasn't there.

"My mother didn't abandon me," I snapped. "She died."

The woman, at least, looked like she felt guilty, but Dick the dick just grumbled and walked away.

"You don't pay them any mind, boy. We're happy to have you here. It's your birthright. Just takes folks a while, is all." She patted my arm and walked away.

Turning toward Isaac, I cocked a brow at him.

"Okay, so maybe I understand why you didn't want to go to the grocery store." Then his eyes widened, and he got this giddy smile on his face. "We should invite our cowboys over for dinner!"

"Um, where did that come from?"

"*Duh.* My busy brain. I'm texting now."

I sure as shit wasn't going to argue with him. I wanted more of Brody's sweet mouth. That man did it for me in a way I wasn't sure anyone had.

We finished our shopping trip and were back home, putting groceries away, when Isaac said, "Walker said they'll be here."

Heat I had no business feeling pooled low in my gut. I was more excited about this development than I had any right being.

The rest of the day flew by. I helped Isaac put together a lasagna for dinner, then showered and changed into a pair of jeans and a T-shirt, right as there was a knock. "I got it," I called out.

I opened the front door to see Brody standing there, Walker beside him. Brody had a rosiness to his cheeks I was pretty sure had more to do with being in the sun all day than anything else. His eyes were tired, though, bloodshot, and his body a little tense.

"No breaking the door down this time?" I teased.

"I wanted to, but Walker said it wasn't polite." Brody smiled, and I felt myself relax, as if everything was okay simply because he grinned. Damn sexy Southern boy was going to kill me.

"Well, he's no fun."

"I'm fun," Walker countered.

"I'll be the judge of that, sugar." Isaac came in and winked. "If you're lucky. And that's right, correct? The sugar. Y'all say that?"

"Stop saying y'all." I thumped his ear.

"Ouch. Be nice."

We all chuckled, and they came in.

Isaac grabbed Walker's hand and tugged him toward the kitchen. "You come with me."

Walker looked over his shoulder at Brody as if he had no idea what to do.

I said, "Isaac is going to keep him on his toes."

"Good," Brody replied. "He needs it."

He leaned against the door and pushed his hands into his pockets. I got the feeling something was wrong. "Everything okay?"

"Yeah, just O'Ralley stuff. Big Daddy's been a little crazier than usual. We got—you know what? Never mind. You don't want to hear that."

"I wouldn't have asked if I didn't."

"Oh, well, what I mean is, they'll kick my ass if I tell you." We both laughed again. I knew he was joking but not. "By the way," he continued, "you definitely haven't done yourself justice as far as your line of work. I googled you, and you're far more business-savvy than you let on. I didn't take a Mitchell to be the humble sort."

"Aw, I'm touched. You were thinking about me?" I said playfully.

Brody's voice was deep, hoarse, and serious when he said, "Yeah."

"Come on." My cock was already starting to plump up. Oh, the things I wanted to do to him would likely make this sweet Southern boy blush.

I led him to the office. The second I had the door closed, I used my body to push him against it, roughly taking his mouth. Brody responded in kind, his hands urgent, wild as he grabbed my hair, then slid them down my back and squeezed my ass, then back up to tangle in my hair again, like he didn't know where he wanted to touch me.

He tasted like mint and smelled like sunshine and barley, something I wouldn't have thought would be so heady until I met him.

We were both hard as we thrust against each other, frantically kissing like we were in a plane going down and each other's mouths were a source of oxygen.

"Fuck." I pulled away and pressed my forehead to

his. "I don't know what it is about you, but you go straight to my head."

He was breathing heavily as he replied, "Yeah, you with me too."

I pulled back, before I ended up on my knees for him. "I, um, don't think I ever thanked you for that night on the porch, for listening to that shit I told you and for keeping it to yourself—and, well, taking care of me when I was drunk and acting like a teenager being given liquor for the first time."

"You don't gotta thank me for that."

"But I want to. It's…a lot. I'm still trying to process it all, ya know? I grew up knowing my mom died when I was young and not knowing anything about my past. I figured my dad didn't know about me or want me, and after Byron found me so easily, I sure as shit knew my dad hadn't wanted me. Then to hear all the stories in town and to read his words about my mom…about me…and to know he did what he did because he cared. Well, it's a lot, and fuck, I'm rambling and embarrassing myself. I'm not on my game. I just wanted to say thank you, is all."

Brody was looking at me, this intense stare I couldn't read. Then he stepped forward, put his hand at the back of my neck, and tugged me closer, pressing a quick, hard kiss to my lips. "You and I are gonna be in a world of trouble, I think."

Somehow I knew he was right. "We're Mitchells and O'Ralleys. We're supposed to be trouble for each other, though I'm thinking not in the same way we are."

"No shit." He snickered. "Maybe we should get out there. Walker will be wondering." He hesitated for a moment, then added, "I don't know yet—and it's not because I don't trust you. It's just all the other shit—but if I can manage it without raising any red flags, would you be willing to look at some O'Ralley business stuff in private and see if you have any ideas to help us?"

Shit. I'd wondered if they were struggling or in trouble in any way. "Yeah, of course. You can trust me to do right by you."

Brody nodded slowly. "I know...just trying to think if it's worth my ass getting handed to me, is all. You Mitchells are nothing but trouble."

"So I've been told, but I'm pretty sure the same can be said about you O'Ralleys. My dad might have not been like the rest of his family and worked to get this place legit, but he also didn't trust a bone in an O'Ralley's body." I assumed, at least, given the whole feud thing.

"I'm crushed," he teased.

"Well, I know there's at least one of your bones I like." I brushed my hand over his bulge, and Brody hissed.

"Be good. You'll get me hard again, and they'll know."

We began walking down the hallway toward the kitchen. I spoke softly, "Now, *that* feels like a challenge. I'm gonna have to spend all dinner trying to make you crazy for me without letting Walker and Isaac know what I'm doing."

Brody's foot caught on a rug, and he almost tripped. "You wouldn't."

"Oh, I assure you I would…and will." This was going to be fun.

CHAPTER TWELVE

Brody

COHEN MADE GOOD on his promise of a little foot-action during our meal. Exchanging glances during this tit-for-tat, we seemed to be making a game out of navigating our feet high up each other's legs as we enjoyed getting away with it around Walker and Isaac.

Cohen was intriguing, beguiling…and just plain fun.

I'd known some sexy guys in my life, but there was something different in the way Cohen Mitchell oozed sex appeal. And apparently it made me ooze enough during our game that Walker asked if I'd spilled some of my drink when he noticed the spot on the crotch of my pants.

What Cohen and I did together—the kiss in the

bar, making out in the kitchen, getting off together in the deer stand, and playing footsie under the table—was this combination of innocence and wickedness that felt so fucking right.

A part of me wanted to stay behind at his place so we could wrestle out another load together...oh, that would be fun...but another part enjoyed how everything we did seemed to happen at just the right time, at the perfect, right pace. I didn't want to spoil it by forcing something too soon.

I'd just gotten home and was passing by Dwain's room, when he said, "Are you fucking whistling?"

I stepped back and peeked through the door. His and Lee's double beds were still in there, just as they'd been when we were kids. Lee had his earphones in, head turned toward the wall. Dwain lay across his covers in his tighty-whities, making it impossible not to notice his cock stretching out across the top of his thigh. He looked up from the book he was reading.

"It doesn't look like Nietzsche is stimulating you very much tonight," I remarked, and he furrowed his brow, like any slighted little bro would.

"I get a hard-on the more I read about Perspectiv-ism," he said as facetiously as he could manage. "Now what the fuck were you whistling about?"

His expression was all suspicion, as if he could read on my face, *I've been doing very naughty things with that Mitchell boy*. And wanted to do a lot more. I said, "Are you the whistling police all of a sudden?"

"Can't you just answer my question?"

"Can't you mind your own business?"

He rolled his eyes, clearly not in the mood to go back and forth with me. "Whatever. I don't give a shit." He glanced at Lee, as if making sure he couldn't hear us over his music, then slipped out of bed and headed toward me.

It was hard not to notice how his dick shifted in his briefs. "Are you getting harder walking over here?" I asked, raising my arms defensively.

"Oh, probably. You know, I wear these because they fit me just right, you know?" He winked.

"Just keep it at arm's length," I teased. I had no desire for him to ruin my own arousal from everything that had happened over at Cohen's.

He shook his head and frowned. "Look, I saw Big Daddy in his office earlier, and he looked… You know how he's getting, and he's not gonna talk to me or Lee about anything. You mind checking on him?"

Ugh. I liked Dwain more when he was acting like an ignorant blockhead, but seeing his worry about Big Daddy reminded me that, at the end of the day, he was the O'Ralleys' ignorant blockhead, with a much softer side than the hard exterior he too often presented.

I agreed to check on Big Daddy and headed back downstairs to his office. I knocked gently on the door and heard him call out, "Come in." When I opened the door, I saw him sitting at his desk, a stack of envelopes and papers in front of him. I could see by his red face and watery eyes why Dwain had asked me to come down.

"Hanging in there, Big Daddy?" I headed to the chair in front of his desk and took a seat.

"Don't figure it matters much how I hang in if I can't hold this place together." He rested his hand on a paper on the table, sighing. "It's nothing, Brodes. Just same as usual. A lot of bills coming in all at once. I had to call the bank and get another line of credit today."

He leaned back and pressed his thumb and forefinger against his forehead, massaging like he was trying to soothe a migraine.

"It'll be okay, Big Daddy. We'll sort it out. We've

been through hard times before, and we can get through them again." It was the kind of thing I said without believing it myself. Not entirely. More a hope than anything else.

He took a long breath. "Yeah…you know, we've had some good runs, but the O'Ralley brand just isn't what it used to be. Distribution has gotten harder and harder as the competition has increased even more, as if it hasn't always been hard enough in our line of work."

He was really not going to be happy once he discovered that I was actually working with future competition, but I also realized our financial problems were more than that.

"And then PR has become something else to me. All these kids have their Instagrams and TikToks and twatters…"

"Twitter…it's Twitter," I said quickly.

"Whatever it is, I don't get any of it. And the further behind I get, well, the more I feel like the horse that falls behind in a race. A whole legacy failing under my leadership."

"Hey." I reached across the desk and rested my hand on his arm. "That's not gonna happen. Just about time to show everyone the dark horse the O'Ralley family really is, right?"

He smirked, but I could tell a little encouragement wasn't going to break his mood.

I noticed his gaze drift and settle on the adjacent wall. I looked to his and Big Momma's wedding photo, set on a shelf. Big Momma's familiar bright smile gazed back, the kind that had the power to put hope into the most hopeless of souls.

When I turned back to him, he looked even more somber than before.

"Big Momma would be proud of everything you've done," I told him. "What we have here is a unique opportunity, right?"

He chuckled. "I think what we have here is the need for a miracle."

"Well, I might just have one up my sleeve." I thought about Cohen. I didn't know if he'd actually be able to help us out, but it was the best I had. "Now I know you've always liked to keep the financials to yourself, but I think it's time you let us kids get in the trenches and see what we can do."

He glanced around the room, clearly struggling with the thought.

"Big Daddy, if you do make this work, we're still gonna be the ones who have to run this place someday. And if we don't, what does it matter?"

I could see the tears shifting around in his eyes, and from this man who rarely showed emotion outside frustration and anger, it broke my fucking heart.

"Brody, it's not that I don't trust you kids with it. Just…honestly, it's a matter of pride." His words caught me by surprise. "Truth is, it's been a combination of legacy and luck that helped us get this far because…I haven't had the sense to figure out how to make this place profitable. Big Momma was always good with the books and managing and navigating the budget, but after she passed, I gave up for a bit, and as soon as I came back to it, I'd made such a mess of things, it just kept piling up on me. I fear she's up in heaven somewhere, looking down on me with such disappointment."

"Big Daddy, we both know she'd probably slap you upside the head for being stupid, but then she'd get on to loving you, same as always."

He laughed again, sniffling. "Yeah, that sounds like her. But you're right, Brodes. I can't do this on my own. So…I'll give you access to the books. See if we can salvage any of this mess I've made."

I could sense his sorrow, his feeling of defeat. I squeezed his arm gently to offer some comfort. As he rested his hand on top of mine and a warm smile pushed across his face, I felt his tension dissipate as he seemed to realize this wasn't just his burden to bear anymore.

Big Daddy made good on his word, granting me access to our QuickBooks and showing me where all the major financial statements were kept in his office. He went through the debts owed and the less than stellar profits we had coming in for the year.

As I should have expected, it was even worse than I'd anticipated, and I could see why he was so stressed out about it. It wasn't something he should have had to carry on his own for as long as he had.

After our chat, I headed up to my room, stewing on the news. I pulled out my phone, looking up No Good Mitchell's number and debating about hitting it. Although, if I'd learned anything that night, it was that it wasn't good to stew on secrets.

So I called.

I was kind of hoping he'd be in bed and not answer, but then I heard that sexy-ass voice. "Missing me already?"

I snickered.

"What's wrong?"

"How do you know something's wrong?"

"I was pretty damn hilarious, and all I got was a chuckle?"

"Just had a…interesting chat with the head of the O'Ralley household."

"Everything okay with Big Daddy?"

"Yeah…and no. I went through the books with him for the first time in my life, and it wasn't pretty. To say we're having a cash-flow challenge seems like an understatement."

"It can't be that bad."

"Problem is, Big Daddy's been running this place same as he has since his dad did before him, and if we want to survive, we're gonna need to make some changes with how we do things. Catch up to the market."

"That's funny that you called me just now. I happen to know a guy who's starting a distillery, and he's pretty good at shit like this. He might be able to help you."

"Oh, really?" I said, laughing. "He any good?"

"I mean, you've had a preview of his work, but you really can't go running home to Daddy after dinner if you expect to know if he's any good for real."

I laughed again, enjoying the relief he offered from my far more serious conversation with Big Daddy.

"He expensive?"

"Real expensive. You have to give him a lot of BJs to get him to do anything."

"I have to give the BJs? What if I just let him give me the BJs?"

"So greedy, Mr. O'Ralley. No, no, you get down on your knees and worship his cock if you want him to help you with anything."

"What if he needs some help from me with this brand-new distillery?"

"Then you guys have to arrange BJs the other way for that. Negotiations. It's the only way to do business."

I rolled my head back as I laughed again, stroking my hand over my crotch, noticing I was already getting hard just thinking about his mouth around my dick again. "Sounds like a lot of dick is gonna get sucked."

"Until I can trick you into giving me some hole."

"Oh, trick me, now? Is that how you're gonna get it?"

"Depends," he said, his voice full of mischief. "Do you enjoy being tricked?"

"Only if I like the guy doing the tricking. But I expect an even exchange."

"Well, that's all going to depend on how good you are at negotiating, really."

God, he made me feel so silly and playful. I fucking loved it, about as much as I loved how he was already getting me leaking.

"Anyway, I'd better rub one out and get going to bed," he went on. "Got a busy day tomorrow, especially now that we're meeting up to chat about the O'Ralley family secrets."

"Do you need to get off the phone so you can rub one out?"

"In business, we call this *leverage*. It means I withhold this thing that you want so I'm more likely to get what I want from you next time I see you."

"This sounds like playing dirty to me."

"Oh, Mr. O'Ralley, don't worry. You'll get to see just how dirty doing business with me can be…"

We shared another laugh before saying good night.

I got off thinking about that pretty mug and all the snark and attitude he'd offered over the phone. As stressful a night as it was after I got home, I had a good feeling that maybe, just maybe, Cohen could help us get this place on the right track again.

CHAPTER THIRTEEN

Cohen

B RODY SAT IN the chair beside me. We were at the desk in what had been Harris Mitchell's office, where we'd spent the last two hours looking over the O'Ralley business. I'd been surprised when he'd come over and allowed me to look at it. We'd joked the night before about it, but teasing about getting your dick sucked was different from actually letting the enemy look at your books, especially when said enemy had admitted that their family had been money-laundering criminals. Not that getting head wasn't pretty fucking important. I quite liked it and took it seriously, but yeah, I hadn't expected him to be so open. Knowing what I did about his family, this wasn't a small thing. Big Daddy would freak the fuck out. Brody had taken a risk. I'd work my ass off to do right by him.

"It's pretty bad, isn't it?" he asked after I went over some ideas and a game plan with him.

I sighed. I respected Brody too much to bullshit him, to sugarcoat it, because somehow I knew that if the situation were reversed, he would do the same for me. I didn't want to be treated with kid gloves, and I couldn't imagine he did either. "Yeah. It's definitely not good."

"Shit." Brody dropped his head back, looking at the ceiling. His throat worked as he swallowed, then looked over at me. "Thanks for being honest."

"It's all part of my evil plan. That's how we Mitchells are. I've got you in my trap now."

He grinned, cocked a brow at me. "What are you going to do with me now that I'm here?"

A flash of different scenes played in my head: Brody on his knees for me, looking up at me with my dick in his mouth. Bent over this desk, and me being the first man to have a go at his ass. Driving him wild with my mouth because last time I sucked him, I didn't get to swallow his load, and I was all about the reward of sucking cock...

"Ooh, must be good," Brody said, breaking

through my thoughts. "You gonna tell me?"

"I don't think I will. I'm going to make you suffer for a little while first."

He chuckled. "Oh, fuck you."

"Fuck *you*? I'd like to, yeah." I saw him tremble, but I wasn't sure if he noticed it. Brody recovered quickly and rolled his eyes, but I could tell I got to him. Was that something he thought about?

"Whatever. You city boys are cocky."

"And you country boys aren't?" I cocked a brow, then forced myself to get serious. "I know it's hard not to think about what it would be like to see me naked, but I want you to know we're gonna fix this. *I'm* gonna help you fix this." The possessiveness in my tone didn't escape me. I wanted to do some good, something that was right. I wanted to be the one to help Brody out of this mess, as if that would help absolve my family of their sins. And maybe because I liked the big, sexy country boy. "I think if you can get Big Daddy to start putting some of the ideas I gave you into action, it'll help. I've got Isaac working on some PR stuff for you guys too. And let's face it, we could also play off this rival distillery thing in a public, carefully controlled way—Mitchell Creek and

O'Ralley Whatever, coming together? I have some thoughts brewing, but I think we could do something with it that'll bring attention our way." I liked the possibility of working with Brody. Maybe I shouldn't. I'd already had one friend use me, but something about Brody...I couldn't even put it to words, but I knew he wouldn't do that. He was honest, and he'd fight like hell for me. Maybe I'd realize one day that I was wrong, but I didn't think so. With Teddy, I'd had a bad feeling but hadn't trusted my gut. It wasn't the same with Brody.

"Big Daddy would lose his shit if I brought that up."

"Then Big Daddy just might lose his distillery. I'm not the rest of my family. I'm not Arthur or Bobby Mitchell." I hated that they'd been dirty, that they spent years using Mitchell Creek for illegal activity. That my dad had been forced to send Mom away to protect us. That my family possibly stole from Brody's. But my dad had changed that, and I sure as shit intended to keep his work going and do some good with what I'd been given.

"I don't want to talk about work shit anymore." His voice was husky and rough. I tried not to show him how much he affected me, but my dick was already starting to swell.

"Oh yeah? What do you want to talk about, O'Ralley?"

"We've done enough talking for now, don't you think, Mitchell?"

My breath hitched when he grabbed my chair, his hands on the armrests, and pushed it away from the desk. Brody stood above me with a very obvious bulge in his jeans.

"Got something you want to share with me?" I rubbed the back of my hand over the lump beneath his fly.

Brody's hand shot out, surprising me. He wrapped it around my wrist, then went to tug me to my feet, but I pulled right back. He stumbled forward, but then the chair rolled. Brody kept going, pushing my seat backward until it clunked against the wall.

"I think you owe me some gratitude, don't you?" My eyes darted down to my erection, achy and uncomfortable already.

"That's how you want it, huh? You want me to suck you off for the first time because I owe you?" He crossed his arms, and damn it, he had a point.

"No, I want you to blow me because you want the taste of my dick on your tongue."

He paused a moment, and I could see the shock on his face. I was sure Brody wasn't used to hearing lovers talk to him like that, but if there was one thing I knew about him already, it was that he could give as well as he could take. Brody matched me that way. "Or choking on your cock the way you'll be doing mine."

Before I could respond, his mouth crushed mine. He tasted like lust, that sharp fucking tongue of his pushing into my mouth, taking control right from my grasp. We battled that way, Brody taking and me giving.

I tried to stand up, but he wouldn't let me. He held me down, kissed the hell out of me, then tugged me to my feet. "You bossy fucker. Stop trying to get everything on your terms."

"Like you're not doing the sam—" His words were cut off by my lips against his, my tongue in his mouth as we stumbled toward the couch, kissing and tugging at clothes that didn't want to come off because our lips were fused together.

When I pulled back, Brody gasped, leaned in, his mouth trying to chase mine. Instead, I pulled his shirt off, then mine. Before I could recover, he pushed me down to the couch. I caught his belt loop with two fingers and jerked him down with me.

I lay down, Brody on top of me. He thrust his jean-covered erection against mine, the simple movement making me nearly beg for more. He went straight to my head, made me feel lust-drunk, desire-drunk, but also curious-drunk and happy-drunk in this strange way I had no business feeling about a guy I didn't know.

"What is it about you?" he asked before nipping at my neck, then sucking.

"Get out of my head," I replied, because he'd been thinking of something so similar to me.

"What?" He looked down at me, his brows drawn together.

"Nothing." I pulled him down so we were kissing again, practically humping each other on the damn couch. I wanted to strip him bare, take him to my room, get him out of all his clothes, and take my time with him, but I was too turned on, too hungry for him to even try.

I growled when he pulled away, then slid to his knees on the floor. Brody's fingers shook as he unbuttoned and unzipped my jeans. I lifted my hips and let him pull them and my underwear off. My cock jerked against my stomach, a pearl of precum at the tip that I wiped off and licked.

"Oh fuck, that was hot."

"You gonna take your clothes off too?" I asked.

He stood, and I leaned forward, worked his pants open and tugged his jeans and briefs down. I stopped at his feet and let him worry about taking them the rest of the way off, while I leaned in and nuzzled his groin. I inhaled, let his heady, masculine scent make me feel drunk that way too.

I looked up at him and lapped at his balls as Brody ran his fingers through my hair. I swiped my tongue across his slit, tasting his precum too. "Now I have both of us on my tongue. You gonna do anything about that, O'Ralley?"

"I'm going to drive you fucking wild."

I had no doubt he was, but I also knew this was a first for him, so I put a hand on his cheek and asked, "You sure?"

"If I wasn't, I wouldn't be here. Don't you know me by now? I'm already in a whole lot of trouble with you, No Good Mitchell, so I might as well go all in."

Brody's eyes didn't leave mine as he leaned forward and licked a strip up my shaft. "Oh fuck." I nearly jolted off the couch.

He smiled. "I'm gonna be good at this."

"Less talking, more sucking," I teased, and he laughed before getting to work again.

He watched me as he sucked me into his mouth. He used his hand in unison, working me up until my thighs started to shake, maybe my whole damn body. I moved my hips a little, thrust into the hot suction of his mouth. My hand knotted in his hair, and Brody moaned around my cock like he was in fucking heaven.

Christ, he really was fucking good at this. My balls were tight, aching. I fought it off, not wanting to give in, wanting to feel his mouth on me all damn day if I could, but then he took me deeper, gagged a little. My hand tugged at his hair, Brody whimpered this deep, rough sound, and that was all it took. I swear it felt like stars and light danced behind my eyelids, this vivid burst of brightness. I cried out, let loose as I shot my load down his throat.

Brody took it, swallowed me down, and damned if that didn't make me shoot again.

My bones melted, but I wasn't done with him yet. He shoved to his feet and went to stroke his cock, but I swatted his hand away, leaned forward, and sucked him.

I was a damn good cocksucker. I took him to the back of my throat, swallowed around him as Brody thrust between my lips. It didn't take long for his thighs to tighten under my hands, his cock to spasm as he filled my mouth with his release.

I swallowed, looked up at him, and winked. "You didn't think I was going to let you have all the fun, did you?"

He was breathing heavily, ran his fingers through my hair, and answered with, "We are so fucked."

Yeah, somehow I knew he was right.

CHAPTER FOURTEEN

Brody

HAVING WORKED UP a sweat with Cohen, I rinsed my face in his bathroom, inspecting myself in the mirror to make sure I didn't have a bit of Cohen sliding off my lips. Not a trace, something I was damn proud of since I swallowed his load like a champ.

We are so fucked.

That was an understatement.

As much as I didn't know what to do about Cohen Mitchell, I clearly didn't have any difficulty making sense of what to do with his cock.

I couldn't get that sensation out of my mind—how it pushed my mouth open as I took more and more, sliding along the base of my tongue. I'd wanted to impress him with how I could blow him, but then he blew me...and I felt like such a goddamn amateur.

Something I'd have to figure out before next time.

Next time?

Yeah, this was definitely a problem, the sort I didn't have any intention of making go away, no matter how angry Big Daddy might get if he found out, which wasn't happening anyway, so what did it matter? But if it didn't really matter, why did I have to keep reminding myself of that fact?

I finished up in the bathroom, and found Cohen in the kitchen. He closed the microwave door, mashing his thumb on a few buttons before pressing Start.

"Did I work up an appetite for someone?" I approached the dining table and put my hand on the back of a chair.

He turned to me, folding his arms and leaning back against the stove. "Just decided you're going to stick around for dinner, so if you have a few other BJs lined up, might as well cancel them."

God, I wished I could have kept from smiling at that. "Gonna have a lot of disappointed dicks waiting."

"Look, greater men than you have begged me to make them my world-famous stroganoff, so a simple thank-you is all I need from you."

"Greater men than me? Now I'm not sure I can trust anything you say." That familiar warm smile spread across his face, so I added, "Well, that smile lets me know I at least made the top five."

"Top five?" He pondered for a moment. "Maybe the top ten."

"Fucking contrarian. Your quick defense must mean I'm all the way in the top three. Damn, I'm good."

He laughed and rolled his eyes. "I don't think egos like ours were ever intended to be in the same room together," he said, and didn't I know it. "A BJ isn't an impressive list to make it on," he went on, not denying my claim, which was good enough for me.

"So what would be the most impressive list?"

He didn't have to think long. "Top Five Ass."

"Well, you've seen my ass, so…"

"Not your actual ass. Like topping and bottoming."

"Oh…oh…" That should have been more obvious to me, but something about the idea…seemed way too much for me at the moment.

He must've noticed my expression because he burst into a laugh. "Don't worry, Brodes. I know you like to take it slow."

"I think you can hardly say that what happened in the office was *slow*."

"No, I would say the pacing was just right. But if you work on your stroke and sucking skills, you could have a chance at the number-one spot."

"Challenge accepted," I said. "So what's it gonna take for me to get to number one in the ass and dick department?"

"Number one? Maybe you should lower your expectations a little, newbie."

"New but ambitious."

He laughed, shaking his head. "I'm assuming this means you don't have an issue staying for dinner."

"You can't just let a guy suck and go? You seem needy."

"This meat is about to go bad, and Isaac and I aren't going to be able to finish it by ourselves."

"Sure, it's the meat's fault that I need to stick around," I said skeptically as I approached him at the stove, assessing his pretty face before leaning in and licking his lips.

"Be careful about tempting a Mitchell, O'Ralley."

I snickered. "Careful isn't going to work for me."

I licked across his bottom lip, and he moved forward for a kiss. I leaned back quickly, turning my lips away, a cruel tease, and he let me know it as he nibbled against my jaw.

It was such a strange exchange, some primal impulses acting out, the animals in us just wanting to tear off our clothes and find out on the kitchen table who was the alpha male. It was the only sort of competition I could think of that would end with two winners regardless of the outcome.

"I should text Walker to let him know I won't be home for dinner," I said, retrieving my phone from my back pocket, and noticed the hard-on Cohen was sporting. I couldn't resist giving it a pat before taking a seat at the table. Cohen found his way into the adjacent chair, checking the timer on the meat as I let Walker know I was busy, hoping he wouldn't press for why.

"You guys always have dinner together?" Cohen asked.

"Not all the time. Some of us work shifts over dinner, and we've got errands from time to time. Unless someone's attending a conference or something, we try to make sure to be there on weekends.

We usually have breakfast and dinner together then. Something we did with Big Momma...a family tradition we like to keep alive."

"That's nice. It was always different in my household. With my adoptive parents, that is. Dad had to work a lot of late nights, and even when he was around, he was mainly talking to me about business. Mom wasn't the type for cooking, so it was a lot of hamburgers and pizza on the couch. Looking back, I think I wound up cooking more homemade meals for them than the other way around. Don't get me wrong, I love them for taking me in. Just...I don't know, when you talk about your connection with your family, I can say it definitely didn't feel like that. And then there's this part of me that wonders how it would have been with my biological mom, a thought I try not to indulge too much because I was one of the lucky ones to get to have kind adoptive parents."

"I would think that's a pretty natural thing to consider," I said, unable to even contemplate a childhood without my parents. Silence stretched between us, like we were both taking a moment for the ones we'd lost. When I felt satisfied with the time we'd offered up, I went on, "When we were younger, Big Daddy used to say that he was going to have to leave this world before Momma because he didn't think he could bear it without her. Guess life showed him…"

"Do you mind if I ask how she…?" He hesitated to say the word.

"I don't know how you feel about it, but I'm fine if you say *died*. I've always fucking hated when people would talk about her *passing…moving on…leaving*. Of all the things, she sure as fuck didn't leave us. Didn't have a choice. And moving on or passing makes it seem…far more painless and peaceful than it was." My thoughts drifted back to the hospital, and then to the hospice. "I think the only thing that made it peaceful were the painkillers they had her on. Pancreatic cancer, by the way. From the time we found out to the end, had about three months."

Cohen's hand slid across the table and took me by my wrist, his thumb moving gently through the hairs on my arm. "I'm so sorry."

Even though words like those usually felt trite to me, I could really feel how much he meant them. I knew they weren't only for my experience, but because of his own loss.

"The reason I'm even over here is that Big Daddy

has gotten the business to this state because of what happened with Momma. We all pitched in to be there for him, as best we could, but for a while, well…we weren't sure he was even going to stick around to take care of the place."

The expression on his face made it evident he got my meaning.

"That said, I think he feels guilty that the finances are in bad shape, even if he was barely holding on to his life at the time, let alone the distillery."

"He clearly loved your mother a lot."

"I think we all took for granted that she was going to be around forever."

"I know the feeling."

His words pulled me out of my own grief, shifted my attention to his.

"I was so young when it happened, though, and I have great memories of her smiling and laughing with me. We lived in this little apartment. She loved decorating it. We'd do crafts together and put them up all over the house. She kept a bunch in a bin too. I always wondered what they were for. Maybe she kept them for my dad." He paused, then continued, "She was always laughing and playing. Once in a while, when she thought I wasn't paying attention, I would catch her looking sad. I'd ask her what was wrong, and she'd say she was missing someone, and then make a joke, and that easy, the subject would be changed. I'm glad that most of what I can remember are those good times, but they definitely leave me wondering about what could have been."

I rested my hand on top of the one he held to my wrist, and we gazed into each other's eyes.

As much fun as it was to see the playful, frisky Cohen I'd come to know, there was something special about seeing this side of him.

I wasn't sure if he was anything like me, but I didn't share shit like that...not with my family, or my friends, or anyone, really. But for a moment, as we held each other, as I felt his comfort and support, I didn't feel so goddamn alone.

He started to say something just as the microwave beeped, interrupting a moment that had gone from being so playful to somber-as-hell far too quickly.

As he retrieved the plate of beef from the micro-wave and placed it on the counter, I checked for a reply from Walker.

Good. Dwain was going to make lasagna. *barf*

It brought my mood up a bit as I imagined my brother's face when Dwain put his watery lasagna down in front of him.

"Based on Walker's text, sounds like I'm dodging a bullet this evening," I told Cohen.

He fished through the cupboards for some supplies, saying, "You guys are clearly very family oriented, but I'm surprised you don't have any families of your own. I would have expected, given your ages, you'd all be married with kids."

"Walker, obviously, has a conflict of interest with that. I just have a great talent for picking out partners who are never all that serious. Dwain and Lee would have to spend five minutes out of each other's sight to get girls...or anyone, for that matter. But we did almost have a little one. Mel got pregnant two years ago, while she was in school. And, life had other plans. Sorry, I didn't mean to bring that up. We were just getting out of the serious territory."

"No, I'm glad you did. I'm glad we've talked about everything we have. You know, sometimes it's hard to remember what an amazing cock you're sucking." He glanced over his shoulder, winking at me, and it lightened my mood once again.

"We O'Ralleys are big on our secrets, as you can probably tell, so it's nice to have someone to talk to about some of these things that we just sort of sit on as a family."

He stopped fiddling with the box of noodles, set it on the counter, and approached me again. "I told you, I trust you, and it's nice seeing that you trust me enough to share this stuff. Sometimes it feels like we have to carry these things on our own, and it's nice when we don't, for even a little bit of time. Anyway, what fun would BJs be if we didn't have something we needed cheering up from?"

The playful expression on his face got me snickering again.

I fidgeted a bit, searching around. "You have to have some whiskey around here. This is not the kind of talk that needs to be had without some of that crap Mitchell whiskey."

He laughed. "Yeah. I'll pour you a glass. I think we could both use a stiff drink after that conversation."

"You guys finished blowing each other or what?" I heard beside us, and turned to see Isaac standing in the doorway.

I froze. Had he fucking seen us messing around?

"Yeah, you know, we got each other off, and then I agreed to make him some dinner," Cohen said as though it were a joke.

Isaac rolled his eyes, which assured me he hadn't actually seen anything. "Whatever. The Wi-Fi at the bookstore didn't work as well as I figured it would, so might as well use my phone hotspot. I'll be upstairs, working."

"Just make sure to get your ass down here for dinner."

"No, I really need to—" His gaze settled on the ingredients on the stovetop. "Wait. Are you making stroganoff? Okay. I'll be down. Just holler for me."

I chuckled as Isaac headed off. "You must make some damn good stroganoff."

He shrugged. "It's aight, I guess."

I couldn't stifle my laugh. "Yeah, you might want to give up the humble act, Cozies. Doesn't really fit you."

He wore a cocky grin as he returned to the table with a bottle and two glasses, and poured one for each of us.

With those beautiful lips curled into a smile and a mix of confidence and vulnerability that was agitating me in all the right ways, I thought about what he'd said when we were messing around—

Get out of my head.

Yeah, I had a hunch I was going to be the one struggling to get this no-good Mitchell out of my head.

CHAPTER FIFTEEN

Cohen

T HE NEXT FEW weeks were crazy. Like, "I couldn't believe how much fucking work we were doing" crazy. Isaac and I rarely stopped. We had government and licensing shit to deal with that was a fucking mess and took up a good chunk of our time. We couldn't get on track to open until we had it taken care of, but we also had to fucking make some whiskey before we could open too, which couldn't start until the other shit was dealt with.

"Can you hand me the list of farmers Brody gave us for sourcing grain?" Isaac asked. We'd put a second desk in Harris's office, so we each had our own space there now. He'd been invaluable, as always.

"Yep." I handed it over. "I was going to do some research. Obviously we want grain from different climates and soils—that adds to the flavor—but I'm hoping to find some obscure...fuck, I don't know, something different."

"Playing devil's advocate for a moment, if we go too different—at least right out of the gate—are we still Mitchell Creek? A lot of people, especially when it comes to this small-town kinda brand, want things to stay the same. Want to be comfortable, see the familiar. Your dad left you those names and recipes. You know how important branding is. People who used to drink Mitchell Creek come to it for something specific. If you change that, some will rebel."

"Yeah, but you also know that staying the same and never growing is just as big a mistake. You have to take chances."

He nodded. "Yeah, agreed. And honestly, the fucking bottling? It's shit. I really want to change that up. We can always consider something like...oh! What about like an Old Timer line of whiskey? It can be the familiar taste and packaging people have known and loved for a hundred years, and then we have...hmm...The City Boy? Start small, with one new bottle, new recipe, different grain, and test the waters."

He was a fucking genius. Outside of loving him like a brother, there was a reason I needed Isaac by my side. "I'm liking this. It's going to cost more, though. I don't know if it's in the budget Harris set aside for reopening, but I'd be willing to front the cost. I mean, we need to figure out what in the fuck we'd even do. I know jack shit about whiskey recipes, but Brody might have some ideas, and we can hire someone."

"Let me do some research, and you talk to your boy."

I let the "your boy" comment go. Brody had been invaluable to us, answering questions, giving us names and data we wouldn't know without him. It was a risk for him, one I didn't take lightly. His family was close, and I knew Big Daddy, Lee, and Dwain would see it as a betrayal if they knew he was working with...and sucking off...the enemy.

"Did you put together those marketing reports I asked you to get for the O'Ralleys? And I was trying to think of a way we can help without them knowing we're helping...silent donation? Secret Angel Investment? If Big Daddy knew it was us, he'd lose his shit, but..." But I knew that while money wasn't a problem for me—I had what Harris left and my own cash, which wasn't chump change—it was a problem for the O'Ralleys.

"Holy shit. You really like this guy, don't you?"

How could I not? He was sexy as fuck, honorable, funny, matched me with wit, spent his days working with his family and his evenings helping me and trading blowjobs. It was rare that a day went by where I didn't see him. Yeah, I liked him. "So? I like you too."

"Yeah, but my dick has never been in your throat," Isaac countered.

"We're friends who like to get each other off. That's it."

"Whatever you say, and yeah, I compiled all the marketing material. It's in a folder on your desk. How does he explain to his dad these new random ideas?"

"I have no fucking clue. And thanks." I let my chair roll over to Isaac's desk. "I want you to know how much I appreciate you. You've uprooted your life to move across the country with me to run a fucking distillery. I..."

He shrugged. "You're my brother, my family. Like I said, where else would I be?"

"Still...I, um...wanted to talk to you about meeting up with Byron and maybe see what we can do about making this a fifty/fifty thing. If you want, that is." I knew what it was like to put your heart and soul into a business only to have the rug pulled out from under you. Isaac did as well, and while I knew he would never think I'd do that to him, I wanted this to be ours.

"Wow...I... You don't have to do that."

"I want to."

"Are you sure you're not in love with me instead of Brody?" he teased.

"Fuck off. You're my family, he's my..." I didn't know what in the fuck he was, so I let it go. "Just something to think about, okay? You know I'll take care of you no matter what."

He leaned in and kissed my cheek. "I know, Cozies." Isaac stood and stretched. "And on that note, I'm going to demand a night off."

"You going to see Lauren?" Isaac was much more of a social butterfly than I was. Where I chatted some with Lauren and Rusty occasionally, he and Lauren were now text buddies, and he went to the Barn to have a drink and hang out with her every once in a while.

"Nope," he replied. "I'm going to shower, and then I'm going to...out."

I frowned. "You're going to out? But not with Lauren?" This wasn't the first time he'd taken off, but usually he said he'd be with her. I didn't always ask, though.

"Yes. I'm in demand. Who would have thought there'd be so much dick around here? My app has been going crazy."

"What am I supposed to do?" I joked.

"You could hang out with Lauren, ya know? She was asking about you. If not, call your boy. Use the folder as an excuse."

And again, I ignored him. "Do you need my car?"

"Yep. And we really need to figure something out so we can get our shit from California," he added, then made his way upstairs without another word.

I didn't take his advice. I kept working as Isaac showered and then left. I considered what I'd mentioned about the O'Ralleys, about finding a way to help, but I knew that wouldn't work. Big Daddy aside, Brody would see it as a handout. Right now, we were helping each other. If I tried to hand over money, that would be a whole different ball game.

With a sigh, I unlocked the desk drawer and pulled Harris's journal out. It was something I did often when I was alone, reading over his notes about Mitchell Creek, his confessions, his letter to me. While I'd told Isaac what the letter said, I hadn't let him read it—any of it. Not even the stuff about the distillery. It all felt too...personal, like this secret I had with a man I didn't know I cared about, one who I grew up thinking hadn't cared about me, and now had conflicting emotions about.

I flipped through it, read the letter again, then tucked it away in the drawer. The house was too quiet, and I was starting to feel edgy. Hell, the only time I left the property was for grocery shopping or on business-related errands. It still felt weird to be in town. Everyone always had their eyes on me, and it was fucking crazy how many different stories about my past, my family, and my mom there could be. I was fed a different one every time.

Shoving to my feet, I went to the kitchen, looked through the cabinets and the fridge. Of course there was nothing to eat. Well, there were things to eat, but nothing I wanted.

Grumbling at myself, I tugged my phone out of

my pocket and sent a text.

I'm hungry. Feed me.

Brody texted back right away: **My cock?**

Well, that too, but food. You busy? Isaac ditched me. I can get away. What do you want?

Your cock, I replied. **But also, pizza.**

LOL. I'll be there soon.

I found myself smiling as I put my phone back into my pocket. Something about him just…got to me, this country boy with the bashful smile and sharp, sinful tongue.

It was only after five, Isaac having left pretty early. Less than an hour later, I heard a knock. I felt a stupid, annoying jump in my pulse that I didn't want to acknowledge or dissect at all.

When I pulled the door open, Brody was there with a pizza box and a smile. "What's wrong?" he asked immediately. Christ, was I that easy to read? I was still thinking about my reaction to his knock on the door.

"Nothing. I'm starving, is all."

"Well, then I guess we better get some sausage in you."

I cocked a brow. "You think so, huh? What if I wanted to feed my sausage to you?"

"I meant on the pizza. Someone always has dick on the brain." He swept inside, obviously completely comfortable there, and went to the kitchen.

"I mean, why not? Cock is great." I waggled my eyebrows.

"You're incorrigible."

"It's my trademark," I said playfully. "Whiskey, beer, water, or sweet tea—I got lemon for you. I know how you like that shit in your tea. I don't get it."

Brody paused as if I'd said something wrong.

"What?"

"You got lemon for my tea? You and Isaac don't use it?"

Oh, well, when he said it like that, it did sound like it meant something. "I needed it for a recipe," I lied.

"Hey, did you know your pants are on fire?" he teased in this almost childish way that made me laugh.

"Whatever."

Brody came up to me, backing me against the counter. "Liar, liar, pants on fire. You like me, and you don't want to admit you got lemon specifically for me."

"You O'Ralleys are cocky motherfuckers." But I

did like him, the bastard.

"And you Mitchells aren't?" he countered, then moved away, and damned if I wasn't disappointed.

We chatted about random shit as we drank and ate—Brody with the damn lemon in his tea. I told him about the folder of information Isaac had put together for him. When we finished, he asked, "So what's up with Isaac?"

"I don't know. He's being shady. I have no idea where he disappeared to today. Fucking sucks, though. We need to get his car. I'm going a little stir-crazy being cooped up in the house."

Brody frowned. "You're not trapped most of the time. You don't go out?"

Damned if I didn't feel a wave of, well, what almost felt like melancholy twisted up with embarrassment, wash over me. "It's nothing really. I mean, I go places. I just…stick out. I haven't stuck out since I was a kid in foster care. For all that Southern hospitality you're supposed to have, people look at me like I don't belong and tell me the craziest shit."

"Aw, I'll protect you when we go out—well, not that I can go out with you." He said it as a joke, but we both paused for a moment, letting that sink in. We legit were hiding our friendship because of a feud from over a hundred years ago. "Come on." Brody shoved to his feet.

"Where are we going? Into town? We can go have a drink with Lauren at the Barn."

"Um, no, but I have something maybe a little better. Do you have a blanket? And towels, we need towels. Grab a bag."

"Yes, sir!" I teased, but yeah, I was excited too.

"I got all the stuff," Brody said, stuffing everything into a backpack, then leading me out the back door and through my property.

"You sure as shit know a lot about the Mitchell land."

"I told you why. Hell, I've explored the whole damn thing."

I followed along as we made our way across the grassy hills, through the field, to the woods.

It took us a good thirty minutes before we reached the foot of a hill and the base of the creek, where a little swimming hole awaited us. It was a different spot from where Brody had taken me last time.

"Last one in is a rotten egg!" Brody ripped his shirt off, then his shoes and jeans.

"Nope. Stop right there, country boy." I walked over, hooked my fingers in the edges of his briefs, and tugged them down. "You brought me out here, I'm damn sure going to enjoy the view. You're going skinny-dipping with me."

CHAPTER SIXTEEN

Brody

"YOU NAUGHTY LITTLE fuck," I told Cohen as he slid my briefs down my legs. I stepped out of them, and he leaned in and swiped his tongue along the length of my cock. Slow, skilled movements that reminded me I had a lot of catching up to do. I was surprised at how quickly I perked up, but I hardly had time to think about that when I was busy enjoying the sensation of him taking my cock into his mouth.

He took his time, and then, in an instant it seemed, let my cock drop from his mouth, the warm air sticking to the saliva he'd left behind. I opened my eyes to see why he'd abandoned such impressive work, but he was gone.

His pants, boxers, socks, and underwear were all that remained, and had I not heard movement behind me, I would have suspected he'd spontaneously combusted while giving me a BJ.

"The hell?" I spun around to see his bare ass cheeks bouncing around as he flung his shirt off over his head.

"Looks like I'm not a rotten egg, after all," he called back to me.

"Motherfucker," I muttered, racing after him.

He was already diving in by the time I reached the pond, but I went in headfirst after him. It was just the right temperature—not too cool, only enough to quiet my lingering annoyance at having been bested by a trickster.

We resurfaced around the same time. Water streamed from his flat bangs, webbing along smooth features that reminded me so much of his father in the photo we'd seen in the tasting room.

"Sneaky fuck," I said as a broad grin stretched across his face.

"Hey, you were the one who wanted a head start, so I gave your head a start while taking one of my own. Besides, this is something an O'Ralley should have expected from a no-good Mitchell."

"Guess it was worth it since I got a good view of these melons," I said, swimming to him. When I reached him, I grabbed his ass and squeezed, thinking about how it had jiggled on his jog to the water.

"You sure do seem to enjoy a man's ass for someone who wasn't sure about his attraction to guys."

"I'm confident I would have known more about my sexuality if I'd seen this ass sooner."

A hint of pink filled his cheeks, and it was enough for me to say, "Ooh, I made you blush."

"What? Pfft. Probably sunburn."

"You always get a little sunburned when you find yourself smitten with me, Mr. Mitchell?"

The pink turned a little darker, assuring me I wasn't wrong. "Shut the fuck up—"

Before he could go on, I stole a kiss. He reeled me right in, just like he had when he'd come to this town.

I gripped both his ass cheeks, nearly gasping at how good his firm muscles felt in my hands.

The water shifted around us as we continued struggling to keep our heads above water through kisses. A splash hit my face just as we had parted our lips for an instant, pushing the water into my mouth, so that I had to pull away and spit it out.

"Damn, Mitchell. You're gonna drown us," I teased as the water around us settled.

There was something almost magical about the moment.

Maybe it was the way the sunlight glistened in Cohen's irises.

Or the way his wet hair naturally settled across his forehead in the sexiest of looks.

Or it could have been that perfect combination of cool water and a warm Georgia afternoon.

Whatever the reason, I didn't care. Just breathed it in before Cohen moved quickly, splashing water my way. I had to laugh at the friskiness of his move, and quickly returned with my own splash-assault.

The littlest of moves turned into an all-out splash fight. And just like everything else that afternoon, it was damn near perfect.

Once we'd settled that neither of us could prove victor over the splashing, I decided to show him Walker's and my favorite spot as kids, taking him to the other side of the watering hole. It was a bit of a climb up the boulder on the other side, and he made sure to give me a little city-boy hell about it, even though I could tell by the smile on his face that he was enjoying the adventure. When we reached the top, we headed along a familiar old path to where we'd jump into the water.

"When we were kids," I told Cohen, "Walker and I used to prank each other. One time I was out here with this girl Meghan, and Walker stole my clothes, so I had to sneak back into the house naked. Well, Big Daddy caught me, and needless to say, he was startled, but very proud of his show stud, as he called me after that."

Cohen busted into a laugh. "Oh, I bet he was."

"I got Walker back, though. He's scared to death of rattlesnakes, so I bought this fake snake at the Dollar General. Looked fake as hell, but put it on the top of this rock, and when he was trying to impress his own girl, oh, she certainly got to hear him sing soprano."

"It sounds like you guys had a lot of fun."

"It was a great time being a kid out here."

I led him to the drop-off on the other side of the boulder, noticing a familiar sight that had escaped my memory until that moment.

"Hey, this might be of interest to you," I said, indicating where part of the boulder protruded up about mid-thigh. It was where we'd usually sit and chat, safely out of view from anyone who might have come out looking for us.

Cohen eyed the spot on the rock, where *HM &
PW* was carved in the middle of a heart.

Considering how much fun we'd been having,
even while griping through the climb up the boulder,
it was unsettling to see how quickly his expression
turned serious.

"I knew that was your dad's, but—"

"My mom too. Pam White."

"Yeah, I kinda wondered if it might be."

He stared at it long enough to assure me there was
a lot going on in that pretty head of his.

"What are you thinking?"

"What do you imagine I'm thinking?"

"God, I don't even know where to begin," I admitted. "That it's nice seeing something that reminds you
of your parents, but then between the way your mom
died and how you never knew who your dad was…
Gotta be a lot of wondering around all that. And then
being adopted and all's gotta throw a whole other
element into it."

His eyes watered as he turned to face me. "See, you
knew what I was thinking after all." He smiled, clearly
fighting back an emotional moment.

He took a seat beside the carving, and I sat on the other side of it, giving him a chance to collect his thoughts.

He swallowed, then said, "It's hard to wrap my brain around it all sometimes. I spent five years with a mom I loved more than anything, who told me my dad loved me while I kept wondering why he wasn't around if he did. Logically, I get it. I was too young to understand, but after she passed, I was even more angry with him for not being there. Then I was adopted, and that came with its own set of conflicting emotions—gratitude, love, but never feeling quite like I fit in. Then guilt for feeling that way when there was nothing they didn't give me. Now I'm here, and still feeling guilty about that, while learning things I like and dislike about my dad and family. It's all twisted up, is all."

I couldn't help myself—I reached for him, put my hand on his, rubbed my thumb over his flesh. "Feel like this is the part where I'm supposed to tell you all the reasons why you shouldn't feel that way, but if I had all that shit going on, I would feel the same. I feel like because of how things are depicted on TV shows and in movies—or maybe because of the way we talk about things like family—we got all these ideas about how life's supposed to play out. But how many of us have simple, easy lives without curveballs that come and fuck it all up?"

"Right?" he said with a bittersweet snicker.

"But as far as your adoptive parents go…if I think about my siblings, Big Daddy and Momma always loved each of the five of us in his own way. Never the same, but I've never doubted their love, even throughout the tough times and all the bullshit life has thrown at us. And I know this might not help and it's just the words of some country bumpkin, but I can't imagine there isn't room enough in your heart to love all that your adoptive parents did *and* love the memory of your mom and dad all the same."

I knew it wouldn't magically make him feel better. Fuck, how could he with all that going on in his head? But I hoped that maybe just knowing I was doing my best to be there for him might cheer him up a bit.

The warm smile that spread across his face made me feel like I'd done that much, at least.

"Pretty smart for a country bumpkin," he remarked.

"And don't forget sexy. Real sexy country bumpkin."

I finally managed to get the chuckle I felt I deserved for my efforts, and it made me smile too, knowing I was able to cheer him up.

"It's a shame," I said, "'cause if it weren't for this stupid feud, I think Big Daddy would really like you if he got to know you."

It seemed like such a random-ass thought, but it was true.

Sitting on that rock beside Cohen, this great guy who had such a big fucking heart and who was so loyal to those who'd been good to him in his life, it was hard to imagine that Big Daddy, in his right mind, could see him as anything other than who he was.

Cohen avoided my gaze. "Seems like a safe thing to say in the middle of Mitchell country, where there's no way Big Daddy can catch the naughty things I'm doing to you."

"These aren't so naughty. You're actually being very sweet."

"Remember how you said you're slow until you're fast…yeah, I think I'm sweet…until I'm really not."

I laughed.

"God, this makes me feel so bad," he said, teasing

in his tone.

"What?"

"That I'm going to use such a touching moment to beat your ass again."

He sprang up and darted toward the drop-off.

"Oh, fuck no," I said, hopping to my feet and racing right behind him.

I grabbed his arm and tugged him back, but only gained on him a little before he threw his arms around me so that we fell off the side together.

A tie.

And when it came to Cohen Mitchell, I could live with that.

CHAPTER SEVENTEEN

Cohen

A WEEK HAD passed since we went to the swimming hole, and two things were getting harder and harder to deny: I was going stir-crazy and needed a night out, and I was beginning to like Brody more than I should.

The first was easier to deal with than the second, yet I'd made no move to do anything about it. The feeling-restless thing probably had something to do with the wanting-Brody thing. Maybe going out would help; maybe getting laid would prove I wasn't catching feelings for my country boy.

Not that he was really mine.

Not that I wanted him to be.

His family would lose their shit. This town would lose their collective shit, and that was fucking with my head.

I wasn't supposed to care what any of them thought. I still didn't know if I did, but I thought maybe a tiny, secret part of me wanted to belong, wanted to fit, which was crazy as fuck and not what this was supposed to be about. All I was supposed to do was open this damn distillery, prove to...hell, I didn't know who, but to someone, how fucking good I was at it, while helping Brody as a friend, no feelings involved, and getting some orgasms out of the deal. Everything else just complicated an already complicated situation. I didn't do complicated, but I was obviously currently obsessed with the word.

This town was making me crazy.

Case in point, I was sitting in my car in the parking lot of an ice-cream parlor, obsessing about what people would think of me and Brody O'Ralley.

About our afternoon at the swimming hole—and if that didn't sound like something out of a small-town dictionary, I didn't know what did.

About him showing me my parents' initials, which affected me more than I'd expected.

About kissing him, and playing around with him, and nearly drowning him, all in good fun, of course.

He'd tried to do the same to me.

And I was *still* sitting in my car like a crazy-ass, weird, obsessive person, so I needed to cut that shit out STAT.

I was losing my damn mind.

Knock, knock, knock.

"Shit." I looked over to see Lauren standing by the window.

"You're late and spacing off in there."

Yes, I was, but I wasn't going to tell her why. She scooted over, and I got out. She was an ice-cream fanatic, so I'd agreed to meet her here because...well, because I liked her and it wasn't as if I had anything else to do.

We went inside, and I bought us each two scoops. She got rainbow sherbet, and I got coffee flavored.

"You're such a city boy," she said, rolling her eyes, as we sat down at a table outside.

"Why?"

"Because coffee doesn't belong with ice cream."

"That's a city thing?" I took a bite.

"Sounds good to me." We were quiet for a moment before she asked, "So what's new? How's the distillery? Isaac? Kissed any more pretty O'Ralleys?"

She only knew about the kiss at the Barn. I could only imagine if she found out what Brody and I were up to. I wouldn't tell her. It wasn't my place.

"Oh my God. You have! You're blushing!"

"I don't blush," I grumbled. And even if I could talk about Brody, I wasn't going to right then because I was already being all *emo* about him. Pretty soon I'd be doodling his name in a heart. "The distillery is going."

We chatted about that for a while, and I was grateful she'd let the kissing thing go. Then she told me about a guy she went on a date with and how he kept burping through their meal. "It was so weird."

"Yeah...so when's the wedding?"

We both laughed, and hung out for a little while longer before she had to go. She was on her way to A Step Ahead, so it was a short meetup.

"See you soon, Cohen. You should come have a beer with me when you can. Also, don't fool yourself into believing I don't think you're secretly kissing an O'Ralley." She hugged me and fluttered away before I could reply.

She was a riot. I was still feeling strange about things, about Brody, and in need of something to cure my social bug that hadn't been fixed with a quick ice cream, so I drove to Murray's to pick up a few things.

I parked, grabbed my wallet and phone from the passenger seat, and got out. That's when I saw *him*— Big Daddy. I didn't need anyone to tell me who he was. He was leaning against the truck parked across from my car. I didn't know how I'd missed him until now. And I couldn't believe it had taken us this long to have a run-in.

Deciding I better get it over with, I walked over. "Good morning. I was wondering when we'd run into each other. I'm Cohen Mi—"

"Yeah, I know who you are," he cut me off.

Even knowing about our family histories from Brody and the other people around town, it surprised me that someone who didn't even know me could speak to me with such disdain in his voice.

"Yes, of course you know," I pressed on. "I just figured, from some of the things I've heard about the Mitchells and O'Ralleys since I came to town, it wouldn't be such a bad idea to have a friendly chat so you can see that, regardless of what happened in the past, we can have a perfectly friendly—"

"I don't want anything friendly with a Mitchell."

His jaw tensed, his gaze shot daggers, the sort of look that made it clear he wasn't looking at me but at some idea he'd already made up in his head.

"You think I'm some damn fool? Yeah, your ilk have always been the sweet-talking kind. We get a rap for our temper, but y'all go on with your fake smiles and friendly manner, gettin' away with hell. Don't think I don't know what you're doing."

Considering how pissed he was acting toward me, a guy he'd just met and wasn't even interested in giving a chance, I couldn't say it warmed me up to him either. But if he was trying to intimidate me, he had another thing coming. "And what is it, exactly, that you think I'm doing?"

"What your family has done for over a hundred years—try and bring down the O'Ralleys. I'm sure you know all about that. From day one they had it out for us—first getting close to Dorothy, making a side deal, tryin' to kill my granddaddy, stealing the recipe. I know your granddaddy was up to no good too, and don't try and deny it. Your mama getting close to me, probably to bring information back to your daddy."

I didn't appreciate what he'd said about my mom, but I took a deep breath and said, "My family is—"

"Always causin' trouble," he cut me off before I could say it was complicated. "Now you're suddenly here, outta the blue, opening Mitchell Creek back up, continuing where your daddy left off. You can cut the cool, slick Mitchell act because I'm onto ya, and don't you think for a second I'm not." His face was slightly red, and I could tell he was getting himself even more worked up, and damned if the old man wasn't doing the same to me.

My pulse raced, and I bit back the angry, sharp reply on my tongue. Instead, I crossed my arms and cocked a brow at him. "Sounds like you got it all figured out."

"O'Ralley has been my family's pride and joy for a hundred years. You're not gonna run us out of business."

"I have no plans to. If fact, if you're willing, I'm sure there are ways we could work together."

He blinked rapidly a few times as if he hadn't expected my reply and didn't know how to answer it. Hell, all these years, and neither family had been willing to work together? Business was business. I got that. You had to fight your way to the top if you wanted to be successful, but damn, I couldn't believe none of them had been willing to even talk to each other before. They'd carried this damn feud on like it was still a hundred years ago and the wounds were fresh.

"O'Ralleys don't work with Mitchells," he practically spit at me.

"I'm not a typical Mitchell. Before I'd been told I inherited this place, I didn't even know what being a Mitchell meant. I didn't know we made whiskey, or who my family was, and I sure as hell didn't know about a damn feud. I'm not here to run you out of business. I'm here to run my own, and I couldn't care less who stole whose woman. As for my mom, I don't think she'd do what you accused her of. I was young when she passed, and hell, maybe I'm wrong, but I don't want to think that's true. If you want to believe it, you go right ahead. Have a good day, Mr. O'Ralley."

Without another word, I walked toward the store. My hands were fisted and my breathing pushing out too fast.

I was pissed at Big Daddy for making assumptions about me. Pissed at my own family for all the dirty shit they did, angry with my dad for never coming for me, with my mom for not telling me, while in the back of my mind, fucking Brody was there with his sweet, mischievous grin and sinful kisses and listening ears. All I could think was what Big Daddy would do if he knew we were spending time together, and how in the hell this whole fucking thing was going to affect us, when that wasn't supposed to matter. Damned if it didn't, though.

After getting myself to calm down, I grumbled the whole time I did my shopping. The longer I thought about it, the more pissed and on edge I got, and the more part of me felt guilty for things I had no control over—for my family's shady past. Hell, if I were Big Daddy, I might hate me too.

But Brody didn't.

I was at the register, checking out, when the cashier said, "So...you finally had a showdown with Big Daddy, huh?"

What the hell? It was fifteen fucking minutes ago. How the hell did he know?

"Cameras." He pointed to the door. "Got 'em in the parking lot too. Georgie saw you guys out there and told Ewing. He went up and watched on the monitors. Said it looked heated. Couldn't figure out what you said, o'course."

"He wanted to welcome me to the neighborhood," I lied. "Said he was baking me an apple pie and invited me over."

The guy paused. His brows pulled together, and then he chuckled. "You almost got me for a second, but we all know that Mitchells and O'Ralleys are like oil and water. You're never going to get along."

I wished I could tell him how well I got along with Brody's dick in my mouth, but of course I didn't. I paid, grabbed my shit, and got my ass back to Mitchell Creek, where it was safe.

"What's wrong?" Isaac asked when I got home. He was sitting at the table, drinking a smoothie.

"I just ran into Big Daddy."

"Oh shit."

"Oh shit is right."

"He doesn't know, right? About Walker and Brody spending time with us?"

"No." I waved off his concern. "Can you imagine if he knew I was sleeping with Brody and you were friends with Walker?"

"Nope, can't imagine. So, what is the plan for today? What do we need to do for work?" He took a drink of his smoothie and looked away from me.

"You're being weird."

"I'm not being weird. You're being weird—you and your Brody orgasm brain. Stop projecting."

"Huh?" I frowned. "I don't even know what that means. And it's Saturday, and I'm losing my fucking mind, so we're not working. We're...hell, I don't know. We're going to Atlanta for the night."

Like I figured it would, that made Isaac perk up. "Really?"

"Yeah. I need to get away." I wondered if Brody would be willing to go, not that it should matter. I didn't need him to go out.

"What about Brody?"

"What about him?" Damn it. He was always in my head. Before Isaac could reply, my cell rang. I knew who it was without looking. Still, I tugged it out of my pocket, and sure enough, *Country Boy* flashed across the screen.

"How's it going, No Good Mitchell?"

I wasn't sure if I should tell him I ran into Big Daddy. Part of me wanted to, but I didn't want to cause any drama between them. If Big Daddy wanted him to know, he would say something himself, otherwise Brody couldn't even mention it to him without Big Daddy knowing I told him, so I decided to wait. "I really hate this fucking feud," is what I landed on.

"Um…okay? Where did that come from?"

"Sorry. I'm on edge. I just…really need a break." Forget that a moment ago I was thinking I didn't need Brody to go to Atlanta. I didn't, but I wanted him to. "You and Walker wanna get out of here tonight with me and Isaac?"

He paused for a moment. "What do you mean?"

"Atlanta? I can take you to your first gay bar."

"Pfft. I went to a gay bar in college, city boy. This ain't my first rodeo."

"Okay, I can't believe you said that, and fine, you might have gone before, but you haven't really experienced a gay bar until you've been there with me and Isaac. Unless…well, unless you can't hang." I figured he wanted to go, but I also knew that would get to him.

"Oh, fuck you. You know I can hang. I'll get Walker. We country boys will show you city boys how to have a good time."

I smiled, feeling a little better. "I'm counting on it, cowboy."

CHAPTER EIGHTEEN

Brody

A WIDE-EYED WALKER ogled the neon-pink *Flirt* sign over the bar. He looked at it as though it was something sacred as he walked through a cloud of smoke from a few guys vaping nearby. The bouncer chatted with the smokers before turning to us and perking up. Isaac and Cohen approached, greeting him with all their wit and charm, reminding me how familiar they were with this world, one that seemed so far removed from what I was used to. I assumed we would have to show the bouncer our IDs, but he waved us in, and as we crossed the threshold, it really dawned on me that we were heading into a gay bar with the enemy.

Our unofficial gay-bar guides effortlessly navigated us through the crowd, to the main bar, where we ordered a round of drinks. I searched around the space, taking it all in as I found myself hardly able to move an inch without rubbing shoulders with one stranger or another. This was definitely a different experience than our little queer nights at the Barn.

"Isaac? What the hell are you doing here?" a voice came from nearby. Isaac turned and caught the gaze of a tall, dark-haired, dark-eyed guy in a white arm sling who was filling out a polo nicely.

"What the hell am I doing here? What the hell did you do to your arm?" Isaac asked him.

"Superass and I were hiking in Peru, and I had a bit of a tumble."

"Is someone talking about my ass again?" a guy with his elbows on the bar asked, turning around. Through a set of glasses, he eyed the guy who'd approached Isaac, a lovestruck expression on his face, which was quickly reciprocated by the man, who seemed to be his partner—my suspicions confirmed by the matching bands on their ring fingers.

"This is Trav and his partner, Gary," Isaac told me. "Met these guys on a skiing trip. Travis has one of the best massage clinics in town."

"The best, according to *Creative Loafing*, thank

you very much."

"If I remember correctly, *Creative Loafing* circa 2018," Isaac added, his expression playful as ever.

"Well, at least someone's paying attention to my Facebook feed," Travis joked, and then they caught up a bit.

As Isaac's friends welcomed Walker, Cohen, and me into the fold, catching us up on their Peruvian adventures, they ignited a mix of eagerness and envy. I'd always wanted to see Machu Picchu, and I was pleased at how willing they were to share their explorations so we could live vicariously through their real-world adventure. On top of their stories, I had to admit, it was nice seeing Cohen in his element, relaxed and enjoying himself.

Although, something about it was unsettling too. My instincts had me believe he belonged in Buckridge, but was that wishful thinking?

I dismissed the thought as much as I could, drinking some more of the vodka Sprite Cohen had ordered for me—since they didn't have any O'Ralley brand whiskey, and I sure as fuck wasn't betraying my family name any more than I already was by being out with a Mitchell.

"Come on," Gary piped up. "The drag show's about to start."

"A drag show?" Walker asked, his eyes growing wider than I'd seen them in a long time, a grin stretching across his ridiculous face.

Isaac hooked his arm around Walker and said, "Come on, my little virgin man. I got a lot to educate you on."

Travis guided us to a set of stairs leading to the downstairs part of the bar, navigating us to where a crowd gathered around the host, clasping their dollar tips in preparation for the show.

"Hope you got a lot of ones," Cohen said as Isaac pulled us closer to the stage.

It was a wild production, filled with songs by Diana Ross, Whitney, Lady Gaga, and some artists I didn't recognize (and definitely hadn't expected to), but I could tell by the way everyone else was singing along, Cohen and Isaac included, that they were more than familiar with the tunes. Cohen turned to me at one point, and I must've been wearing a similar expression as Walker, since he noted, "Oh, didn't even do this at the gay bar you went to? Pfft. Amateur." He winked, his smile broadening.

I wasn't sure if it was the drink, or the liveliness of the cheering bar patrons, or just that damn pretty mug of his again, but I went right in and took a kiss. I didn't give any more shits than I had that night at the Barn. And Cohen didn't give me any reason to think that mouth wasn't mine just then as he moved in closer.

Another song came on, turning our attention back to the show. When the performances came to an end, the lights dimmed, and the wall-mounted TV screens started playing music videos, the crowd filling the space that had been used for the drag show, turning it into a dance floor.

Cohen took my hand and guided me into the crowd, while Isaac, Travis, and Gary swarmed around Walker, helping him cut loose a bit.

"God, my brother's gonna think he was in an orgy tonight," I joked as we settled into an open space. Nearly as soon, Isaac started grinding up on my bro, making him blush.

"He's not the only one having a good time," Cohen said, smiling brightly as we found our way into the beat.

"It's aight."

"Tell me this is not better than when you came out here with whom I can only assume were your straight college buddies."

"Hey, whoa. That is totally untrue."

He glared at me.

"We had a bi friend, and it was his birthday, which is why we went to a bar."

"What was it called?"

"I couldn't even tell you. It was over on Glenwood Avenue. Doubt it's even still there."

He rolled his eyes overdramatically. "That's horrible that you have to make up fake gay bars to seem cool."

"To be honest, we didn't realize it was a gay bar. Just looked fun."

"There wasn't a disproportionate number of guys?"

"Yeah, but half the straight bars we went to were like that. Most of us didn't know, but I'm pretty sure my friend knew what he was getting us into."

He busted out laughing. "Well, now you're learning just how fun these gay boys can be."

He moved closer, his hand sliding around my waist as he pulled our hips together. It was fucking effortless to find the rhythm with him, which shouldn't have surprised me, not when we kissed the way we did.

"Technically, I think I'm just learning how much fun one gay boy can be."

"Just doing my best to represent. You never told me you were interested in going to Peru, though."

I nearly stopped dancing, and my response seemed to catch him off guard...nearly as much as I'd been caught off guard by his remark.

"How did you know I wanted to go?"

"I guessed by the look in your eyes and your overly enthusiastic questions about Machu Picchu when Travis and Gary were talking about their trip. Clearly, I was right."

Of course he was right, but the discomfort rising from my gut to my chest made me want to change the subject.

"What's this song?" I asked.

He eyed my curiously before listening.

While he was trying to figure it out, I grinded up on him, hoping to distract him from his line of questions. It seemed to work. He busted some moves, and I made sure to show him that, despite where I was from, I knew how to dance. And after proving that I could drop it low just as well as he could, we both got to laughing. Hell, it might have been the hardest I'd ever laughed.

We kissed once more, both of us seeming to get lost in the moment. It was nice to let loose, to forget about all the stress and Big Daddy's worries, and to feel Cohen's lips against mine, without shame or fear, in public—the same as the first time we'd kissed.

It was different now, though.

It had been hot before, it had felt amazing, but now, after getting to know this special man who was Cohen Mitchell, there was something else there too.

I hooked my arms around him, my hand navigating to the back of his head. He pulled away for a moment, looking between my lips and my eyes. I was waiting for his usual jokes or some quip, but he maintained this intense expression before letting me draw him in once again for another kiss.

And another…and another.

His hand slid down my back, cupping my ass firmly.

I couldn't help smiling. "Somebody's curious."

"More than curious," he confessed.

"It's okay. I'm curious too." There wasn't a joke there. I was deadly serious, and as I felt his lips curling upward against my cheek, I could tell by the way he kissed me again that he knew it.

His grip on my ass firmed even more as I licked up the middle of his lips. He bit gently at my chin, then nibbled my bottom lip.

Just like with every kiss, and our dance moves, there was something innate about this chemistry we had. Like wolves who'd stumbled upon each other in the forest, exploring, testing one another before wrestling and fucking for hours.

Where the hell did that come from?

I stumbled at my wayward thought and felt an arm at my side. I hardly had a chance to turn before a cold sensation crawled down my side.

"Oh fuck, sorry," a guy beside me said.

It took me a moment to notice the drink running down the side of my tee and jeans. I cursed, but seeing the guilty expression on the guy's face, quickly assured him it was fine, before telling Cohen, "I'll fetch some napkins."

Cohen took my hand, coming with me as we navigated the bar. A spot opened up, but there weren't any napkins close to us, so we had to travel farther down the bar. I started to grab a few from the holder, when I noticed a familiar face a few feet away, near the corner of the bar.

"Lee?!"

His eyes popped open, then shifted toward the wall, where I saw the back of my other giant-ass brother, who had his arm around a guy.

"The fuck? Dwain?" I approached him, still in disbelief of what I was seeing.

He didn't seem to hear me—too busy making out—so I grabbed his shoulder. "Dwain!"

He turned, looking between me and the guy in his arms, whom he released. "Oh…um…this isn't what it looks like?"

"You have a boyfriend?" asked the guy he was making out with before huffing and storming off.

"Boyfriend? What?" Dwain was clearly disoriented, and by the smell on his breath, I knew it was from more than the tongue-swap with the guy who'd just ditched him.

"What in the hell are you guys doing here?" I asked.

Dwain's expression shifted from disoriented to angry in an instant, the veins in his neck pushing forward. "I knew you and Walker were up to no good.

I could see it on your faces when you were heading out. Then Lee and I got in the SUV and followed you to the Mitchell place."

"You followed us?"

"Of course we followed you. Headed a little farther down the road past the Mitchell place and watched to see what mischief you were up to. I knew you guys were lying when Walker said you were frog gigging. When was the last time either of you even had frog legs for dinner? You think I'm an idiot? Don't answer that."

"Well, you asked."

"No. I mean...oh fuck..." His gaze trailed off as his face flushed. "I'm gonna be sick."

Lee grabbed Dwain and pulled him toward the restroom.

I turned to Cohen to find that Walker and Isaac had come over to see what all the fuss was about.

"The hell?" Cohen said.

"We were fucking followed," I explained.

"I think you guys might need to be studied for the supposed gay gene," Isaac noted, which would have been much funnier if I wasn't still seething from discovering that Dwain and Lee had followed us.

Goddammit.

After some fussing and discussion, we all agreed it was best to call it a night. Walker, Isaac, Cohen, and I had Ubered from the Mitchell house, and on account of Dwain having commandeered Big Daddy's six-seater SUV, and Lee not having anything to drink, Lee acted as DD while we lugged a moaning, sickly Dwain back to Buckridge.

Walker and I flanked him on either side in the middle seat, ready to call for Lee to stop the car if he needed to throw up again, as he'd done three times back at the bar.

"Running around behind our backs, making out with a Mitchell. Don't think I won't tell Big Daddy."

"Yeah, you ready to tell Big Daddy about your little boyfriend tonight too?" Walker asked.

"Shut your damn mouth, traitor."

Despite our "betrayal" against the family, I knew Walker was right, and that, considering what Dwain had been up to, it wasn't likely he'd expose us, since he'd have to give up the reason he knew what I was doing to begin with.

"Hey," Isaac called from the front of the car, turning back to Walker. "Does this one talk?"

Through the rearview mirror, I saw Lee open his

mouth to speak when Dwain interjected, "Of course he talks!"

Lee pressed his lips together, which I knew he was perfectly happy to do anyway.

An amused chuckle came from Cohen in the back seat. Damn, he was really getting one hell of a crash course in O'Ralley family dynamics.

"Oh, here I go again..." Dwain leaned toward Walker, who scrambled to open the window.

"We shouldn't have put him in the middle," Isaac warned belatedly.

After that we had to rethink our strategy and stop a few times for Dwain, but we finally managed to get back to the Mitchell house.

It took most of us to get Dwain through the front door, but he had a bit of a fit, drunkenly thrashing about before falling to the floor.

Isaac pitched in to help him back on his feet. "Jesus, there are four of us. How can it be this hard?"

"Easier than tipping a cow," Walker said.

Isaac's jaw dropped. "I'm pretending that's a metaphor for something else."

Walker and I eyed one another, chuckling.

"He's a traity-traitor," Dwain told Lee as he and I helped him onto the sofa. "I can't believe we're in the enemy's house."

"We're only here," Walker began, "because you're rambling like a buffoon and we can't risk you blabbing everyone's secrets, including your own, bro."

Dwain growled before making a familiar sound that prompted me to warn, "Don't you dare throw up on me."

He looked to me, an indignant expression on his face. "You touch me, you get thrown up on!"

I was certain that made sense in his drunk brain, but considering I already had my arm around him, I couldn't make heads or tails of it.

As he landed back on the sofa, he muttered, "That guy said I'm a bear...a sexy bear? What the hell? Bears aren't sexy, are they?"

"Oh, they can be," Isaac assured him, all smiles.

Dwain's eyes just barely opened as he looked at Isaac. "Howdy, I'm Dwain." He reached for Isaac, but Walker slapped his hand. "I think you've touched enough boys for the night."

"No homo," he muttered, before smirking. "Maybe a little homo."

"Big Daddy's gonna wonder where you guys are," Cohen said.

Walker pulled out his phone. "Yeah. I'm messaging Mel. We're gonna need someone to cover for our asses before we get back over there tomorrow morning."

"What's she gonna say?" I asked.

"It's Mel. She'll think of something. How many times have we covered for her ass?"

I laughed. "Fair point."

We figured out sleeping arrangements so Dwain could sober up before the morning. Walker and I would share a spare bedroom, and Lee would keep watch over our wasted brother in case he needed additional help during the night.

I was still wearing the drink that guy from the bar had spilled on me, so Cohen offered me a shower in his room first.

When we made it inside the bedroom, I relaxed against the door, closing it behind me. We both let out a sigh of relief before cracking up.

Maybe we were still a little tipsy. Or maybe we were just so damn relieved to have made it back after the drama. Whatever the reason, I felt the weight of everything lift off me, and Cohen's lips seemed like the perfect way to loosen up even more.

And damn, he tasted as good as ever.

CHAPTER NINETEEN

Cohen

G OD, I WANTED him. Brody tied me up in knots, in such an unfamiliar way. Like I wanted to hold on tight, but I was scared to, only the thought of letting go was even more frightening. Fucking country boys had me feeling all kinds of things, but the truth was, I knew it wasn't just any country boy.

It was this one.

We kissed as I tugged him toward the bathroom. I tried to lean down and turn the faucets on without breaking contact, and almost fell into the tub. Brody laughed and caught me. "Good thing I was here. I just saved your life," he teased with that drawl that was so hot and that mischievous tone he had.

"But I wouldn't have almost fallen in the tub and died if it wasn't for you."

"Semantics." He nibbled my bottom lip, then sucked it into his mouth. "Now get that shower going."

My dick twitched. "Well, shit. I don't know why, but that was kind of hot, you cocky motherfucker."

"I didn't even say anything, but I guess when it's me saying it…"

We laughed again, and I got the water on. We stripped each other out of our clothes, before kissing and almost getting wrapped up in the curtain while we tried to get in the shower.

"We're gonna make a mess," Brody said.

"I don't care."

He looked at me strangely, his brows furrowed as if in thought, before his mouth crashed down on mine again.

We finally made our way into the shower, and I pushed Brody against the wall as water ran down over us. He was bigger than me, his tan lines from working in the sun more noticeable than they usually were.

"Fuck you feel good," he said.

I squirted soap in my hand and wrapped it around his cock. Christ, he was thick. I wanted him in my mouth again, wanted in his ass, but even though I could tell there was curiosity there, I didn't know if he would be ready. "We don't want you finishing too soon, then." I let go of him, and Brody gasped.

"Touch me, you fucker."

I slid my soapy hand around him and teased the crease of his ass. "Say please."

"Oh fuck." He closed his eyes and dropped his head back. "Please…"

"That was easier than I thought it would be." I pushed a finger between his cheeks, testing the waters. Brody spread his legs farther, his breathing sped up, and he opened his eyes and looked at me. "Too much?" I licked at his lip. "I want you, whatever way I can have you. I'll give up the ass, and I don't usually do that on a first date."

He didn't chuckle like I expected him to. I went to pull my hand away, but Brody grabbed my wrist. "No…I want…"

Hell, I was so fucked. My cock twitched as I saw the heat in his stare. "You're curious," I said, and he nodded. He was going to wreck me, this man. He was so damn full of surprises.

"You couldn't tell?" he asked. "Aren't you supposed to be good at this?"

"Oh, fuck you. I just didn't want to make assumptions." I leaned in again, sucked his lip, felt him tremble. "I'll take good care of you. It's a mighty fine ass. Is that how I'm supposed to say it?"

"Goddamned city boys," he teased.

I sobered. "Seriously, though. I'll make it good for you. You'll be running around begging for my dick in your ass after this."

"Well, I don't know. It's a little smaller than mine, sooo…"

"Fuck you." I laughed. Damn, he did it for me. There was nothing like laughing with Brody O'Ralley, and for a moment, I got unexplainably sad. I thought about the history between our families. The rage in Big Daddy's eyes when he saw me, the anger in Dwain's words. Hell, the fact that we had to go to Atlanta just so we could be in public together.

"What's wrong?" Brody asked.

I shook those thoughts away. "Nothing. Come on. If I'm taking you for the first time, it's definitely going to be in a bed."

We rinsed and turned the water off.

I tossed him a towel, which Brody caught before saying, "You better be good at this, No Good Mitchell." There were nerves in his voice, which I could understand. It was always scary the first time.

"I was nervous too, ya know?"

"Don't know what you're talking about."

"I'm just saying if you are."

"Shut up and fuck me," Brody countered, and it was all I needed. We weren't completely dried off, but I didn't give a shit about that. I grabbed him, pulled him toward me as I took his mouth slowly. We backed up toward the bed. When we got there, I turned us around so his back was to it and pushed him onto the mattress.

"Lie down."

"Who's bossy now?" Still, he did as I said, lying on his back, head on the pillows, legs spread, and slowly stroked his thick cock. "Like what you see?"

"Eh, you're okay," I teased, crawling toward him. I sucked his dick to the back of my throat, and he jolted off the bed.

"Fuck, that feels good."

"Mm-hm," I replied, licking him, before grabbing the lube and a condom from the nightstand. I squirted some in my hand and winked. "Now it's time to play."

Lowering my mouth to his dick again, I let my

fingers slide back behind his balls. Brody spread his legs wider as my fingers circled his pucker.

"Fuck...that's..."

"Have you ever played back here before?"

"No."

I kissed his inner thighs, his balls, his shaft, still rubbing him. When he was gasping and writhing, I pushed the tip of a finger inside.

"Oh..."

"It'll get better." Lick, suck, finger. I teased him and played, worked more inside his hot body. Then I angled my finger toward his prostate and rubbed.

"Oh fuck!" Brody thrust into my mouth, his dick hitting the back of my throat. "Sorry."

"It's okay. I can take it. You ready for another one?"

"If you rub that spot again, I'm pretty sure there's nothing I'm not ready for."

"Methinks Brody is going to love him some ass play."

"Shut up and put another one inside me."

I lubed up a little more and did, working two into his tight channel as I enjoyed myself—sometimes playing with his prostate and watching his reaction, others using my mouth on his cock. Brody's hand tightened in my hair as he looked down at me, sweat beading on his brow, his stare intense and hungry.

"Shit...fuck...God, that feels good." His eyes began to roll back. I could tell he was close to coming, so I slowed down, pulled out. "God, I hate you."

"That's no way to talk to someone who's making you feel so good."

"You were until you stopped."

"Roll over, country boy. Let me see that ass."

He did, and damn, it really was a nice one, his cheeks and upper thighs white compared to his back and lower legs. "Haven't you guys ever heard of tanning beds out here?" I joked.

"That's what you're thinking about right now? With my fine ass in front of you."

Leaning in, I chuckled before I bit.

"I like that...your teeth."

"I'm planning on doing a whole lot of things you like." After slicking my fingers again, I used two on him, stretching him. I watched my digits breach his hole, disappear inside, before teasing them out again. My balls were aching as Brody thrust against the mattress.

"Do it...don't make me beg," he finally said, and I silently thanked God.

"Get up on your knees."

I put the condom on and lubed up, before squirting some more in the tight, pink hole that might actually kill me. I wasn't sure how I'd survive fucking Brody O'Ralley, but I figured it would be a good way to go.

I spread his cheeks, rubbed my thumb against his rim, and watched as goose bumps chased each other down his back.

"Please..."

"You're fucking hungry for it, aren't you?"

"You're just realizing that?"

I pressed at him with the head of my cock. "Push out a little, okay? It'll make it easier."

He nodded, did as I said, and I started to ease inside.

Every curse word in existence ran through my head. He was so damn hot, so fucking tight, I didn't know how I was going to keep myself in check. I would, of course, because I wanted this to be good for him. I wanted it better than good for him.

"A little more," he said when I paused. I kept going, following his lead, the signals his body was giving me and the things he told me, until my groin was against his ass as I knelt behind him.

"Fuck…Brodes…" I ran my hand down his spine, trying to get myself under control. Christ, I wanted to spill right then.

"You can move a little. Just go slow."

I leaned over, kissed his upper back, then cautiously pulled out some before pushing in again, over and over, at his pace, until I felt his body loosening around me.

"More," he begged, and I gave it to him, hands on his hips, nails in his skin as I worked him harder, faster, making sure it wasn't too much. Brody was panting, moving against me, sweat on his back, both his and mine that dripped from me to him.

I was fairly certain this was the best moment of my life, like maybe we could find a way so I could just stay here, in this bed, dick in his ass all the time.

I drew him up so he was kneeling without weight on his hands, his back against my chest as I fucked up and into him. He turned his head, and I took his mouth, pushed my tongue between his lips the same way my dick breached his ass.

"You gotta come, Brodes," I said when we broke the kiss. "Otherwise I'm going to embarrass myself."

"As fun as that sounds, I'm not willing to pass up an orgasm for it."

I squirted lube into my hand. With my arm wrapped around him, I jerked him off as I fucked into his ass.

"Yes...God yes. I'm almost..." His hole tightened, his body tensed, and he cried out as his hot load spurted all over my fingers.

I kept jacking him, kept fucking into him, my whole world melting away, turning fuzzy. I shot into the condom, wished it was his ass, which tightened again, making my dick spasm, and another spurt pulled from my balls.

Brody fell forward, and I went down on top of him, my heart beating frantically as quick breaths escaped my lungs.

I kissed his nape, his shoulder, smiled against his skin. Christ, I liked him, maybe too much. I thought maybe I wanted dinners at his house, and to walk with him in town, and fuck, was I getting ahead of myself. I'd never gotten so sappy after sex before.

I pulled out, moved over. "And?" I asked.

Brody was on his stomach, his face away from me. He turned, looked at me, and grinned. "Eh. I've had better."

"Shut the fuck up." I went to roll off the bed, but his hand on my arm stopped me.

"It was, um... I think I might end up being a bit of a power bottom after this."

I kissed him and laughed. "I think we can work with that."

I got up, tossed the condom, and got something to clean us up. When I climbed back into the bed, he said, "I should probably go to the other room..."

"Don't." My arms tingled with the need to hold him, to feel his breath against me and figure out if he snored or moved around a lot or talked in his sleep. I wanted all the moments I could have with him.

He hesitated, and I held my breath, thinking he would say no, but he gave me a quiet, "Okay."

I pulled him into my arms, and we went to sleep.

CHAPTER TWENTY

Brody

STRETCHED AS I felt myself waking up.

My hand bumped into something, and I heard, "Hey, hey, watch it. You're not alone in this bed."

I chuckled as I opened my eyes to see Cohen lying beside me, a tablet in his hand.

"What are you reading?"

"I was catching up on the latest from the *Times*."

I leaned over, trying to get a peek at his screen. "Did they already print 'Power Top City Slicker Drills Innocent, Curious, Straight Country Boy'?"

"Um...this is the *Times*. I'd like to think they would have done enough research to know that that Country Boy isn't so straight or so innocent."

"Very curious, though, and of course they'd say that. You know the news never gets it all right."

He shook his head, unable to fight that smirk. "You might want to cover up there, mister. You don't want to tempt me again."

"Huh." I followed his gaze, glancing over my shoulder to see the sheets tucked just under my exposed ass. I pushed my hips against the bed a few times, tensing my cheeks together to show off the skills he'd already gotten a preview of.

He growled. "Be careful. You make it too inviting, you're gonna be feeling some pressure in a minute."

"That a promise?"

I didn't know why I felt so goddamn frisky, but I couldn't help it. The sensations Cohen had worked up in me the night before... He'd taken me on a whirl-wind of a ride, introduced me to things I was feeling fucking greedy for.

Because of him.

I pushed up on my forearms, leaning into him and kissing his neck before biting down gently.

He twisted his head and kissed my hair before shifting toward me, his hand finding its way to my ass and gripping firmly, my cheeks flushing as my mind raced back through everything I'd experienced with him the night before.

"I feel like you're just wanting to get fucked so you can pretend you don't have to deal with your cluster-fuck family shit that's waiting for you downstairs."

"To be fair, that's only half the reason."

I wanted to pretend we could enjoy each other a little longer without having to deal with the less fun parts of the night...or wondering what Big Daddy would have thought if he knew where most of his family had spent the night.

"I didn't realize you'd be so hungry for my dick inside you."

"I told you I go slow until I go fast."

"And when you go fast, damn."

I beamed with pride. "Just needed you to show me how to do it so that I can show you how much better I am at it than you."

"Oh, really? So cocky, and you've never even fucked a man before."

"I have a pretty good teacher." I pulled away from his neck, looking into his pretty eyes as I ran my finger and thumb along the side of his cheek. "Looks like I'm gonna have to teach you to take it as good as you give it." I winked, and as I leaned in for a kiss, a loud clanging sound came from downstairs. Followed by some more.

"The fuck?" I asked, both our heads turning toward the door.

What was my family up to down there?

Whatever it was, it was time to face the music, so Cohen loaned me some clothes, and as we got dressed, I accepted the cruel fact that I would have to deal with this morning wood later.

When we stepped out of the bedroom, I glanced over the upstairs hall banister, into the living room, expecting to see Dwain and Lee, but they weren't there. Chatter came from the kitchen, and as we made our way there, I could see the familiar neon-pink hair near the stove.

"Mel?" I approached the kitchen and noticed Walker, Dwain, and Lee at the table. Dwain looked as hungover as he must've felt, considering how he'd behaved the night before.

"Sorry, I hope I didn't wake you guys," she said. "I didn't know that the pots and pans would be such a booby trap." She picked a pot off the floor and added it to a stack on the counter.

"What are you doing here?" I asked her. "Aren't you supposed to be making excuses with Big Daddy?"

"Already covered that. Big Daddy's convinced you're having some brotherly bonding time in the woods. He thought it was a great idea. And it's half-truthful, at least, so I don't have to feel like the lyingest liar who ever lied once he finds out. Now, I'm making eggs, so what do you want, Brodes? Omelette or over easy?"

Cohen leaned close to my ear. "I took care of the over easy, so you might want to go with the omelette."

I knew he was just trying to get me to chuckle, but my stomach was twisted in knots now that I was having to confront so much of what had come up the night before.

"Lee, can you grab me some things from the fridge?" Mel asked. "Whatever you find that I can make work."

He hopped up from beside Dwain and headed for the fridge.

"Dwain was telling me you guys went to a fun bar without me," Mel went on, "so…I accept deets and apologies."

I aimed dagger-eyes at my treacherous bro. "As loose-lipped as last night, I see."

He glared right back. "Don't even start with me,

traitor. I have a hangover like nothing." He pressed his hand against his forehead.

"How did you even get that drunk?"

"I just wanted one. Thought it was going to be enough to calm me down, since I wanted to fucking go up to you and put you in your place for how you were dishonoring our family. But then one drink turned into two...and then this kid got me started on shots 'cause it was his birthday. And then he wanted a birthday kiss."

"You didn't think we'd see it?"

"I thought it was going to be a little peck."

"That was more than a peck," I assured him.

He got a dreamy look in his eyes. "Damn right it was."

"Jesus, Dwain, you are a dummy," Walker said.

"Oh, are you the one in charge of smart drunken decisions, is that how it is? Besides, I haven't gotten anything in a long time."

Lee, who was helping Mel at the stove, glared at him.

"Look, it's been a while for me," he said before Lee had a chance to speak up. "Tucker and I haven't seen each other in months. That's where I was really going, not Angela's."

"Ooh, what a very queer turn of events," Isaac said as he headed into the kitchen in just a pair of white side-split boxers. "I hope I haven't missed breakfast, especially all the tea you guys are spilling."

His gaze shifted from Cohen to me before he winked, obviously intuiting what we'd been up to the night before.

"Just in time for the tea," Walker assured him as Isaac made his way to the table to join the others.

"Oh, that reminds me," Mel said. "Lee, we need tea and coffee."

Isaac guided Lee while I returned to the issues at hand. "Wait. Mel, you aren't even acting surprised that Dwain had his tongue down some guy's throat last night?"

"It's my magical pansexual powers," she said, totally unfazed. "We can sense these things."

"*Really?*" I asked.

"Yes, of course. You didn't suddenly start mind reading after you discovered you liked dick?" I could tell by the annoyed expression on her face and her overdramatic tone that she was putting me on. She shook her head. "No, Mr. Gullible. Dwain told me.

Everyone tells me everything because I'm good at keeping secrets. You guys are the ones who can't even do a good job of keeping your own."

"All I know is," Cohen said, "Big Daddy is in for a very busy Pride next year."

The room erupted in laughter, Dwain cringing through it because of what must've been a massive hangover.

"But just wanna make sure we're all on the same page," I went on. "No one tells Big Daddy anything about what happened last night."

I noticed Cohen eyeing me uneasily. I was sure he was wondering, if not now, then when the hell we would, but I had to figure out the best way to deal with that. It was all fun and games that we'd made a bunch of fools of ourselves, but for now, it needed to go no further than the Mitchell place.

"I know, I know," Dwain said. "You're worried Lee will say something. Fucking blab that he is. But seriously, Brodes, why did you have to go and start fucking around with a Mitchell? This is so like you."

"What is that supposed to mean?" Cohen asked.

"Like me?" I jumped in. "Dwain, you have to see that this feud is absurd. It always has been."

"It's not about the feud. It's about family. You know as well as I do how important this is to Big Daddy."

"He's not upset over some guy he's never met before. He's upset because the distillery is hurting, and he's struggling to keep it afloat. And if you'd open your eyes, you'd see that this is something he's clinging to because he can't control the rest."

Dwain's gaze settled on the table. "Even if that's the case, I don't see why you can't do this for the family. You never wanted to be an O'Ralley. Admit it. You went on to college, and then Mom got sick and—"

"That's enough, Dwain," Walker said.

"Mom's the only reason you came back, and she's the only reason you stayed. And you wish you could have gotten out of the distillery, far away from your own blood. You think any of us see it any different than that?"

For a room that had been full of arguments and laughter, it had quickly turned silent.

I could tell by the way my siblings turned to me, knowing expressions without a single damn protest, that Dwain wasn't the only one thinking that. No, it had been hanging in the air since I'd first gone off to college.

I felt a warm hand on my shoulder...Cohen's. Nice as it was to have his support, it reminded me of all the support I didn't have from my family.

"Is that what you all think?" I finally asked, already knowing the answer.

"Brody, it was just a hard time," Mel said, and it was impossible not to notice the lack of an outright denial of Dwain's remarks.

Even Walker didn't come to my defense.

"Well, maybe I don't want to be a fucking O'Ralley anymore," I spit out, feeling utterly betrayed by my own. I couldn't think straight, the blood rushing to my face as I dashed out of the kitchen and through the front door.

Cohen was right behind me. "Brody, come on. Come back inside. That's not how you want to end a fight with your brothers and sister." He firmed his grip on my shoulder.

I was all tension, nerves, tears forming in my eyes. "You heard them. I don't even want to be a part of this family. I've just been waiting for my chance to bail on them...after everything I've done. And even this one thing I'm enjoying—and they *know* this feud is stupid as hell—to just live my life is a betrayal to them. It isn't right."

He rubbed a thumb gently against my shoulder, the sort of sensation that I knew, if there had been any hope of him soothing my pain, *that* would have done it. But I was clearly too far gone. He added, "This is something you guys need to talk out."

I ran my hand through my hair. "Cohen, I had a lot of fun last night, and I really do like you, but I think I'm going to take a walk."

I felt like such an ass, seeing so much sympathy in his expression. He was trying to be there for me, but I couldn't let him. Not while I was so pissed at my siblings…and Big Daddy.

And the past.

And myself.

Cohen relaxed his hand, and I pulled away.

"I'll call you later, okay?"

He nodded, and I turned and darted off, the sting in my chest burning like a motherfucker.

In a moment—a fucking instant—that innocent, playful, delicious night we'd shared had been spoiled.

Fuck being an O'Ralley.

CHAPTER TWENTY-ONE

Cohen

I WAS SO damn angry, I couldn't stop shaking. I wasn't pissed at Brody, even if I was a little hurt that he'd walked away—I got it. No, I was pissed at this. At this whole fucking situation, the stupid goddamned feud and his family.

Without letting my logic talk me out of it, I spun and went back for the kitchen. Isaac was talking to Walker, but the second he saw me, he rushed my way. "Excuse us! We're going to go chat for a minute!"

He was trying to help, to diffuse the situation, but I shook off his concern.

"Co...it's not your place," he said, but the words wouldn't penetrate the anger flushing my system. Brody was...fuck, Brody was incredible. He was kind and funny, and there wasn't anything he wouldn't do for people he cared about. He was helping us with the distillery when we were the enemy, but also helping his father when the guy didn't even know or appreciate all the work Brody put into O'Ralley's.

I walked around Isaac and didn't stop until I got to Dwain. The rest of them, I was pissed at too, but he was the worst. "You're a real fucking asshole, you know that?"

Everyone in the room went silent. Seriously, it was so fucking quiet, I wasn't sure anyone was breathing or their hearts were beating. Everything went in slow motion from there.

Dwain's head lifted until his eyes were on mine, murderous and hard. For one second I doubted myself because he was a big motherfucker and I was sure he might kill me, but then I thought about the look in Brody's eyes when he'd left and the pain in his voice, and fuck that. I wasn't letting this shit go.

"'Scuse me?" Dwain said, and I rolled my eyes.

"You heard me. Christ, I'm so fucking tired of hearing about this stupid feud, Mitchells and O'Ralleys fucking bullshit. Grow the hell up! That shit happened a hundred fucking years ago. Newsflash, none of us were involved. I didn't even know I was a

Buckridge Mitchell until a couple of months ago. And I could deal with it if it was just me, but he—" I pointed to the door as if Brody was still there. "He doesn't deserve it. Brody's better than all of it. He's better than all of you, and there's nothing he wouldn't do for his family. And fuck you all if a no-good Mitchell can see it and you can't."

I turned and went for the back door, shoving it open so hard, it slammed against the house. My hands were shaking, I was so pissed. I wasn't wearing any shoes, and only had on pajama pants, but I didn't care. I made my way across the property to the distillery I couldn't even get into because I didn't have the damn keys.

I sat down on the stoop and leaned against the door. This whole thing was so fucked up. Just last night I was balls-deep in Brody, and it was all...well, I wasn't going to say perfect, because that was a little sappy, but it was really fucking good. And then, just like always, life was right around the corner, this world I didn't understand. I grew up so differently. My family wasn't like theirs at all.

It wasn't long before I heard footsteps. I didn't have to look up to know it was Isaac. He sat beside me and rested his head on my shoulder. "Hi."

"Hey." I turned and kissed the top of his head.

"Everyone left. Dwain's head nearly exploded. It was all good fun."

I groaned, rubbing a hand over my face. If I'd wanted to make his family like me more, I'd royally fucked up, but I couldn't help it. I'd been quiet through most of the morning and even the night before, but I was tired of it. Why should they give a shit if Brody wanted to spend time with me? "Thanks for staying until they left."

"It's fine." He waved me off. "So...I have a question."

Part of me knew that whatever Isaac had to say, I really wouldn't want to answer, but he was my best friend, the closest person to me in the world, so if I couldn't talk to him, who could I talk to? Plus, I knew him, and he wouldn't stop until he got his way. "Shoot."

"Did you know you're in love with Brody O'Ralley and just decided not to tell me, or were you not aware? I didn't just give it away, did I? Oops!"

I couldn't help but chuckle at the last part, before I got serious. "I'm not in love with him." I would know if I was in love with him, wouldn't I? "I'm *in like* with him. The more time I spend with him, the more I like him." Which was why the situation with his dad got to me so much, and that we could never be seen in town together, and his family didn't know we hung out, or that I was helping with the money issues, or a hundred other things. But that wasn't love. It was…because he was sexy as hell to look at, and he had a nice, smart mouth I liked to fuck, and he made me laugh, and talked to me about my family, and would do anything for those he loved.

"Well, that's a start. I'm not going to push harder than that. I honestly thought you wouldn't even admit that much."

"It'd be pretty hard to deny. Oh, and I ran into his dad yesterday, which is why we ended up at the bar in the first place, and then, well, a gentleman never tells."

"This gentleman heard the bed hitting the wall and Brody calling out your name. God, you must be a good fuck, Mitchell. I'm a little sad we're only besties."

Laughing, I nudged him with my elbow. "No comment about last night, but yeah, after that and then Dwain this morning, I was fucking done. Even if it's true and Brody only stayed or came home because

RILEY HART & DEVON McCORMACK

of his family, he still fucking did it. That's what matters. He would do anything for them, and Dwain is a dick. They don't realize how lucky they are to have him as a brother."

Isaac patted my thigh. "My dear, sweet, not-in-love-but-totally-in-love Cohen."

"Oh, look. It's a gay bear. Go get it."

"Where?" he joked, his eyes darting around. "That was a mean, mean trick, Cohen Mitchell." Isaac rested against me again. "What are you going to do?"

I shrugged. "There's not much I can do. Keep having fun with him and see what happens. He has more to lose than I do." All I could think was how good we could be together—how good Brody and I could be, and also, how strong Mitchell Creek and the O'Ralleys could be together too.

"You should tell him how you feel."

"What? Say I have a crush on him and ask him on a date to the diner to share a milkshake with me? Isn't that what people around here do?"

"So judgy."

"Learned it from you."

"Lies. No, just tell him you like him. Also, maybe hide because Dwain is a scary motherfucker and I don't know what I'd do if he killed my bestie. We should maybe get the locks changed, and I don't think you should leave the house on your own... I can't go with you, of course. He'd crush me. Do we have enough in the budget for a bodyguard?"

I laughed again, starting to feel better. "I'm not scared of him. If he keeps giving Brody shit, he's going to have me to deal with."

"*Aww!* You are so sweet when you're in love!"

"Fuck off. I'm not in love."

"Yes you are."

"No I'm not."

"Yes you are."

"Shut up."

Isaac sighed. "Those O'Ralleys...they're something special, aren't they?"

"Yeah, they really are. Fucking country boys, right?" I joked.

We laughed again, then leaned against the door. We were both quiet for a moment before I said, "As crazy as it sounds, and as gossipy as this town is...I like it here."

"I like it here too. It feels like..."

"Home," we said together.

It felt like home.

CHAPTER TWENTY-TWO

Brody

M Y THOUGHTS WERE all over the place.

Every O'Ralley kid, except Lee, was queer. Cohen knew how to dance and work a cock in my ass, and apparently, I fucking loved it. And now I'd been betrayed by my own blood, who had to go and ruin the best night of my life.

Betrayal, yes, that's what it was, and it hurt like hell.

In times like these, I found myself gravitating to a familiar space near the old shed, half a mile from the house. Dwain and Lee had already collected wood in a nearby pile, so I chopped it up on that same stump we'd chopped wood on since I was a teen.

Having discarded my shirt so I could feel the harsh summer sun beating against my back, I was working up a good sweat when I heard the sound of a four-wheeler.

Surely Mel or Walker searching for me, I assumed, so I didn't bother to look. I didn't want to talk to either of them, or see their expressions, which had already given away too much in Cohen's kitchen. That none of them had stood up for my loyalty was enough to fuel my rage.

The four-wheeler engine shut off, and I heard, "Need a hand?"

I nearly jumped at the sound of the voice, turning to see Cohen hopping off Walker's four-wheeler.

"You must really be in my head to have known where I was," I said, his ride already making me suspect that wasn't the case.

"Eh, it was kind of unfair. Got tipped off."

"Which rat told you where I'd be?" I asked, which came out more bitter than I'd intended.

Cohen neared, and something about him being close helped soothe me in a way he couldn't have after I'd blown up that morning. Fucking lost it in a way that had even surprised me.

"I'm sworn to secrecy, especially now that I'm behind enemy lines and liable to be shot by Big Daddy himself."

"Big Daddy's not too keen on guns. He'd rather fuss at you to death."

As I said that, he got a strange look on his face, but he shook it off before looking me over. "Speaking of guns, you always come out here shirtless and chop wood when you get a little angry? Maybe I need to be in charge of the O'Ralley Instagram account, after all."

I hadn't really thought about it, but as I glanced myself over, I felt a little cocky. "Must be nice to get a wet gun show. You should see these muscles in action when I get to chopping."

"I could see them from afar, but happy to watch them work up close."

I showed off on the piece I'd been about to chop before he arrived, then relaxed the head of the maul on the ground and wiped the sweat off my brow. I, of course, made as big of a production of it as I could manage, taking Cohen's eye roll as a slight and compliment all at once.

"If you keep eyeing me like that, gonna be a different sort of wood I'm dealing with," I warned.

"Looks like you've already got that covered too," he said, eyeing my crotch since my cock had apparently already perked up.

He smiled, and as much as I wanted to keep brooding, I couldn't help laughing. He had a way of making me crack up even when I was pissed.

"Wanna talk about it?" he asked.

"My hard-on?"

"I'm being serious. And don't worry. We have time to deal with the hard-on later. Now, do you want to talk about the prime-time drama breakdown you had over breakfast?"

"Probably about as much as you wanna chop wood."

"How about a trade? You hand me the ax and show me how to make this happen, and then you tell me whatever's on your mind."

"Lesson one of chopping wood: what I'm holding is a maul, not an ax. But since you were so generous with skilling me up last night, I guess I can do the same for you here."

I wasn't eager to chat about anything that had happened that morning. Hell, I'd planned to do the O'Ralley thing and just keep all that anger stored up for weeks, maybe months, if I could manage. But it was hard to resist Cohen's charm or natural ability to

269

make me want to open up.

"Okay, I'll see what we can work with, but take off your shirt. No city-boy farmer tans out here."

"Just trying to get me out of my clothes again. I mean, if you need me to take you against a tree to get some of this anger out of your system, I'm all yours." He winked, and sexy as it was, I knew he was just being playful. I clearly was beyond being cheered up with a quick fuck.

He threw off his shirt as I removed my gloves and retrieved a mini bottle of sunscreen from my pocket. Handing him the gloves, I went ahead and got to work lathering him up with sunscreen.

"Look at you, being so considerate," he noted.

"Trust me, this pasty flesh of yours will regret it if I miss any spots. Gotta take good care of your skin down here. You don't think all this beauty is kept up by being careless, do ya?"

"Apparently not," he said, laughing, as he glanced over his shoulder.

Had I not still been all wound up, I would have leaned in and kissed him, but the tension made me feel a certain distance between us, even with my fucking greedy hands groping him up and down, taking liberties as I enjoyed massaging my fingers across his body. I finished with a good rub of his abs before telling him, "Now I'm gonna make you show me how you think you chop wood first, so I can make fun of you, and then I'll show you the right way."

"Sounds like a good way to make you laugh."

He gave it a whirl, doing all the wrong things I'd already suspected, even making it big and overdramatic, like he wanted to give me a good chuckle, pull me out of that O'Ralley shell I'd crawled into.

It was working.

I didn't allow him to make any more of a spectacle of himself. I grabbed a log and showed him the cracks to follow on the sides, then how to hold and swing the maul to get the best cut.

He got better after a few logs, continuing until he was panting. "Yeah, I can see why you like this."

Sweat glided down his chest, making a path between his pecs, down his abs.

"You just gonna treat me like a piece of meat?" he teased with a wink. "Now, how many more of these things do I have to chop before you tell me what's up?"

"You ready to fill the shed?" Realizing I was stalling, I sighed. "I love my family," I said, almost too defensively, as if Cohen didn't know that, hadn't seen it for himself.

He rested the head of the maul on the ground, his hand on the tip of the handle. "Do you think I doubt that?"

"Seems everyone else does."

"I don't think that's true, but I'm not them, so whatever you tell me, I'm gonna listen."

"Haven't you been able to tell that this talking-about-things business isn't exactly a skill we O'Ralleys possess?"

"Oh, really? It was hard to tell during Dwain's coming-out party last night."

I would have laughed if it hadn't been so goddamn true.

He dropped the maul and approached, moving into me so effortlessly, his body pulling close to mine as if by some magnetic force. His hands rested against my hips before gliding around to my back.

He didn't say anything else. He didn't have to. In his hold, I felt his support and encouragement as I worked up the nerve to talk about those things that had been burning in my chest since the morning had been so thoroughly ruined.

"When I was a kid, in elementary school, I used to cut out pictures of places...the Northwest Territories, Machu Picchu, the pyramids of Giza. I'd tack them to this board in my room. Big Momma called me her little explorer since I had all these dreams of traveling the world...adventuring. On Halloween, I'd always be a pirate or explorer...some type of costume where I felt like I could see it all.

"Just got worse as I got older. Added more places. Bigger dreams. After I started attending college, I was saving up to go to Australia that summer. Then spring came, and we got the news about Big Momma's cancer. She encouraged me to finish the semester, and I traveled back and forth on weekends. The plan was college, major in business, help out with the distillery, and work traveling into my schedule. But as Big Momma got worse, it was all hands on deck. I managed to finish the semester, but by the time I got home full-time, Big Momma was going downhill fast. And it was so fucking hard, watching her deteriorate before our very eyes. Hoping that all that work...chemo and radiation...would be for something, but then in the end...just to watch the life get sucked right out of her. It was excruciating. We all were so broken by the time she was gone."

Cohen's hand moved up to my face, his thumb stroking my cheek. "Of course you were. That's a horrible thing to have to go through. You have every right to feel that way."

I thought I was doing a good job fighting back the tears, but then I felt Cohen's thumb travel through one, the warmth spreading over my flesh.

"Goddammit," I snapped.

"Brody, you're not broken now. It's okay."

Something about hearing my name, about Cohen telling me it was going to be okay, made me really believe it. Pulled me out of the dark past I'd let my mind drift to. But his words left me with a bitter realization. "The O'Ralleys are still broken. Maybe I'm just mad Dwain went and finally said what I already knew. Nothing's been right since she's been gone."

"But you guys are still together, and you have each other."

"Apparently that doesn't mean as much as I thought it did."

"You don't mean that. You know they love you. You're all hurting. And you have every right to hurt. That's a horrible thing for any family to go through.

But you know your mother wouldn't have wanted you to be like this."

"Then she shouldn't have fucking left us!" The words spit out before I had a chance to stop them in my throat, and the moment I spoke them, tears rushed from my eyes. "No, I know she couldn't do anything..." Shame and guilt overtook me as I pulled away from Cohen. "Fuck me. Fuck." The tears continued, no matter how much I fought them back. "I'm so sorry, Big Momma."

I wasn't even sure there was a place she could have heard me, but I was so fucking sorry for speaking those words, to her, to her memory.

I could hardly think straight, but I grabbed hold of Cohen, who pulled his arms around me, holding me close. "I shouldn't have fucking said that. I know in my heart that if she'd had a choice, she never would have let anything pry her from this world, but sometimes I just..."

"Brody, you don't have to explain that to me. We're in the same boat there. You think I haven't cursed my mom or dad a time or a thousand growing up? You're hurt. It's okay. Just got a lot bottled up in this big body of yours. I have a feeling if Big Momma were here, she'd rightly 'bless you out' and then get back to loving you as much as ever."

I laughed through the tears and pain. "Damn right. Where the fuck did you learn 'bless you out'?"

"I've been around for a minute. Picking up this small-town thing pretty damn well."

I pulled away, wiping my eyes. "This is what happens when you get some of that sunscreen in your eyes," I lied.

He glared at me.

"I know she didn't choose," I iterated, feeling so ashamed for having let those errant words escape my lips.

"I don't think for one moment that Big Momma would ever think anything else, but I do think she would want to know why you haven't been going on these adventures you were talking about."

I shook my head as regret swelled in my gut. Didn't I know it? "I put all those pictures away a long time ago. Buried them in the basement. And after all that, my brothers and sister still don't think I love them. What more could they need?"

"I sure as fuck understand feeling that way. Hell, just being here makes me feel like I'm betraying my adoptive parents for wanting to know about my dad. If I bottled all that up, that'd be a fucking lot to deal with. But don't you think you can travel *and* be with your family?"

I quieted as I faced this part of myself I pushed away most days. But clearly, Cohen had already seen me at my most vulnerable, so I didn't see a reason to hold back. "I don't like to admit it, not to anyone, but…Cohen, I'm scared."

He neared, resting his hand against my hip, his soft thumb contrasting with the rough material of the fingerless glove as he massaged my skin. "What are you scared of? You can tell me."

"All those days when I was at school while she was sick. I should have dropped out of the semester and come back to be with her as much as I could before the end. Each day was a day I lost. Now I know how fast you can lose someone you care about, and I don't want to be gone and then find out I missed all this time with the only thing that really matters in this world— family. Nothing else means shit. And the fact that they can't see that—that everything I do is because I want to cherish all the time, what limited time we have on this earth together—makes me feel like they're the ones turning their backs on me. Don't they see that I would fucking deprive myself of everything, I would give my last breath, would starve myself so that they could eat?"

"But do you think your family wants to sit there, watching you starve?"

It was a sobering remark, the sort that could only have come from outside my own brain, where I was right and justified in all my fury and pain. As I reflected on the expressions on my siblings' faces in his kitchen that morning, it made far too much sense. All this time they'd been watching me love them, but with all this pain in my heart still…a self-imposed suffering. "Well, it's all we've got," I said, unwilling to accept any alternative.

I could tell that wasn't satisfying for Cohen, and while I appreciated him being there for me, he couldn't help me with that. Mistake or not, it was my choice to make.

"Big Daddy would be pleased to know you have his stubbornness," Cohen said. "Come on. We're not gonna figure out all the O'Ralley problems in a day, so let's have some fun. Wanna play a game?"

I eyed him curiously. "Game?"

"Yeah, it's called: I take sexy videos of you swinging that ax...or maul...or whatever the hell, and then we blow up Isaac's phone with them and get some hits on the O'Ralley social media."

The way he had the power to diffuse all that tension so quickly filled my chest with a soothing, warm sensation.

We gazed at each other, his smile comforting me in a way I hadn't expected.

No, I wasn't going to find all the answers in an afternoon, but something about having a no-good Mitchell there with me made me feel like I didn't have to.

CHAPTER TWENTY-THREE

Cohen

WE STAYED OUT there for a good couple of hours. After we finished with the photos and videos, we sat in the grass, Brody with his head in my lap, a weed sticking out of his mouth. He had that mischievous grin of his plastered on his face, all that golden, tan skin on display. I wanted to strip him bare and fuck him hard. Remind him of what it felt like to have me inside him, hoping maybe it would help wipe some of that other shit away.

But the thing was, I liked talking to him too. Liked looking at him, and teasing him, and God, I was so fucking into this guy. What was wrong with me?

"You're such a country boy." I tugged on whatever the hell it was he was chewing.

"You like this country boy."

"I like his ass."

"Nah." Brody shook his head. "I mean, you like that, but you like me too. You liked me before you had my ass."

I couldn't argue with that, and even if I did, we would both know it wasn't true.

It surprised me that he was so chill about the sex, though. He didn't seem to have any qualms or regrets, which I was glad about, but… It was hard to put into words, but I worried I was in too deep and taking this more seriously than him. That it was only a fun experiment for him. Don't ask me how I got that by him letting me fuck him, but it's where my thoughts went.

"What's wrong?" he asked, grabbing my hand and intertwining our fingers. It was such a simple thing, but it felt heavy. Made me feel closer to him in some ridiculous way. I was pretty sure the country air was fucking with my head, and the crazy part was, I just wanted to inhale more of it, wanted to hold it in my lungs and make it last.

"Christ, it's hot out here." I wiped the sweat off my brow, thankful he couldn't hear my thoughts. The Georgia sun beat down on us, the sounds of bugs and wildlife all around us.

"Oh no you don't. If I didn't get to change the subject, you can't either."

He was right, of course, but the truth was, I didn't know exactly what was wrong. I just… "I've been thinking a lot, is all."

"About what?" Brody grinned up at me from my lap. I didn't know what in the hell was so cute about it, but something was.

"I don't know…everything. What you said earlier about Big Momma is making me think about my adoptive mom. I haven't talked to her nearly as much as I should have since I got here. It's all a mess in my head."

"That's understandable. Don't give yourself such a hard time." He reached up and wiped his thumb beneath my eye. "Make a wish."

I closed my eyes, didn't know what to hope for, so I said the first thing that came to mind. "I hope we're able to get O'Ralley out of the hole." I blew the stray eyelash off his finger.

Brody frowned. "You're making a wish for us and not you?"

I shrugged. As excited as I was about this, it was a

new goal for me. It was different for them. "This is your legacy but not in the same way as it is for me. This is your family's dream."

Brody was quiet for a moment before saying, "What am I gonna do with you, No Good Mitchell?" He sat up, tugged whatever he was chewing on out of his mouth, leaned in, and pressed a slow, soft kiss to my lips. He tasted like salt and Brody.

When he pulled away, he stayed sitting up. I figured I should take the opportunity to tell him about my run-in with Big Daddy before he heard about it somewhere else.

"So...yesterday morning..." Christ, I couldn't believe it had only been yesterday. It felt like a week ago. "I didn't get a chance to tell you I ran into Big Daddy."

"You what?" Brody rushed out. "Does he know? About us? No, he can't. He would have said something."

Not gonna lie, the fact that his first concern was whether or not his dad knew we were...whatever the fuck we were, stung. "Nah, I don't think so. He did tell me he knew what I was doing. I asked what, and he went on about the past—the feud, my parents. I'm pretty sure he thinks my mom was a secret agent for my dad or something. It's all fucked up." Plus, it didn't help that he'd dated my mom. That likely left some residual issues he wasn't talking about.

"Shit. I'm sorry."

I shrugged. "It is what it is. Not sure what we can do about it. I did mention the possibility of working together, and his head turned so red, I thought it might explode, so I took my leave and went inside the store. That's when I found out everyone had been sitting around watching us on the cameras, talking about how the Mitchells and O'Ralleys would never get along."

That bothered me more than it should. I wasn't sure I could tell him that, though. I was pretty embarrassed by it, and thought maybe I should go to the doctor and get my brain checked. Then I reminded myself that not five minutes ago, I wanted to savor this thing between us, had all these crazy musings about holding it into my lungs or whatever the fuck.

I shook my head, before falling onto my back and looking up at the clear, blue sky. The sun stung my eyes, so I turned my head a bit.

Brody lay down beside me, rubbed his hand over

my dick, and said, "I don't know about you, but I think this Mitchell and this O'Ralley get along pretty well. I mean, I had this big dick in my ass, so I think that's even better than *pretty well.*"

I knew he expected me to chuckle or say something sexy. It was on the tip of my tongue, and I wished I could let it out, but I didn't.

"Okay, I just joked about sex and didn't get a response. I'm confused."

That made two of us. I was being all mopey, and I didn't do mopey. I blamed Brody. It was all his fault.

"So, you know those cheesy made-for-TV movies where the big-city guy goes to small-town America and he's wooed by—well, a woman, because society is still homophobic as fuck, but I digress."

"The ones I pretend to think are cheesy, but I really eat them up like candy and I have a feeling you do too? Yeah, I know the ones."

"How the fuck did you know? But anyway, I love that one where they get trapped in the snowstorm and the hard-ass CEO just ravages the fuck out of the woman stuck with him for days on end. And they're magically in love in a weekend and it all works out?"

"I don't think I've seen that one, but why is the sex

never hot enough?"

"No shit," I replied.

"What does that have to do with running into Big Daddy, though?" Brody asked.

I paused for a moment, not sure if I could tell him, but fuck it. "Well, I never got it. I mean, I watched the hell out of them, but in the back of my mind, my logic was always telling me it wasn't reality. Either that, or small towns sprinkle some shit in the air, and we city boys don't have any immunity to it." I stalled, breathed, pushed the hair off his forehead. "There's something in the air here, and I'm not immune to it."

Brody stilled, as if he got what I was saying.

"Don't freak out. I'm not saying I'm in love with you or anything, but you got me feeling some kinda something, and then I saw Big Daddy, and...fuck, he hates me. I don't think he ever won't hate me, and the residents of Buckridge watch it like some reality-TV show. We can't even be seen in public together, and it's all fucking with my head."

Brody was still watching me. My heart was thumping, and I closed my eyes.

"I can't believe I just said that. What do you guys put in the air? I'm that guy—the movie guy. Can we forget I said that?"

"No...don't think I can," Brody replied, then damned if he didn't get that smirk that said he was up to no good. "Are you sayin' you wanna date me, city boy?"

"First, don't enjoy this so much. I've never been the first to say...whatever I just said. Second, I don't know what in the fuck I'm saying other than you've twisted my brain all up and those movies aren't as far from reality as I always thought they were."

"Well, I mean, it's me, so I'm pretty hard to resist. Don't know that I think it's realistic. I'm just that hard to resist."

Damned if I didn't laugh. "You cocky motherfucker." I rolled over, Brody going easily with me until I lay on top of him. Playfully, I nudged my face in this neck and bit him, sucking at his salty skin. The second time I bit him a little harder, and he pinched my side. "Ouch."

"That's what you get," Brody replied, then leaned up and kissed me. We both sobered. He ran his fingers through my hair. It was longer than I'd ever let it get before. "I like you too. I don't know...where we go from here. I gotta... You know how my family is, so I got some stuff to sort through, but I like you too."

I let out a heavy breath, feeling more relief than I should.

"Never had a guy ask me to go steady before."

I rolled my eyes. "I didn't ask you to go steady. Stop being so full of yourself. And I don't think people say that anymore."

"Are you saying I'm not hip and trendy?"

"Strike two. Who says that either?"

"The man you just asked to go steady with you. We say those things round these parts."

I laughed, and he did too. Our bodies were vibrating against each other. Brody was so much fun. But then my brain started spinning again. "I don't want to come between you and your family." Christ, why had I said anything to him at all? After what he told me and how I already knew he felt with them…

"We'll figure it out, No Good Mitchell. For now, I think you need to kiss me."

So I did. We lay in the grass and made out like a couple of teenagers, before he drove us back to my house on the four-wheeler.

Brody dropped me off, and I watched him ride away. I didn't go straight inside. Instead I ended up on the screened-in porch with my phone to my ear. "Hey, Mom," I said when she answered.

"Hey, you. How's it going out there?"

We talked for close to an hour. I told her about the distillery and some of the things I found out about my family. We spoke about Isaac and how well he was fitting in too.

"It sounds like things are going well there."

I thought about Brody…the distillery, the land, random conversations with Lauren or Rusty. "Yeah, they are."

"We sure do miss you out here, but I'm glad things are mostly going well."

"I miss you too." I really did. I was lucky to have her, to have them both.

"I'd like to see it sometime. Maybe we can plan a visit. I'm sure your father would love to come too."

The thought made me smile, but I knew with his schedule, it wasn't likely, at least not for him. "I'm not sure exactly what will happen, but we should plan something."

We chatted some more, about her yoga class and a charity she was working with.

Eventually, I said, "You know I love you, right?

Even though I'm here? I know you're the one who pushed me to come and all, but I want to make sure you know that no matter what, it doesn't change the fact that I love you and you're my mom."

"I know, you sweet boy. You have two moms and two dads, and that's okay. I know your heart."

I smiled, thankful to have her. Grateful for my past, the present, and hopeful for the future.

CHAPTER TWENTY-FOUR

Brody

A S MUCH AS I wanted to see Cohen again some more, our week quickly got busy as we each became consumed with our distillery crises. We texted and kept up with each other, but I had to admit, I was getting a little agitated about the time we weren't together.

"I'm not saying I'm in love with you or anything" kept playing over and over in my head.

I walked through the distillery, clipboard in hand, running my usual inspection checklist, when Walker headed in. "Hey, bro. You need anything from the store?"

"Still not talking to you."

"Yes you are."

"No I'm not. Not that it would even matter, since

you seem to be scarce lately."

"This is talking."

"Says you." But as much as I wanted to bite my tongue, I couldn't help myself. "I figured of everyone, you would have said something. Stood up for me when Dwain said that. You think I can't tell that something's been off with you? I know you too well for that. Ever since Cohen came to town, you've been…distant. Enough so that you took this long to really try to talk to me about this."

He quieted, his gaze shifting to the floor. "Brody, you know I don't doubt your loyalty to the family. I would never have stood by that comment, but some of the things he said, about you wanting to leave for and after college…you can't say that wasn't true."

"I wasn't trying to get away from the family, and I'm here, aren't I?"

"Yeah, you're here. A part of you, at least."

Fury burned like a hot poker to my chest. "What the hell is that supposed to mean?"

"We've had issues since Big Momma died, but it's gotten worse since Cohen came to Buckridge. Now I'm not saying that's on him or you, but it's just added to the secrets and confusion and anger. We're less of a family than ever before."

"So this is my fault?"

"Jesus, sometimes you are worse than Big Daddy, Brodes. We all got shit weighing on us, that we struggle with, now as much as ever. We need to come together, not turn on each other like this."

I couldn't deny that he was at least in part right, but it felt so goddamn hypocritical. "Funny thing to hear from the guy who turned on me."

Walker sighed, clearly disappointed that despite his attempts, he couldn't break through to me. "Fine. How about you text me if you decide you need anything from the store."

I didn't say anything as he retreated. Surely it was for the best, since if he'd stayed much longer, I would have probably wound up saying some things I'd regret.

I hated not being on good terms with my siblings. I loved them to death, would've done anything for them, but I couldn't magically wish away the sting of betrayal. And it was hard for me to get past, even if just to swallow my pride and talk to them again, which I hadn't since that breakfast at Cohen's. Aside from the sort of discussions necessary to coordinate our daily tasks, I continued giving my siblings the silent treatment.

It broke my heart, though; I didn't know how Lee managed to keep so goddamn quiet all the time.

In the empty distillery, I found my thoughts shifting back to the man I hadn't seen for too many days.

I thought about all the fun we'd had...all the fun I *wanted* to have with him.

And about the fact that I hadn't had my morning jerk-off session.

There was no reason for anyone else to head in there, so I found a nook behind the electric kettle. I reached down and stroked my hand against my crotch, the way I might have as a teen. I enjoyed the sensation of pressure against my shaft as I closed my eyes and thought about Cohen's pretty face...

I imagined him deep throating my cock, taking it the way he showed me before...hearing him practically gag on it before pulling it out so I could fucking shoot on those beautiful lips.

My thoughts shifted to having him pushed up against a wall, my cock buried in his hole.

I could see his fucking face...I knew exactly what it would look like when I was inside him...didn't even know how I could have known, but it was like I was a goddamn psychic.

The way his mouth hung open. The way he called out my name. Down to the way he'd sound when I'd make him come.

"Fuck," I growled as I felt myself getting close.

"Brody, where in the hell are you? Family meeting!" Big Daddy called in an all-too-familiar tone.

Shit.

I stopped pleasuring myself, my arousal quickly subsiding as I headed into the main part of the warehouse, where I saw Big Daddy with Walker and Mel already at his side, Dwain and Lee not far behind.

"Everything okay?" I asked.

I looked to my siblings, wondering what the hell they'd told him, if they'd ratted me out.

But their wide-eyed expressions suggested they were just as confused by this scene. Dwain and Walker, in particular, looked white as ghosts, as though they feared somehow Big Daddy might have found out their secrets.

Whomever Big Daddy had a problem with was about to get their ass handed to them.

He turned his intense gaze on me. "You!"

"Please, Big Daddy. Can you just tell us what's

going on?" I said, trying to keep a level head as he killed the good time I'd been having with myself before his arrival.

"Don't you play with me like you don't know."

Fuck. It was about me and my Mitchell.

He added, "I've been getting emails coming in all week long. And I didn't know what the hell they were on about, but then this morning, my email was flooded. I thought I was getting Spam from the Soviets or…"

"Dad, you know there are no Soviets anymore. What are you on about?"

He shook his head and pulled his phone out, fidgeting with it before showing me the screen. It was one of the playful vids Cohen had filmed while I was chopping wood. I chuckled as soon as I saw it. "This is what you're concerned about? Look, I didn't even use our regular social-media accounts. Created this TikTok thing so it wouldn't bother you. I can take it down."

"Take it down? Are you out of your mind? You have two thousand views on this thing. I'm lucky to get three likes on a post on our Facebook page."

"Two thousand views? Really?" We'd gotten a

couple dozen when I'd checked the day before, so something must've happened between then and this morning.

"This TikTack..."

"TikTok."

"Whatever it is, it's something we really hadn't considered as a marketing tool. I'm getting emails and calls about when we're having events. We really should be working this. We've always been lagging in this area. It would be great if we could find a way to monetize this."

"Wait. What are you suggesting?" Walker asked.

"I mean, Brody is..." Big Daddy began, then added, "What can I say? He's got my body when I was younger."

I threw back my head for a good laugh. "You are so full of it, Big Daddy."

"Wait, wait," Walker said. "You want to use your own son's body to sell our product? Is that what you're saying?"

"Hey, like with a good whiskey, we don't get to decide what the people want. They know what they like, and obviously, they want to see Brody chopping some wood."

"Oh, please," Walker said. "Everyone knows I'm the hot O'Ralley. What did he get? Two thousand? I can make that four."

"Um…I'm pretty confident I'm the hot O'Ralley," Mel piped up. "I mean, I'm not doing this because I'm so hot, I don't have anything to prove, but this man-beef show is going to be hilarious when I get to see which of you doesn't get the most views."

"See, it's like a game," Big Daddy said, clearly trying to get his sons excited about additional promo for the distillery.

"Well, I'm not being used for my body," Dwain said, folding his arms in protest.

"That's not what you were saying weekend before last," Walker said, and Dwain gave him a nasty glare. "No one wants to see what's going on under there anyway."

"A lot of people want to see—"

"Oh, come on," Big Daddy said. "I think we need to look into making our image a little more fresh. And if that means a little tease here and there to get people excited about our product, it could really give us an advantage. Just wish I knew more about this stuff…" He looked at the phone as though that in and of itself was enough of a challenge for him.

And an idea sprang to mind. "You know, I think I might have someone who could help us with this."

"Who?" Big Daddy asked, sounding desperate.

"You may not like it, but that Mitchell brought a friend with him."

"That Isaac guy."

"Yeah, and this is his area of expertise. We could meet with him, talk to him about what we're trying to do, and get his advice."

"He'd talk to that Mitchell about it, though."

"Well, what does that matter? I don't think it's such a big deal, really. We'd be the ones sort of poaching Isaac from him."

That phrasing seemed to sit well with him as his expression shifted. "Yeah...that's right."

Walker was glaring at me, but then he smirked, like he knew exactly what I was plotting by steadily easing Big Daddy into the idea of working with Cohen.

"You think you can make that happen?" Big Daddy asked.

"I have a good feeling about it."

Big Daddy nodded. "You can't fight results. So

let's give it a try."

We chatted a little bit more about it before Big Daddy excused everyone from the family meeting. He played on his phone for a minute, so I said, "Big Daddy, I just don't want you to get your hopes up and think that some silly social-media thing is going to turn things around magically. That's not really how the world works."

"I know, son. I just... Honestly, I watched it and saw you laughing and having a good time, and it really made me think that if we're gonna be in a bind, it wouldn't kill us to make the best of it. This meeting was the most fun we've had talking shop in a while. And I could use something going well while I'm navigating the rest of this mess. Unique opportunities, right?"

I could see the skepticism in his expression too, but was relieved to at least see that he wasn't being unrealistic about what any of this could lead to.

"Just go steal this social-media whiz from that no-good Mitchell, will ya?" he said with a wink and a pat on my shoulder. "That in and of itself will be worth it."

The sadistic pleasure in his expression didn't

soothe my concern about how difficult it was going to be to really persuade him that Cohen was a decent guy and had nothing to do with any old feud or the reasons for the O'Ralleys' failings.

Big Daddy headed back to his office while the rest of us got back to work.

When I was finished up, I texted Cohen. I knew he'd be around since he was working on repairing a broken fermenter. So on account of not having seen him all week—and of having found an excellent opportunity to propose something to him—I decided to surprise him and headed over on my trusty El-liecomb. After tying her to a post, I entered the distillery, and discovered Cohen in a dirty tank, a stack of tools at his feet.

"Oh, hey, man," he said, dripping with sweat.

"Seems like you're having some issues. Could have called."

"Rusty said that too. It's good. I'm watching YouTube videos. Trying to learn how to figure this shit out on my own."

"And looking good while doing it." I winked, moving in for a kiss.

He didn't deny me that. We'd been apart too long

during the week.

As we pulled away, he asked, "The O'Ralley family playing nice now?"

"Not as nice as we could be, but since you brought them up, I've come to see if we can arrange a meeting with Isaac."

"Isaac?"

"That video we posted to TikTok really impressed Big Daddy, so now he wants us to up our game in the marketing department."

"Oh, so more shirtless Brody O'Ralley for marketing? I think Isaac would be happy to help."

"Apparently, it's a bit of a competition which O'Ralley will be stripping for the brand, but...pretty much that idea."

He laughed. "That sounds fun."

"So you think he can make some space in his schedule for us?"

"Of course. He just ran off to the store to grab some tools to help me with this, but I'll get him to text you about it when he gets back."

"Good. Then we can go ahead and schedule a date night for us this weekend."

He froze for a moment, as though it took his brain

a moment to process what I'd said. Then he smiled. "Oh, you're asking me on a date?"

"You're the one who said you're in love with me."

"That's not what I said. I said I *like* you."

"You said, 'I'm not saying I'm in love with you or anything.' And I think we both know that's something only a person who's kinda in love would say."

"Or someone who's very good at being clear about where he's at, and *like* is the best word for it. In strong like, but like."

"*Strong like* sounds like the exit you get off at a couple of miles before the exit for *love*."

"But you can stay at one exit for days...weeks...years, before ever getting to that next exit."

"I'm sorry," I said. "This is so mean of me, calling you out on how hard you're falling for me. But don't worry. I'm getting some feelings for you too. Feels hot, almost burning."

"That's probably something you need to get checked out before we mess around again."

"Face it, Cozies, I'm helping save you the heartache of fearing the rejection of asking me on a date."

"Am I being tricked into a date?"

"Depends…do you like being tricked?"

I winked at the reference to his previous remark about tricking, and he rolled his eyes, unable to keep that chuckle in. "I'm supposed to be the cocky top here."

"You can be the cocky top until I decide to show you what a cocky top really looks like."

He couldn't have grinned any harder if he'd tried, I just knew it. "I can feel the hate our ancestors had for each other right now."

"Well, save some of it for our date tonight, then."

"Is that when you're gonna show me these topping skills?"

"Depends on how the date goes, I imagine. I'm a Southern gentleman, so I gotta take good care of you…before I take care of you."

"Oh, wow. So you're taking me on this date, but I'm pretty sure under the circumstances, I'm the one who'll be hosting."

"Yeah, that's the plan," I admitted.

"What if I say no? That I don't want to date this cocky asshole O'Ralley, for all the obvious reasons." It was clear by his expression he was just teasing, and I fucking loved the way he teased.

"Then you can text me and let me know how it feels to be alone when you're all in love with a guy who's just trying to ease your pain by dating you."

"Oh, now it's to ease my pain too? Wow. You're the most generous man in the world, aren't you? And again, strong *like*...but fading with each new dick comment you make."

"Or is it getting stronger, like you're getting closer to that next exit?"

He narrowed his gaze, shaking his head, as I moved closer to him. He slipped his arm around my waist effortlessly, and that let me know all this tit-for-tat was just in good, hot fun.

"So what did you have in mind for this date in my home this weekend?"

"You'll only find out if you say yes."

"Then yes, but just out of curiosity and not at all because of my like for you."

"Perfect," I said before taking another kiss of his warm, wet lips, but not granting myself too much time with them.

No, I was gonna save that for when we really had time again.

But as soon as I pulled away, he said, "Wait. What?

That's it?"

"For now."

"Okay, so we'll chat and see each other...say, this Saturday night, around seven?"

"Works for me, Cozies."

"Guess we can catch up on whatever Isaac's helping you guys with, and then I've had some ideas—"

"Nah. We'll have another meeting for that."

"Meeting?"

"Yeah. Sure. The date's just us. Clearly, I gotta train you not to mix business with pleasure."

"Oh, now you're training me?"

"Only if you like being trained," I said, winking again. "Text you later." I waved goodbye and headed out.

God, I was smiling like the biggest fool. I had a feeling I knew which exit was coming up next for me.

CHAPTER TWENTY-FIVE

Cohen

I T WAS RIDICULOUS to be nervous about a date. That hadn't happened to me in…hell, ever, to be honest. Because it had never really mattered before, but this one did. Probably more than I was ready to admit.

Fucking Brody O'Ralley and his stupid grin and adorable jokes and…fuck, I was so close to that damn exit he'd mentioned, I didn't want to think about it. Even the metaphor made me grin like a damn fool— one who had no business feeling much of anything, considering we could only go on a date in my house, because we lived in a made-for-TV movie where everyone in town had their eyes on us and Brody's family would never accept me.

Well, Big Daddy and Dwain wouldn't. The rest I could work with.

Brody's family meant so much to him, were an integral part of his life in a way I was unfamiliar with, but one I maybe wanted. If it came down to it, he would choose them, as he should. I would expect nothing less, and I sure as shit didn't want to come between them.

Isaac stepped into the office, where I was pretending to work instead of thinking about Brody. "Oh, hey. FYI, you have an hour to get ready, and then you need to leave for an hour before coming home to meet Brody here. I'm letting him in, then making myself scarce so the two lovebirds can have a night to themselves."

"We're not lovebirds," I gritted out, when inside, my pulse might have been dancing around at the thought of it. I was ridiculous about this guy.

"Okay, yeah, sure, and I'm not the sexiest twink in Georgia, with the most fuckable ass. Obviously, we both know I am, in fact, the best, and the phrase *power bottom* was coined for me, which means you're also really in L-O-V-E with your country boy, so stop denying it and go get ready. Fifty-eight minutes."

I rolled my eyes. Sometimes I didn't know if I wanted to strangle him or...nope, strangle him. That was the only thing I wanted to do.

"I'm going, I'm going."

"I mean, it's your choice. If you want to look like that." Isaac pointed at me, his finger roaming up and down my body.

"Hey, fuck you. I'm hot."

He patted my arm. "I know, sweetie. Of course you are."

"Why do I put up with you?"

"Because we're family, and we love each other, and that's obvious by the fact that I'm here with you, no matter what?"

He was right. I leaned in and kissed his temple. "You're all right, I guess. What are you going to do tonight?"

Isaac looked at his fingernails and began to pick at one. "Oh, I don't know. I'll figure it out. I was thinking about getting a hotel room. It might be nice to have some time to myself."

"You mean have some time on Grindr?"

"Who? Me? No way. I actually took the app off my phone. There's…something about the town air here."

I frowned. "What's going on with you?"

"Absolutely nothing. You're down to fifty-three

minutes, and there's a lot of work to do. Go shower."

I laughed. There was no one in the world I would let talk to me the way I let Isaac do.

I went to my room, showered, shaved, and got dressed. I wore a pair of shorts and a T-shirt. It wasn't as if we were going out, so I didn't need to dress up.

When I was done, I said goodbye to Isaac. I thought about heading to the Barn to see if Lauren was around, but then it might be hard to leave to make it back to Brody on time, so I drove to this little park on the outskirts of town. I didn't want to see anyone who would ask me questions or remind me that they couldn't know I was close with Brody.

I parked, got out, walked over and sat under a bushy maple tree, and…nothing. I fiddled with my phone for a while, wondered again if I should have gone to see Lauren…maybe pouted a little because I was sitting under said tree, acting like a big baby who had their favorite toy taken away just because we couldn't go out in public yet.

Today was supposed to be a good day. I had a date with a sexy man, who'd hopefully end up naked in my bed all night.

I still had some time to kill, so I walked through

the park. As I got closer to the other side, it got busier as I went, before I noticed what looked like a small farmer's market.

With each step I took, there was either someone watching me or I'd get a, *Cohen Mitchell, right? Hi, Cohen. How's Mitchell Creek? Any idea on an opening date?*

The last question was something Isaac had been asking me about as well. We were nearly ready, so we needed to set a date and do some hardcore marketing beforehand. As he reminded me nearly every minute of the day, he couldn't do his job unless I did mine and chose a date. I didn't want to admit I was waiting to see if things got sorted out with the O'Ralleys. What they did shouldn't have mattered unless I was trying to one-up them and do better, but the fact was, I wasn't. I wanted to give them air to breathe a bit before we came in and took some of their business, even if part of it was simply because Mitchell Creek was open again and there was mystery behind it.

I browsed around, grabbed some peaches—I mean, I was in Georgia now, so I had to. There was a flower stand toward the edge. They had a mix of daisies and marigolds that were the brightest orange I'd ever seen, so I grabbed that too.

The woman at the booth smiled at me. She looked kind, with freckles all over her face and red hair piled on top of her head in a messy ponytail.

"Cohen Mitchell, right?" she asked as I started making my way back to the car.

"Yes, ma'am," I replied, hoping I got that right.

"I knew you were back in town, of course, but I wanted to give you a little space. I know how overwhelming Buckridge can be."

Well, damn. That was different. No one else in town had offered me that yet. "Thanks. I appreciate it."

"No problem." She picked dead leaves off one of the plants. "I, um…I knew your mama." Immediately, I tensed up. "Uh-oh. That bad, huh? I wondered if it might be. I'm not going to harass you or give you any crazy stories. I know how many of them go around."

For the first time since someone random mentioned my mom, hell, my family in general, I breathed out a sigh of relief. "Thank you."

She looked around before her gaze found mine again. "My name is Amelia, and your mama…well, she used to be my best friend. Pam was one of the best women I've ever known."

My pulse began to race in the best way. This was the kind of thing I wanted to hear. Not horror stories or rumors. "Really?" There was a neediness to my voice I wasn't even embarrassed of.

"Yep. And you, oh boy, when she found out she was pregnant with you, she was so damn happy. Pam always wanted to be a mom, and she loved Harris so much. You were her dream."

My eyes began to pool slightly, a calmness settling into my chest I hadn't felt...maybe ever. "I was?"

"Yep. You sure were. I was the only person she told when she was leaving. Your daddy and her, they didn't want me involved because Bobby Mitchell was a mean sonofabitch, so she said goodbye and didn't tell me where she was going, just that she was going to raise her son away from Bobby Mitchell. Broke my heart when she passed. Harris told me about it. Damn near broke him."

My heart was thudding so hard, so fast, I was worried I might pass out. "Did he say anything about me?"

"He said you were safe, that he loved you, and that you were better off without him. He didn't say it, but I

313

don't think Harris thought he deserved you. I think he felt like he let both you and Pam down."

Her words nearly sucked the air out of my lungs. It was the first time someone had said something positive to me about my parents.

"Crazy as it is here, your mama loved Buckridge."

"I think I do too." The words shocked me. Sure, I loved the property, the house, the idea of getting Mitchell Creek off the ground, Lauren, and yeah, the townspeople made me crazy, but...I almost felt my mom here too, in a way I didn't in San Francisco. Even the weirdness of the people could be endearing sometimes.

"Good. I think your mama would have liked that. Listen, I'm about to close up shop, and it looks like you have a date or something too? If you'd like, we can exchange phone numbers, and I can share some Pam and Harris stories with you sometime."

"I'd like that." I maybe needed it. We swapped numbers. When I tried to pay Amelia for the flowers, she turned it down.

"Your mama loved marigolds too."

"Thank you. You don't know how much this means to me."

"I hope you plan on sticking around, Cohen Mitchell."

"I do." With one more smile her way, I headed for the car.

I pulled up at the house at five till seven. Brody's ass better be ready because that was all the time I could give him.

As soon as I got inside, the scent of garlic and the sound of sizzling oil met me. Flowers and peaches in hand, I leaned against the entryway to the kitchen, feeling giddy over him, over Amelia. Maybe that was a sign. Maybe things would get better. Maybe we could figure out the whole Big Daddy and Dwain issue.

Brody had his back to me. He was wearing jeans and a tee, along with an apron over it. He was busy flipping food and stirring things a little frantically, to be honest. It was cute as hell. I didn't know what it was about him, but he was like this constant pulse beneath my skin.

"Ouch. Shit!" Brody jerked his hand back, shaking it.

"Something wrong?" I asked, and he whipped around to face me.

"You're early."

"Less than five minutes by now."

"Still early. I get that you missed me and all, but I'm trying to make you dinner, and it was supposed to be done before you got here. I was a little worried it might be the tipping point for you to find that exit, but I was willing to risk it."

I cocked a brow at him. "Willing to risk it, huh?"

"It's inevitable anyway. I'm what most people call *irresistible*."

A laugh tumbled from my lips. "You're pushing it, O'Ralley. Also, I'm fairly certain it's the other way around. I'm the irresistible one."

"Eh, you have a great cock."

I chuckled again. He was good at making me do that. "You burning my dinner or what?"

"Oh shit. I forgot." He turned around again and started plucking fried chicken out of the skillet. "I'm making you a very Southern meal. These are all Big Momma's recipes, I'll have you know. I had to steal them from the box in the kitchen. This may look like simple fried chicken, mashed potatoes and gravy, and fried okra, but she had a special touch. I'm not only fraternizing with the enemy, I'm sharing O'Ralley secrets with him again."

"That's because you like me." I kissed his cheek. "Smells good. And look, I brought you flowers."

"What? No one's ever brought me flowers before. You must really want to get lucky tonight."

Or like, right now. That would work too. "Eh, I kind of like you, remember? You need help?"

"No, sit. This is my date."

I put the flowers in a vase before doing as he said. He finished up the food, and I told him about Amelia.

"Wow...that's...that's incredible."

"Isn't it? I'm excited to get to talk to her. It makes me feel...I don't know, a tie to my mom, and I think to my dad too."

"You deserve that." Brody walked over and kissed me.

I noticed the scent of apples, and looked over to see the oven was on. "What's in there?"

"A Ferrari."

"Funny guy."

"Dessert." His cheeks got a slight pink to them. "Isaac might have told me you have a thing for apple crisp."

It was my favorite. I couldn't believe he'd gone through all that trouble for me. It was...sweet. Brody

O'Ralley had a romantic streak.

He pulled the dessert from the oven, then nodded toward the door. "We're eating out here."

"We need to make our plates."

"I'll do it."

Smiling, I followed him to the screened-in porch, and froze the second I stepped out. The table was covered with a red-and-white cloth, with candles in the center. He'd hung red LED light strips around the porch where the wall met the ceiling. And going vertically along the ceiling were twinkling fairy lights.

"Can't take you to a restaurant. I know you want that—you deserve that—but I hope bringing the restaurant to you will do for now."

Christ, Brody O'Ralley was going to fucking ruin me.

I cupped his face, leaned in, and pressed another kiss to his lips. "It's perfect. You do realize I'm going to have to show you up for our second date, right? I can't have you being better than me."

"I'm counting on you tryin', city boy. Not sure you can do it, but I'll sure as shit enjoy watching you give it a go."

"Challenge accepted."

"Now move out of the way so I can wine and dine you. I better get laid after this."

He could count on it.

Brody pulled out the chair so I could sit down, which I did. He went back into the house, and a few minutes later came out minus the apron and with two plates. He put one in front of me and the other in front of him.

He leaned over, and I noticed a cooler. Brody handed me a beer and then took one for himself. "I was going to go with whiskey, but then I remembered you're a lightweight. Wouldn't want you passing out on me tonight."

"You're never going to let me live that down, are you?"

"Of course not. You wouldn't either."

We each opened our bottles, then clanked them together over the candles.

"To temptations and rivalries," I said.

"Temptations and rivalries," he replied.

CHAPTER TWENTY-SIX

Brody

THAT COHEN HAD even mentioned a second date made me feel like the efforts I'd gone to so we could have an actual date made it more than worth it. He took a whiff of his plate, which was stacked in the way Big Momma might have fixed it for guests back in the day.

"Don't know that I'll be able to eat all this," he said, eyes wide.

"Momma was big on always having enough for leftovers throughout the week, so really, this is the only way I know how to cook. Now get to trying that fried chicken. And don't forget to put some gravy on it."

"Already trying to get your gravy inside me, Brody?"

A soft growl slipped past my lips. "Just be careful

not to look too sexy while you're eating it, or I'm liable to dump this nice dinner on the ground and fuck you on the table."

"I'll try my hardest to avoid such a cruel temptation."

He poured some of the white gravy onto his fried chicken, and I waited in anxious anticipation for his response. Everyone loved some good fried chicken, but I just knew I'd be pissed at myself if I went and fucked it up.

He slipped the chicken into his mouth, a bit of the gravy sliding onto his lip, which his wet tongue swept in quickly. He closed his eyes and offered a familiar moan, like the one I'd heard when he was shoving that thick cock up inside me.

"Now you're just being mean," I insisted.

"Mean? I wanted to show you how good it tasted." He winked in that mischievous way I had a feeling was a genetic trait—this ability to look so very innocent and oh-so-guilty all at once.

He started to cut into his chicken again, so I grabbed mine and bit a chunk out of the meat. "That's how you eat good fried chicken, Mitchell."

As he swallowed, the way his Adam's apple shifted

had me fantasizing about what he looked like swallowing my load. He set his fork by his plate, grabbed a piece of fried chicken, and took another, much larger bite that way.

"See. Told you I was good."

"Yeah, for a guy who only burned some of the chicken a little, I'd say it's pretty good."

The look on his face told me all I needed to know—the wink, the corners of his lips curling into his cheeks, and some other quality I couldn't quite place, something in that expression reminding me I still didn't know him as well as I wished I did.

After we finished dinner, I cut us each slices of the apple crisp, adding vanilla ice cream on the side.

"Here, gonna make sure you don't fuck this up," I told him as I cut some of the crisp and spooned some ice cream with it. "Close your eyes."

He eyed me suspiciously. "What?"

"Come on. Like when you were a kid. Here comes the choo-choo."

"What the hell are you on about?"

"Just close 'em."

He glanced at the spoonful of dessert and then at me before obeying.

"I want you to enjoy it as much as possible," I told him. "Open nice and wide."

"This is so fucking dumb." But he did just that.

"Here it comes," I said, keeping the spoon in place as I licked along his bottom lip, the fragrance of beer lingering on his breath. He started to kiss back, but I pulled away.

"That's cruel," he said, but I could tell by his expression that he was fucking loving it.

"What's cruel is you not being able to follow orders, Mitchell. Close 'em again."

He rolled his eyes, and I figured he didn't have any complaints about my surprise move, because he did just as I'd said. This time, I fed him the spoonful.

"I'll grab you some more," I said as he chewed and swallowed.

I scooped up another spoonful and slid it into his mouth, watching the frozen lump melt on his tongue before he swallowed, his Adam's apple bobbing up and down. As he sat there, his mouth hanging open, his expression full of eagerness and curiosity, his wet lips proved impossible to resist.

I lurched forward and took a kiss.

The combination of my dessert lingering on his

tongue, with the beer, and the faintest hint of that fragrance so specific to Cohen, drove me fucking crazy.

He started to kiss some more, but I pulled away.

"Are you refusing my advances, O'Ralley?"

"I made a promise to myself that I wouldn't let either of us fuck this up with sex."

"I think the point of sex is to fuck something…"

"I'm serious. We gotta finish our date, or I have a feeling we'll just be spending the rest of the night in the bedroom. Let me take this slow," I added, and kissed him again, rubbing our bottom lips together before pulling away once more.

"As long as you promise not to edge me all night without actually being able to get off."

"Oh, there's gonna be edging, all right. But then there'll be the rest too. Don't worry. You'll like it."

"For a guy who didn't fuck around with guys until me, you sure are confident about this." He kept his eyes closed.

"There's only one way for me to prove it to you, I guess."

I slipped his shirt off over his head, tossing it aside before carefully moving his plate and silverware to the other side of the table. Then I got up from my seat and hooked an arm around him and the other under his legs, lifting him up. He chuckled as I said, "No peeking," before setting him down on the table. He didn't fight me as I unfastened his fly and pulled his pants down his legs until they reached his shoes. I didn't rush to get the rest of his clothes on the floor with his shirt.

There he was, lying on the table, the LED lights glistening off his smooth skin.

I took a sip from his glass of ice water, catching a piece of ice between my teeth, then set the glass down. I crawled up onto the table, my foot on the chair, my knee on the table as I moved the ice up Cohen's happy trail, traveling through the lines in his abs.

He gasped, rolling his head back, clearly enjoying the tease as I maneuvered my way to his pecs, then ran the melting ice around his left nipple. A drop of water rushed down the side of his chest. His hand pressed against the back of my hand as he stroked, encouraging my work. I inspected his hard cock, moving back down and running the ice along the shaft.

Battling against Cohen's warm flesh, the ice didn't last much longer before I had to fetch another piece from his glass of water.

He was all gasps and moans as I probed him with the ice, making my way down his balls, to between his legs. He raised them for me so I could rim his hole with the ice.

God, it looked so damn tight, too tight to take me, but obviously there had to be a way, same as Cohen was able to get inside me.

"Fuck, Brody," he said, giving me the encouragement I needed to press the piece of ice into his twitching hole.

I swallowed it as it melted before kissing and licking his hole.

I was controlled by emotion and instinct, this same wild impulse that had pulled me right to Cohen from the start. I grabbed my spoon and depressed it into the vanilla ice cream, pulling a chunk out and landing it on Cohen's abs.

He laughed, his body trembling from the cold. "Naughty little O'Ralley," he said as I moved the scoop around his belly with my mouth, watching as it painted his abs with the cream. I let it settle in his navel before lapping it up, then took my time navigating for the rest around his torso.

Once I'd finished cleaning up the mess I'd made, I

kissed his navel before nibbling at the edge. Kissing up his body, I reached his mouth, and his eyes popped open. He had this satisfied expression on his face as we kissed. He helped me pull my tee off. We laughed and played as I stripped down with him, and soon we were both lying across the table, just enough room for us next to the dishes we'd pushed aside.

I retrieved a condom from my pocket and slyly displayed it for Cohen. He started to take it when I pulled it back and shook my head. "My turn now."

"You gotta go real slow. It's been a long time since someone's been back there."

I slid off the table, crouching down as I lifted his legs, spread them, and inspected the hole I'd been familiarizing myself with just a few moments earlier.

I offered a kiss just beside it. "Is that true, lil' Cozies? You haven't had anyone inside you in a while?"

I kissed it again.

And again.

Tenderly, to prove to Cohen just how good I could be to his ass.

He laughed. "What the hell are we doing?"

"Don't worry. I'll take good care of you," I spoke to his hole before running the tip of my tongue along his slit, earning another wave of shivers, goose bumps pricking across his thighs.

As I rolled on the condom, towering over Cohen, I loved the idea of dominating his body, having him begging for more. Stooping down, I spit against his hole a few times, then opened the packet of lube attached to the condom, and put some on my cock and his hole.

He spread his legs more, allowing me closer to the edge of the table. As my cock got closer to his ass, I noticed it stiffening even more. And then I noticed Cohen's expression.

"What are you so smug about?"

"Just how badly you want this ass."

"You gonna pretend you don't want my cock?"

He shook his head. "Get in here."

"Bossy bottom. Yes, sir."

I pushed the tip against his hole, carefully maneuvering inside him, my gaze shifting between his ass and his expression as I tried to ensure he was enjoying every moment of it.

He took deep, pensive breaths, his expression so much more serious than before. We were on a fucking mission.

We were as patient as we could manage as we worked together through my own eagerness about wanting it all in a moment and his nervousness about me being inside him. But by the time I got in deep, it was evident with each moan that escaped his mouth, his head rolled back, his hands behind his head, that I was giving it to him right.

"How do I feel?" I asked him.

"If I answer that, it'll only make you more conceited than you already are," he replied between my thrusts.

"Here," I said, guiding him as I stepped on the chair and got onto the tabletop on my knees.

He scooted back, accidentally hitting his plate and sending it crashing to the floor. "Shit."

"Fuck it all." I shoved my dishes off the side of the table to give us space. "Always time to clean up later."

He didn't fight me on it, not as I kept pushing inside him, his body shifting about wildly before me.

"Let me on my knees," he told me.

"You don't like this?"

"If you're gonna give me a run for my money in the top department, then I get to show you my bottoming skills too."

I was excited as I forced myself out of him and he got on his knees so I could push into him from behind. My hands navigated around him, feeling his taut stomach as we kissed over his shoulder. I licked at the vanilla flavor still lingering on his tongue, keeping my hand against his neck as I held him back in this position while he worked that ass in a way that made me feel like I'd been the worst bottom in the world for him.

"Fuck…" I moaned into his ear as that ass took me higher and higher.

I bit at his neck, then licked before caressing my face against his flesh.

As we both seemed determined to impress the other, we found ourselves shifting into one position after another, as though we were filming a Kama Sutra documentary.

Even as I had him pinned with his front against one of the porch support beams, his feet on the ground for a change, his forearms against the wood, he was working that ass, working my dick like his entire existence in that moment was for nothing more than to worship my cock.

We'd kissed so much, my lips were starting to hurt.

And yeah, it was humid as hell in Georgia, but that should have given me an advantage rather than turn me into a fucking fountain of sweat.

"I bet I can make you come first," I told him as I grabbed his shaft.

He winced. "Oh, really? Make it happen."

As soon as I started stroking, I didn't know what kind of bottom magic he was working on my dick... "Where the fuck has this move been?"

"Saving it just for this," he told me, glancing over his shoulder like he wanted to see how close I was.

I sped up my strokes on his dick. "You're just as close."

"But I'm not gonna be the loser who comes first."

"We'll see about that," I said, pushing up against him, kissing and licking behind his ear.

Another moan mixed with mine as he did some sort of ass-fuckery that sent my cum roaring through me at a rate that made me worry it would breach the condom inside him.

Both our guttural sounds came out at once as I felt him shoot.

As he continued coming, I pulled out to make sure the condom hadn't broken, and fortunately, there it was, all my cum at the end.

But damn, I hadn't just thought that climax could tear through latex, but Cohen himself.

Cohen whirled around, his smile broad as ever. "Nice of you to let your date win that one, loser."

Between the smile and the wink, I wasn't sure I'd ever wanted to lose a game so much in my goddamn life.

"Too bad for you we never negotiated an award," I remarked before kissing him.

"I think that means I get to be big spoon while we watch a movie."

"Big spoon? But I'm always big spoon…"

"Tonight you're just a loser with a good dick and a pretty face."

"Then I guess I'll accept my punishment, but I get to decide what we watch."

"Hmm…on second thought, maybe I'll be little spoon."

We shared a laugh before our lips slammed together again.

"Rematch," I demanded playfully.

"Maybe if you're a good little spoon, I'll consider it."

And each kiss after promised that there would definitely be a second date…and that this was totally going to blow up in our faces at some point.

But for now, I just needed to lick his cum off the side of my hand and his cock's head.

A second round of dessert, really.

IT WAS LATE when I got back home. I figured it was late enough that I'd be able to slip into my room without being noticed, but I was halfway down the hall before I heard a voice behind me call out, "Brody!"

I stopped.

I was really hoping I could let those amazing things I'd shared with Cohen linger through my dreams, rather than being interrupted, but it seemed Dwain wasn't going to let that happen.

By the time I'd turned around, he was right behind me.

"I think I have a good idea where you were tonight."

"Will you keep it down?"

He glanced around, whispering, "How long do you

really think you can keep this up without Big Daddy knowing? You've pissed everyone off, but Walker and Mel are still covering for you every night."

I got up in his face. "Maybe you're right, Dwain. Maybe I just don't give a shit about this family anymore." I felt like such a goddamn coward, because my voice cracked even saying the words, but I held firm. "Maybe I should just go tell Big Daddy now. Let him know his son's getting boned by that no-good Mitchell." I pretended to start toward Big Daddy's room when Dwain set his hand on my chest, stopping me.

I pushed back, glaring at him with contempt.

"You think I don't know you well enough to know when you're bluffing?" He eyed me suspiciously. "You think you're the only one in this family who has problems?"

"No. I'm just pissed that you all seem to believe that's what I think."

"Brody, you need—"

"No," I interrupted, so fast that he froze with his mouth still open. "You don't know what I need, Dwain. Good night."

He pursed his lips, and I whirled around and did

my best not to stomp down the hall.

He's not spoiling my amazing night.

But that wouldn't have been the first time I'd lied to myself, I guessed.

CHAPTER TWENTY-SEVEN

Cohen

N O MATTER HOW many ways I dissected it, I continued to come to the same conclusion.

I was fucked.

I couldn't stop thinking about Brody or wanting to be with him. We had so much fun together, just talking or working, and yeah, obviously fucking, but it was the fact that I liked the other stuff as much as the orgasms that told me I was screwed.

I'd spent the last few days thinking about our date and the way we laughed together, oh, and the fact that we couldn't leave the house as a couple and his dad wanted to kill me. I was fairly certain if it were possible, I too would be challenged to a duel the way our ancestors did. Considering I didn't know shit about guns, Big Daddy would kill me, and then Brody would be heartbroken, and I would have done the one thing I really didn't want to do: come between Brody and his family.

That was my main concern. The O'Ralleys were all so different from any family I'd ever known. Brody had already sacrificed so much for them, and they still didn't understand or appreciate it. If Big Daddy found out about us, I would be the wedge that made him feel even more separated from the people he loved most in the world.

It got to the point where I was seriously considering halting all plans to open Mitchell Creek. I didn't *need* to own a distillery. I had options. The O'Ralleys didn't, and maybe that would somehow endear me to the grumpy old man so I didn't, you know, tear his family apart the way our families had been hurting each other for generations.

I grabbed my dad's journal off his desk. With a sigh, I stood, stretched, and made my way out of the house, heading for the distillery.

Isaac was gone again. He was up to something, but I couldn't put my finger on what it was. All I knew was it had to be important because Isaac and I didn't keep secrets from each other.

I made my way across the dense, green property that seemed to glow under the sunlight. I tugged the keys out of my pocket and unlocked the door. The air smelled like a mixture of corn, rye, barley, and wheat. I thought maybe it was engrained into the wood after a hundred years' fermentation, and turning from grain to whiskey.

I went to the newly renovated tasting room and sat at one of the tables. It really did look good. Isaac and I had gone back and forth over the decor, deciding on furniture that was all made from logs and gave a true rural feel, but also with a modern flair. We wanted to stand out, not be the same old brand everyone was used to.

I opened the journal. There was something comforting about reading my dad's words and seeing his handwriting.

Still, I couldn't make myself read it. I'd gone over it a hundred times since I'd been home—shit, home? When had I started thinking of Buckridge as home? But yeah, I'd been through it a hundred times since Byron gave it to me.

My eyes scanned the pages, but it wasn't holding my attention, so I tucked it under my arm and walked around the distillery—my distillery.

My family had been planning to start one with Brody's...then the feud, the missing recipe, the duel, and a hundred years of drama. I somehow felt both part of it and distanced from it. These walls hadn't been built with clean money, but Dad had done his part to fix that. Still, it felt like I could do more.

My footsteps were heavy across the wooden floors before I found myself unlocking the office door in the back. I walked around the space, knelt next to the old desk, which was falling apart. It was odd that this room hadn't been kept in as good a shape as the rest of the building.

I opened all the drawers, but of course they were empty. I had no idea what I was even doing, but something was fueling me in that moment. I remembered Isaac's teasing about false bottoms, and checked for those as well, laughing at my ridiculousness.

Maybe I was a glutton for punishment, looking for something I didn't want to find, or maybe I wanted to find some kind of something to save the day, to prove to Big Daddy that although my family had done bad things, they hadn't stolen that damn recipe. If I could prove it, maybe that would make things easier. Maybe that would mean Big Daddy would somehow accept...whatever the fuck this was between Brody and me.

What in the hell am I doing? I shook my head. This wasn't an episode of *Scooby Doo*. I didn't know what I thought I'd find.

I stood and took a step. My foot caught on something...a loose floorboard, I realized. My eyes darted around the room, as if someone was somehow playing a trick on me. That loose-floorboard thing wasn't really something that happened, was it?

Still, I knelt back down and tried to lift it. The damn thing wouldn't come straight out, so I went and found a hammer, and then, bending down, I began removing nails from the wood. I took the loose board off, then another and another. I didn't know what in the hell got into me, but it was when I removed the fourth board that I found it—an old tin box with photos inside. I didn't recognize the people, but someone had written *Arthur and Randall* on one with two men, their arms around each other and huge smiles on their faces. There were a few photos of them together, some where they were laughing, others with a mason jar full of whiskey between them. There was even a photo of them with someone I assumed was Dorothy.

At the very bottom was an old piece of paper. I unfolded it carefully. The damn thing felt like it could rip apart easily. The lettering was faded, but when I squinted, I was able to read it.

Randall,

I remember the first day we met. My pa had beat the shit out of me, and I took off to the creek and met you there. You took me home and got me drunk for the first time, off illegal whiskey. I fell in love that night, both with you and the damn bottle.

I never told ya. How could I? I knew about you and Dorothy. Was jealous but not of you, of her. I asked her to marry me when it was you I wanted. That started the downward spiral of it all, didn't it?

But I couldn't admit it. How could I? They woulda had me committed, or killed.

I will always regret everything I did after that. The duel, shooting you, taking what was yours. And having done that, I could never get myself right again. Just kept fuckin' up, hating everyone and everything around me.

Mitchell Creek should be yours, but I don't know if I have the balls to ever say it. Haven't told a soul I stole that recipe from you. Don't know if you'll ever read these words. You were right. I'm a coward.

I'm sorry.

Art

My hand couldn't stop shaking. The letter dropped from between my fingers.

Proof that Mitchell Creek, everything that my family had built, was a lie. It came from a stolen recipe that never belonged to us in the first place. My grandfather had loved Brody's, and he'd stolen from him, lied to him, and hurt him, all because of a broken heart.

I crawled backward, away from the letter, as if it were a venomous creature poised to attack.

It was a lie. Christ, it was all a fucking lie. The O'Ralleys had every right to hate us. *I* hated us. We were liars and thieves and criminals.

Bile crawled up my throat, and I shoved to my feet. I dry-heaved but didn't vomit. All I could think about was Brody, the O'Ralleys, their struggles over the years, and this feud Big Daddy held on to, how they sure as shit wouldn't walk away from it now. How could they? Because I had to tell them. There was no way I wouldn't.

I grabbed the letter and journal, shoved them into the box, then picked up the box and stumbled out of the room.

The second I did, I heard, "Mitchell! Get out here!"

Big Daddy.

Not gonna lie, part of me wanted to stay right where I was, maybe hide and never come out. Well, at least until I could figure out how to unpack the information I just discovered. Even thinking about it made my chest clench to the point my breath could hardly escape.

But the truth was, that wasn't me and never would be. I wasn't the type who could lie or hide, not from something this big.

"Mitchell! Where the hell are you, you coward!"

If there was one thing I wasn't, it was a coward, so I made my way toward the door just as Big Daddy stepped inside the distillery. All I could think was, *he knows.* Whether about the recipe, or me and Brody, but he knew something.

Big Daddy was breathing heavily, a vein throbbing in his forehead, his hands fisted. I could see the punch coming, but I wasn't going to do anything to stop it. Hell, I probably deserved it, if not for any reason other than I was the last Mitchell left and I came from a family of lying thieves just like the O'Ralleys always knew I had.

His hands were both in tight fists, his right one opening and closing, but he didn't make the move to hit me. "I'm this close, Mitchell," he gritted out.

"You want to kick my ass? Go ahead and do it. I'm not fighting you back."

He took a few deep breaths, his whole body trembling slightly, hands loosening. Even though he had the right, it was clear he wouldn't hit me. I didn't believe for a second that Big Daddy was the kind of man who would hurt someone who wouldn't defend themselves.

"'Course you won't. Mitchells have always been cowards," he spat at me, and I just shrugged. From what I'd heard of my family, he wasn't wrong.

"I'm not like them, and I don't believe my dad was

either."

"Hogwash. Your daddy was just like the rest of 'em. He used your mama to get at my family, then sent her away and didn't take care of his own son."

My heart seized, his words finding every one of my insecurities and pumping blood through them, making them feel bigger and more alive. "You don't know…" I tried, but couldn't find my words. They were all tangled with the truth I just found out, one my dad hadn't known either.

"You think I don't see through your act? You think I don't know what you're playin' at? Comin' to town, pretending you're not like the rest of them. Your great-granddaddy weaseled his way into the O'Ralley world only to lie and steal from 'em. Your granddaddy was a no-good criminal. The whole damn Mitchell business is built on a lie, on something your family stole from us. Your daddy tried to *use* your mama against us, and now here you are, worming your way into my son's world. I won't let Brody be hurt by you, damn it. He's my son, and I'll protect him!"

I flinched.

"That's right. I know what you're doin'. You're tryin' to use Brody. I heard 'em talking. My own son went behind my back to share family finances with the enemy he's sleeping with."

"No." I shook my head. He was turning something beautiful into something ugly. "He didn't go behind your back in a vindictive way. There's no one in the world who loves his family as much as Brody does. All he wants to do is help, and I know you have no reason to believe me, but I do too. I would never—"

"Liar!" he cut me off. "You're using my own flesh and blood against me! What is wrong with you people?"

A week ago I would have blown off his question. Hell, an hour ago I would have, but the truth was, we were everything he said we were. Sometimes it didn't matter that you tried to make things right. My dad had fought to make the distillery legit, but underneath it all was the truth that it never should have been ours to begin with. "It's different with Brody." It was the only excuse I had. I wouldn't hurt him. I wouldn't lie to him. Which meant I had to tell him what I found. I had to tell them all what I found. Things could never be right any other way. I could never live with myself if I didn't.

Anger flared on his face, the red of it deepening.

"You stay the hell away from my son." And then...then he sobered, pain mixing with the anger in his stare. "Hasn't your family done enough? You gotta come here and take my son away from me too? My family is all I got, the only thing I didn't think a Mitchell could steal from me."

"Big Daddy—"

"Don't you call me that."

"Mr. O'Ralley. I wouldn't. I would never hurt Brody. I love him." As soon as the words left my mouth, I knew they were true. Holy fuck. If I wasn't in the middle of a crisis already, I sure as shit would have been sent into one then.

I was in love.

With Brody O'Ralley.

I'd never been in love before.

I was in love with the guy my family stole a legacy from.

I took the letter out of the box and handed it to him. "And that's why...that's why I have to tell you the truth." Because if there was ever any chance of this working, I had to be honest. If not, I wouldn't be able to live with myself. "You were right. Almost everything you said about the Mitchells was right. My dad...he didn't try and use my mom against you. He just fell in love with her. That's all. But we were criminals. The rest of my family was everything you said they were. But my dad wasn't. He tried to fix it. He tried to make things better. That doesn't change what my family has done, though." I paused, took a deep breath, ignored the voice in my head that told me not to do this. "It doesn't change the fact that a hundred years ago, my great-grandfather stole the recipe for the Buckridge Deluxe Scotch from your family. Everything that we have should be yours."

It felt like an eternity before Big Daddy said, "You sonofabitch. What are you playin' at tellin' me that?"

"Nothing. I just want to tell the truth because it's the right thing and because of Brody."

He shook his head. I could see the thoughts form-ing in his brain. "No, you want to use this by lookin' like the good guy. You wanna get your claws into us even more. I know how you Mitchells work. Every Mitchell has somehow hurt an O'Ralley. If you cared a lick about Brody, you'd walk away and leave him be. He's got a big heart, that one, and he's always wondered what was out there. He'll fall for you, and he'll hurt his family because of it, which will do nothing but hurt him. If you love him like you say you do, you'll leave him alone. You owe us that."

Without another word, Big Daddy turned and walked away.

I stood there, trying to tell myself he wasn't right.

CHAPTER TWENTY-EIGHT

Brody

I RAN A brush through the fine hairs along El-liecomb's neck. Spending time with her was always soothing, even more so since I'd started pulling away from my siblings. I was still having a hard time overcoming my pride.

The door to the stable opened, and Walker came in, his gaze shifting about uneasily.

"What broke?" I asked, though going by his expression, I figured this didn't have anything to do with work.

As he approached, I was tempted to be a smartass but stopped myself, since it seemed important, given his hesitation. I might have been mad, but I knew Walker better than anyone, and I knew when something weighed on his mind.

"I don't know how to tell you this, Brodes…"

I wanted to tell him to stop using a name he was only allowed to have for me when we were on better terms, but I bit my tongue, realizing how petty that would be.

"I'm having a hard time believing it, really," he added, "but Isaac just sent me a text. Cohen's packing up over at the Mitchell place."

"Where's he heading?"

Walker's downturned gaze and tense jaw told me everything I needed to know.

"What the hell happened?"

"Sounds like he had a change of heart."

I knew he meant about the distillery, but that wasn't the change of heart that concerned me.

"It sounds like he's planning to leave…very soon."

Fuck.

I didn't even remember I had a damn brush in my hand, dropped it right in Elliecomb's stall, and rushed past him toward the door, stopping myself as soon as I reached it.

"Walker…thank you for coming to tell me that."

At the end of the day, stubborn as I could be, he was still my brother. We could be at each other's throats, but we were on the same side. Deep down, I could never forget that.

I fetched Elliecomb from her stall, disregarding a saddle in my hurry to get to Cohen, fearing I might be too late. I rode through our woods, then slipped through a familiar spot in the fence between our land and the Mitchells', where a tree branch had made space for one rebellious O'Ralley to get to his Mitchell in a hurry.

By the time I was heading from the woods to the house, I had to practically recall how I ended up there, it all happened so goddamn fast.

I thought back on the time I'd spent with Cohen. We'd had so much fun...more than fun...and he was taking to the place like an old pro. What in God's name would have possessed him to pick up and leave now? And why hadn't he even mentioned it to me first?

When I reached the house, Isaac opened the front door like he'd been anticipating my arrival. "He's in his room," he told me as I passed him at the door. He looked as concerned about his friend as I was.

Something wasn't right. I could feel it in my gut. This wasn't where things had been heading, not even close.

I went upstairs to Cohen's room, where he stood at the foot of his bed, placing a stack of clothes into his luggage. I stopped in the doorway, and he caught my gaze and froze in place.

"Going on a weekend getaway?" I asked facetiously as he finished setting the clothes in his suitcase.

"Fucking Isaac," he muttered. "I was going to call you."

"When? When you got to the airport?"

He didn't respond, just stood there, staring at me, not like a man who was regretting his decision, but like a man who'd made up his mind. There he was, the guy I'd thought was so fucking hot the night I'd kissed him at the Barn, who opened up to me so easily as we'd come to know each other, and now I could see in his eyes how the door that had been open for me had slammed shut on me.

But *why*?

"I've been doing a lot of thinking…a hell of a lot of thinking. Brody, I didn't even know what the fuck I was looking for when I came out here. And I thought I could maybe find myself by taking on this part of my family's history. But then…I was going through some of my family's belongings, and I guess you could say I found out that I'm not cut from the same stock as the Mitchells who built this place."

"Sounds like bullshit to me."

"Bullshit or not, I realized it's time for me to go."

"So you bust into town, invest all this money into the distillery, and now you're gonna pick up and walk away from it? I know enough about you to know you ain't some quitter."

"It's called a sunk cost, Brody. I poured some into this, but nothing I can't get back. You know as well as I do that I don't know what the hell I'm doing here. I can hire the right people, watch all the goddamn YouTube videos in the world, but who the hell was I to think I could trek into an old distillery and get it up and running, ready for business, having never even picked up a book about this shit before getting here? This whole thing has been some desperate attempt at figuring something out that I'm not going to figure out here. This isn't me."

No. *This* wasn't Cohen. Not the guy who came out here and picked it all up so easily, the guy who approached this work without any trepidation or worry. The words...they made sense for someone, but not the guy I was coming to know.

I could tell he was holding back.

I approached him, heartbroken as I saw the inside of that suitcase, which was too goddamn full for my tastes.

"Cohen, if something happened, you can talk to me. Why can't you just talk to me as easily as you have the past few weeks?"

His mouth was open slightly, as though the words were on his tongue, but he sealed his lips nearly as quickly, tensing his jaw as if struggling to keep it all in.

"There's nothing specific to talk about. I just... You know my future was always up in the air. Plus, I'm missing my mom, and she's missing me. I figure it's time to head back."

As much as he'd talked about the distillery, it was hard that the thing weighing on my thoughts hadn't come up. What about the time we'd shared? The laughs we'd had? It fucking meant something to me, and I didn't believe it hadn't meant anything to him.

"And what about us?"

"I think you're incredible. God, I don't deserve someone like you. One day you'll see and—"

I held up my hand, cringing. "Okay. You can stop

there. I don't need this talk. What you're doing says all I need to know."

"Everything that matters to you is right here. You have an amazing family, and they'd do anything to protect you from getting hurt. Don't ever forget that."

It was an odd comment for him to make, but it didn't change that I was hurt. Even worse, it was evident that nothing I said or did was going to change his mind.

I nodded, resigned, before extending my hand.

He eyed it for a moment, sorrow in his expression; surely, he had to realize this seemed to be what all we'd shared had amounted to.

He took my hand, and we shook firmly.

I held on a little too long...or maybe he did...or maybe that was what I wanted to believe. But I took a breath and forced my hand back.

"Thank you for all your help," he said.

"And thank you for yours...and everything."

"If you guys do need anything..."

"We'll sort it all out, but thank you for offering. And I do genuinely appreciate everything you did to help out, Cohen."

"I'm sorry I wasted your time on the distillery."

"No, that was an even trade. Don't ever think otherwise."

We stood in silence as I accepted our fate. "I'll head out and let you get on your way."

I went to the door, set my hand on the doorframe. I should have left, but the sweltering anger in my chest...at Cohen, or just this damned situation...stopped me in my tracks.

"Guess we were at a different exit than I figured," I blurted out.

I glanced over my shoulder. It was clear he was about to say something, but I knew I wouldn't be able to handle whatever it was.

"Sorry, that was a low blow," I went on. "I think now's my time to bail...speaking of sunk costs and all. Goodbye, Cohen."

"Goodbye."

Just like when heading over to his place, I had a hard time recalling how I'd wound up back on Elliecomb. I was being guided by my emotions, by the anger pulsing through my veins, but then I realized...no, I wasn't angry. I was heartbroken.

This was something deeper than my heartaches of the past. It seared right to my core.

Tears pushed from my eyes, and I cried all the way home.

Cohen was leaving…tomorrow, for Christ's sake.

Somehow I found my way into the basement, and sat on a box, looking through old photo albums. I stopped on a picture of Big Momma hosing off her mud-soaked kids, Dwain and Lee, in the yard. Beside that photo was another of Walker and me playing in the sprinkler. I turned the page to see an image of us swimming in the pond. With Big Momma and all the siblings in it, I knew Big Daddy must've taken the photo.

How the fuck did I wind up going from being so fucked up over Cohen leaving to looking at these photos?

But I couldn't deceive myself. I knew the reason.

Another loss. Never enough time spent with the ones I wanted to spend it with.

I knew one day the hole in my heart would heal, but I'd never get rid of the scar.

CHAPTER TWENTY-NINE

Cohen

JESUS, I FELT like a piece of shit. It had been two days since I left Georgia, and I still couldn't get Brody's look out of my thoughts—the hurt I'd seen when he came over to find out why I was leaving, when he told me we were at different exits. The worst part was that we weren't. I wanted him so damn bad. Wanted him more than anything I'd ever wanted in my life, but how could I be that wedge between him and his family? Brody already felt enough guilt where they were concerned. Big Daddy would never accept Brody and me. All it would do was hurt him, and my family had done enough of that over the years. This pain would be short-term. He'd get over it, but losing them, risking them, for me, was something Brody would never get past.

My bedroom door pushed open, and Isaac was there. I didn't know what I'd do without him. I couldn't imagine making it through this without him by my side.

"Lying there thinking how much of a dumbass you are?" he asked.

Yeah, yeah I was. That and how much this fucking hurt. "Now isn't the time."

Isaac came into the room and lay on my bed with me. "God, I'd forgotten how comfortable the beds are at home. We need new beds in the Mitchell house."

"We're not going back to the Mitchell house."

"In fact, we just need to get rid of all the furniture. No offense, but your bio-dad had shit taste. Maybe I can get it cleaned out while we're gone and call in a decorator so it's very us when we get back. Plus, we left your car there. That was stupid, by the way."

"I'm not going back," I said again, knowing he heard me the first time. I didn't know why he was so intent on heading back there—well, other than I was sure he could tell I was miserable. "And the furniture has grown on me. It's...very Mitchell and Buckridge."

I tried to get out of bed, but Isaac grabbed my wrist.

"Are you going to tell me what in the hell happened? This isn't like you—the whole running thing. We were fine. We were happy. We were moving forward with the distillery, and you were in love for the first time, which you still totally are. Don't try to deny it. You gave your cold, dead heart to that country boy, and he brought it back to life, Cozies."

I rolled my eyes, though he was right. Every damn word Isaac had said hit the nail on the head, and even that stupid saying made me think of Brody because it was *so* him.

"If you cared a lick about Brody, you'd walk away and leave him be. He's got a big heart, that one, and he's always wondered what was out there. He'll fall for you, and he'll hurt his family because of it, which will do nothing but hurt him. If you love him like you say you do, you'll leave him alone. You owe us that."

Big Daddy's words tumbled around in my head, in my damn chest too, in that place where Brody was. My country boy had found a home there, all right.

"It never would have worked out," I managed to say. But I'd wanted it to. God, I'd wanted it to. I still did.

"Oh, and you know that how? Your magic crystal

ball? Why didn't I know about this ability of yours? Wait, did you go back to the Barn for a reading I don't know about?" I sighed, and he added, "What in the hell happened that you aren't telling me?"

This time when I pulled away, Isaac let me. I sat on the edge of the bed, with my back to him. I wanted to tell him, wanted to let it all spill from my lips. What I'd found, my conversation with Big Daddy, but I wasn't sure Isaac would understand. He didn't know Big Daddy the way I strangely felt like I did. He didn't know Brody the way I did. This was all too much of a clusterfuck for it to end any other way. "Nothing. There's not a damn thing I'm not telling you. But we do need to figure out what our next move is. We should try something totally different. We both have savings." I needed to sell Mitchell Creek and find a way to get the money to the O'Ralleys. It wasn't mine, wasn't ours. We didn't deserve any of it.

"You might have to fly this one solo," Isaac said softly behind me.

I froze, my heart stopping as the hairs on the back of my neck stood on end. I turned to look at him. "What do you mean?" Isaac's gaze wouldn't meet mine. He never avoided me this way. It made my chest get tighter and the feeling of emptiness inside me grow. "What is it?"

"I just... I know it sounds crazy, but it felt right there. It's weird, and quirky, and most people have zero fashion sense, and sometimes I still feel like I'm in a cheesy small-town flick, but...I don't know. It felt right. Like I was doing something I was supposed to be doing. I've never had that, ya know? And I love you like a brother. I always will. You're the only family I've ever had, but I...I think I'm in love with Walker." The last sentence was said so softly, I almost couldn't hear him.

"What?" I was shocked so stupid, I could have fallen off the bed. "You guys are..."

"I haven't told him that. Oh God, do you think I'm crazy? I would never say it first, and he's not out to his dad and not ready to do that yet. I've never known anyone like him. He makes me feel *wanted* in ways I never have. We've been...fucking around, secretly, and I probably shouldn't have even told you, but I need you to understand. When it's the two of us...it's perfect. I can't walk away from that."

I sat there, unable to find my voice. I knew Isaac was attracted to him, obviously, but they'd been sneaking around? My best friend who was anti-love and never wanted to settle down thought he was in love with Walker O'Ralley?

He hadn't told me, but then, I had things I hadn't told him either. Now the secretiveness made sense, when he would disappear and I didn't know where he was.

"I think he was hurt when I told him I was leaving with you. That's what made me realize I love him—the way it felt to hurt him, and thinking about saying goodbye. But it's you, and we're us, and how in the fuck do I live without you? But...I don't think I can do it. I don't think I can stay. I don't even know if Walker will have me, if he'll want me, but I have to try."

In that moment, for the first time since we'd known each other, I was filled with jealousy toward my best friend.

My brother.

Because Christ, I loved Brody too, and I wanted him, wanted him so damn much, it hurt to breathe. So much, I was afraid I would never be happy again, and apparently Isaac felt the same way about Walker, yet he wasn't running. He planned to go back and fight for what he wanted.

Our situations weren't the same, though. Big Daddy could eventually accept Isaac in ways he never could me. Isaac's family hadn't stolen from them. My whole family business was based on a lie I didn't know how to come to terms with.

"Cohen, say something."

I grabbed him, pulled him to me, and hugged him. "I'm happy for you. Christ, of course I'm happy for you. And he'd be stupid not to feel the same. You're Isaac fucking Connors. Did you really think I would be angry with you?" I had to admit that hurt, but only because I wanted what he had. I wanted to be with Brody, and I couldn't imagine my life without Isaac in it every day.

"No, I just didn't want you to feel like I was choosing him over you. We'll always be us. Walker is just a really good fuck."

I laughed, knowing Isaac was trying to lighten the mood. If he was thinking of heading back to Georgia, Walker had to be a whole lot more than a good lay.

"You're in love with Brody too. As crazy as Buckridge is, you like it there. Why are you running? I've never seen you run in your life. You're doing it to protect Brody somehow, aren't you?"

I closed my eyes, even hearing his name twisted me up. "I'm doing it because I don't know that I want to be a Mitchell. I don't know if I fit." But the truth was, I'd never completely felt like I fit here either. That was why it had been so easy to drop everything and go to Georgia, to decide to stay there. "Fuck, this is such a mess. I don't even know who I am." How could I not know that?

I wasn't a Mitchell, not really. I wasn't a Sorenson really either.

"Get over yourself, man. A past doesn't define who you are. You're Cohen Mitchell, and who that person is has nothing to do with who your family is or who your adoptive family is. You're you. You've spent your life looking for something outside of you—whether it was wondering about your biological family, or trying to find your worth by fitting in with your adoptive family, trying to be who you think they want you to be, when none of that shit matters. You're not going to find what you're looking for until you look inside yourself."

"We stole it!" I shouted, surprising myself. I shoved to my feet and began pacing the room. "We're thieves. My family not only took part in illegal activities, but they stole the damn recipe. None of that should be mine. It should all be the O'Ralleys'." And I would make sure to pay them back for that.

"Okay, well, so? That's shitty that your great-grandpa, or whoever the fuck it was, was a janky-ass thief who stole something a hundred years ago, but that wasn't you. Sell Mitchell Creek, give the money to the O'Ralleys. Do whatever you have to do to make yourself feel better, but that's not why you're running from Brody. You're running from him because you don't feel good enough for him and you're scared of losing him, even if you don't want to admit it. You're scared he'll decide you're not worth it and walk away because your mom died and your dad didn't come for you. And I'm sorry, C. You know that. I can't imagine how it is to feel that way, but as much as I love you, you're being a coward. That's not the Cohen I know."

Without another word, Isaac walked out of the room.

I stood there, unable to move, unable to think, except one thing—he was right. I wasn't worth Brody screwing up his whole family for, and sooner or later he would realize that.

CHAPTER THIRTY

Brody

W E SAT ON the back patio at breakfast together, most of the family. I could never say the whole family, not when one of its most cherished members couldn't be there…ever again.

The silence was palpable, broken only by clinking silverware, sips, and chewing. Sounds that were fairly typical were grating on my nerves, as even Mel didn't attempt to disturb this unnatural quiet.

We'd all pulled away from one another over the past few weeks, a rubber band stretching, but this time I wondered if we'd snap back or break. It was hard to even think about eating without imagining that first dinner date with Cohen…

I wanted to fucking tear him from my thoughts so that this burn in my chest and the constant tears percolating from my eyes would stop. It was something I'd wished with Big Momma too, but hated myself for even thinking it would ever be better to go on without having her in my thoughts.

It was stunning how a person could feel such unbearable emotional agony, the sort that made it feel like your heart was going to explode, but then kept you right on going all the same.

"Can someone pass me the butter?" Big Daddy asked, like everything wasn't wrong and like he didn't know goddamn well that the butter was right next to me.

I understood why my siblings were on edge around me at the moment, but even Big Daddy had started acting strange, to the point where I had to wonder if any of them had blabbed on me like when we were kids. He was distant, but also, it was as if he felt guilty about something. I thought maybe it was business-related, but we certainly weren't worse off than before.

I grabbed the butter and passed it to Walker, who passed it on.

That simple exchange with Walker reminded me that I hadn't lost just Cohen. I'd lost my best friend, the brother I could always confide in about shit like that. And just as shitty, he seemed as out of it as I was…and to think he couldn't come to me with whatever was on his mind… It was the sort of thing that made my misery shift to downright anger.

"Maybe we should do something as a family today," Mel said. The way she spoke the words, light and cheerful, it was as if everything was the same as always, but the nervous expression on her face suggested otherwise. "Maybe go out to the pond. Go fishing or…"

"I was going to go to the Feed & Seed to pick up supplies for the horses," I said curtly.

"Come on," Dwain chimed in, which took me totally by surprise. When the hell had he ever cared about me hanging with the family?

"Yeah," Big Daddy added. "It would be good for us to have a day without stressing about work or chores. You can take some time for your family."

I could take time for my family?

Seriously?

Between his words and the horrible feelings I was still processing since Cohen had packed up and skipped town…I. Fucking. Lost. It.

"I don't want to hear another person at this table

say anything about me needing to make time for the family."

"What?" Big Daddy asked. I'd never seen him look so shocked, scared even, by anything I'd said.

"Maybe you're the one who needs to spend time with your family, to talk to us about who we are, who we've become. Do you even know any of us anymore?"

"I know you much better than you realize." He sounded so confident about that, as though there was something he knew that I somehow wasn't privy to, which only pissed me off more.

"No, you don't know us, Big Daddy. Not anymore." I bit my tongue, but just for a moment. I didn't have a damn thing to hide anymore. "Did you know I'm bi, or pan or something...I don't even know, I'm so goddamn confused right now."

He was quiet, his brows tugging closer as his forehead creased. "Do you really think that would mean a damn thing to me?"

"It should mean something to you that your own kid didn't feel like he could come to you and just say it. It should mean something to you that I couldn't talk to you about the important things in my life right now. The things weighing on my mind."

I wasn't just talking about myself, but about Dwain and Walker as well. Clearly, all of us were trying to figure shit out, and none of us feeling like we could just be open.

"I've never done anything to make you feel like you couldn't talk to me, have I?" Big Daddy asked, looking around the table.

I scoffed. "Nothing? You don't think you and your stupid feud with the Mitchells made my life easy, do you?"

"Brody," Walker said, glancing at me as though wanting me to rethink where this conversation was going.

In my periphery, I noticed Lee and Mel eyeing one another uneasily. This was not going to be pretty.

"Brody, there's no reason for us to get back to that—"

"Yes, there is. Because I'm tired of carrying this stuff around on my own. It's this fucking weight I'm carrying around, and about to get crushed under. Cohen and I were seeing each other. And it was serious." I stopped as I reflected on seeing that suitcase on Cohen's bed. "At least, it was for me. And all that time, because you were so caught up in family honor and loyalty, you betrayed me. Because you cared more about that than my happiness."

"I've never meant to get in the way of your happiness."

"You know what kills me most about Big Momma? That time in college when I wasn't here as much as I could have been. I could have watched dumb shows with her or helped her cook…or talked to her about her vintage horseshoe collection, but I was robbed of all that time. By the time it was over, all I wished was that I'd had more of that. And now, here we are, all these years later, and here I was, running around in secret, stealing time here and there for the only thing that has made me feel alive in I couldn't even tell you how long, and if it hadn't been for your dumbass feud, I would have been over there every day. I would have been bringing him over here to talk to my family, who loves me and supports me. I would have been able to take him out on a date in town, not hiding him like he's something I should be ashamed of."

Now it was really quiet, my siblings' gazes down-turned, Big Daddy's mouth agape. But there was no holding anything back anymore. "I fell in love, Big Daddy."

Hearing myself say it shocked the fuck out of me,

but it was true. The moment I said it, it felt like the truest thing I'd ever said. I loved that no-good Mitchell.

"And you weren't there," I went on. "Your stupid, stubborn attitude toward him stole time and memories I can't get back. And I shouldn't even be yelling at you about it because I should have been the one to stand up and say *screw it* to it all, but I was a coward. I'm not hiding from the truth anymore. Excuse me."

I threw my napkin onto the table and stormed into the house. No one tried to stop me, which was for the best, since I needed a moment to collect my thoughts.

I found my way back into the basement, like when I'd pulled out all those old pictures, but this time, I pulled out the corkboard Big Momma had encouraged me to make. It was tucked behind a bunch of old furniture, which meant it was one of the oldest things down here. I pulled it into the light, settled on a crate, and glanced it over: all the places I'd wanted to see, all the places she would talk to me about, that she wanted me to take pictures of on my travels.

I heard the door open at the top of the stairs and then footsteps. I'd been in this house long enough to recognize the sound of Dwain's footsteps, the pace, the way they hit my ear. I fought back my tears before he came down and saw me.

His expression was hard to read, and I was curious what he would say.

"Can you just go? I'm still not talking to you."

He found a nearby crate and plopped down on it.

"Dwain, I need some fucking space right now."

"Well, I'm about the only member of this family who isn't going to be butthurt over you not liking me, so I figured I'd take one for the team." He winked, but I didn't so much as crack the sort of smile I might have, had I been in less of a mood. "Any rate, your little stunt at the table really did a number on Big Daddy. But hell, you made Walker's and my life easier. We went ahead and outed ourselves, so there's that."

As disoriented as I was from my own confession, I was relieved to hear that. "I'm glad, Dwain. You deserve that. We all deserve to be able to be who the hell we are and love who we love, even if we have all these dumb family rules around shit. But now you guys can all be happy. Cohen's gone. It's what you and everyone else wanted—you practically wanted to get out a rifle and chase him out of town as soon as he got here—and now you got your wish. Hating on him for no goddamn reason other than this stupid feud that don't mean nothing. What is the point of all this fucking hate when you only have people in your life for a short time anyway?"

"If you coulda seen the way Big Daddy looked after you left, I don't think you'd feel this way."

"How's that?"

"Sad. Whether you believe it or not, the last thing in the world he wants is to hurt us. And that shit you said about Big Momma, damn...I think that fucked with all our heads. I knew you were crushing on that Mitchell, but if I'd thought it was that serious, I wouldn't have been so pissy about it. You might not know it, but I want you to be happy too, Brodes."

"Since when?"

He grabbed the side of the corkboard, stroking his thumb across it. "Since I watched my big bro walk away from his dreams...and himself."

"I thought I'd done the right thing, sacrificing it all for my family, and now I'm just so fucking mad at everyone. But mostly mad at myself."

"Well, I fucking hate your guts, and I'm down here trying to cheer you up, so at least you know you can be mad at me and it don't change a thing."

I finally cracked a smile. "I don't hate you, Dwain."

"Hey, don't start being nice to me now. All those wrestling matches we had when we were younger were the only thing that got people to stop teasing me before my growth spurt."

I laughed as I reflected on the little scheme we'd devised when he was being bullied in school.

He set his hand on my shoulder, pulling me close.

"I didn't know life was gonna be this tough," I said. "Falling in love with people, only to lose 'em."

"Yeah, it sucks balls. But it'll suck a lot less when you finally stop trying to take it all on yourself and remember that's what family's for."

I pulled away and glared at him suspiciously. "When did you get so fucking smart?"

"Eh, I read it in a book."

I laughed, and he returned it with a grin.

Dwain's sympathy reminded me of just what was so goddamn special and irreplaceable about family. His words did make me feel better, made me realize I needed to get past my stubbornness.

But I knew it wouldn't make this pain magically go away. There was no quick fix.

And I knew as much as anyone that deep wounds took a lot of fucking time to heal.

CHAPTER THIRTY-ONE

Cohen

I WAS AT the home I'd lived in from when I was adopted until I was eighteen years old. It was in Pacific Heights, with a prime view of San Francisco.

We were outside in the back, eating catered food and enjoying the view. This wasn't the first time I'd seen Mom since I'd been back, but it was the first time I'd seen Dad. He was always busy. Oftentimes it was just her and me when I was growing up.

"Have you put the place on the market yet?" Dad asked before taking a drink of his wine.

"No, sir." My stomach clenched at the thought of it.

"You don't have to rush," Mom assured me. "That's your history, Cohen. You don't have to walk away from that."

I both appreciated her words and wished she'd never said them. I didn't want to lose Mitchell Creek, but I also didn't think I deserved it. I didn't want theft to be my history, but there was no way to get around the fact that it was and there was nothing I could do about it.

"We'll see."

"It's worth a lot of money. If you're not going to live there or open it, there's no reason to sit on it."

I shrugged, not sure how to explain the situation to him. Hell, even if I did, I wasn't sure he would understand. Dad wasn't real good at the sentimental stuff.

Sometimes I didn't understand it myself, but then, I wasn't sure I was much better than him with the heart stuff either.

We all chatted as we finished our meal. The food was delicious but somehow tasted fake, almost manufactured. Not like the Southern meals I'd had in town. The last one Brody had made for me had been—Nope. I wasn't going to allow myself to go there. Damn it. I had to figure out how to get him out of my head, out of my heart.

"What are your plans now?" Dad asked.

"I'm not quite sure yet." I could always go work for him full-time again.

"Well, I'm sure you and Isaac will figure it out. You always do."

"It'll just be me. He's actually planning to go back. He met a guy while we were there. He hasn't told him how he feels. I think he's stalling because he feels bad leaving me, but he's going to." And he should. At least one of us should be happy. I would never begrudge him that.

"Oh, wow. The two of you have always been a package deal. I can't quite think of one of you without the other. How are you feeling about all this?" Mom asked, and I shrugged. "What about that young man you were spending time with while you were there? Brody, I think you said his name was."

"It was just a thing," I lied, just as Dad's cell rang.

"Shit. Sorry to cut dinner short. I have to take this. I'm probably going to need to run into the office. It was good seeing you, Cohen." Dad walked over, kissed Mom, and then was on his way. The scene wasn't unfamiliar. He didn't love me the way Mom did. I'd always felt like I hadn't been loved by two fathers.

Once the car started in front of the house, Mom

said, "Now, are you going to tell me what's really going on?" Her question didn't surprise me.

I averted my eyes from hers. I'd already gone through this more than once with Isaac. I couldn't imagine doing it again with her. "Nothing. I just realized it wasn't where I belong."

Mom reached over and put her hand on mine. "I don't think that's true. It doesn't have anything to do with me, does it? Children move away from their parents all the time. No matter how many times we talked about it, I know you worry that by having a part of your biological past, you're betraying me. That's not how it is at all, Cohen. I love you. I will always love you, and I know you love me. That's not going to change because you move or because you run a business that was left to you by your biological father."

The thing was, I knew that. I was a smart guy. In my head, I knew these things. It was my heart that struggled with it, struggled with accepting that I was lovable. It was a whole lot easier to hold on to any and every reason I could not to let Brody in.

Mom sighed. "I know your dad and I aren't typical parents. I always look back on our past and wonder if I did something wrong. Should we have changed your last name? Looked into your history when you were young? There are so many questions. And I know you and your dad struggle to connect outside of business stuff. I'm sure that wasn't easy on you either, but we all did the best we could. You're our son no matter what."

"I know that. I do. And you're my mom no matter what too." God, relationships were complicated. It didn't matter what kind of relationship it was. It was all part of being alive, of being human. "I just... I found out some things, and I don't know if that's where I belong. But being here, back in San Francisco, doesn't feel right either. Nothing does, and I'm questioning myself in ways I never have. I don't even know who in the hell I am." I groaned. "I don't know if any of this makes sense. If my thoughts or feelings make sense. I just feel..."

"Lost?"

"Yeah, I do. And I think I always have." My eyes darted toward the table. I'd always felt like that, hadn't I? Untethered, like nothing was connecting me to earth. Sure, Mom did in some ways, and Isaac did in others, but without them, it was like I could float away, with no real direction, and no one would notice.

And maybe *I* wouldn't even notice because I'd always felt lost anyway.

Then I surprised myself by adding, "I fell in love." And as much as those words hurt, it felt good to say them to her.

"That explains a lot. It's different looking through our own eyes once we fall in love with someone. Makes the world a little brighter, but it makes our insecurities brighter too because it means we have something to lose, something that really matters."

That was exactly it. That was how I felt. "It's...complicated. His dad hates me."

"Well, you're not planning on dating *him*, are you?" she teased, and I smiled.

"I don't want to get between Brody and his family."

"It doesn't sound like you are. You would never do something like that. If Brody's father allows it to cause problems in their relationship, that's his fault, not yours."

"That doesn't change the fact that it would hurt Brody."

"Losing you probably hurts Brody too."

I rolled my eyes. "He'll get over it."

"Why? Because losing you is insignificant? Oh, Cohen. You really think that, don't you? You try to come off so confident, but you don't feel it."

I fiddled with the tablecloth, unable to answer. Hating that my reply would be yes.

"Sweetheart, I know you have a lot to work through, between losing your mom and your dad not being around, foster care and adoption, and then finding out your biological dad knew about you. I'm sure your father and I played a part in all that too. We didn't always make the right decisions, but you are not insignificant. You don't have to be afraid people are going to walk away from you. You don't have to run before they get the chance. Love doesn't always go away."

She was right. Logically, I knew that. Hell, I knew if Brody felt similar to how I did, I'd tell him he was being ridiculous, but it was a lot easier to say words like that than it was to believe them.

"I don't think I deserve him." That was the difference between Brody and me. He always thought of other people. He put his family first. He'd never hurt anyone. I'd been selfish quite a bit in my life.

"You do. I can promise you that. Don't live your

life with regrets. If there's one thing I want you to have learned from me, it's to fight for what you want. And if you don't think you deserve something, work your ass off to make sure you do. This boy, do you think he loves you too?"

I thought about the look on Brody's face when he found out I was leaving. The sound of his voice. The way he laughed when we were together, and the way I caught him looking at me when he didn't know I was watching. "I think he could."

"And he's worth it? Fighting for?"

"Hell yeah," I answered automatically. Brody was worth everything.

"Then all you have to do is see that you're worth it too. I can tell you that until I'm blue in the face, but no one can make you see it but you."

As I sat there letting her words seep in, the truth dug itself deeper into me, becoming a part of everything that made me, *me*. I wanted to see what she told me about myself. I wanted to feel worthy. I wanted to do the right thing.

I wanted Brody O'Ralley.

Now I had to figure out if I had the balls to do anything about it.

CHAPTER THIRTY-TWO

Brody

I TOOK ANOTHER swig of bourbon from my flask, sitting on my ass and gazing out across the pond at the Mitchell property—the pond we'd sneak off to as kids so many times, the place where Cohen and I had enjoyed such a good time. The sun was setting in the distance, a cruel reminder of the memories I would have to leave here.

Elliecomb nudged her face against the side of my head, and I turned, stroking her neck softly. She'd always known my moods so well, could sense when I was hurt or in pain.

Thinking about my losses.

We'd hardly had time for goodbyes, and even worse, I'd put so much on him.

It wasn't his fault if he didn't feel for me the way

I'd come to feel about him. Maybe it was best for both of us that he'd picked up and moved along so quickly. Certainly made it easier than him telling me he didn't feel the same and staying, and then, knowing that, we'd have to continue our relationship of exchanging tips and tricks in our areas of expertise.

I told myself he'd done me a favor, even though I knew it was only a justification to soothe my pain. No matter what I told myself, it couldn't magically change the way I felt. Losing someone was never easy, and there were no shortcuts to getting to the other side.

As the sun finished setting, I did my best to accept the light that had set in my heart...then rode Elliecomb back to the stables and headed home.

Walking up to the house, I noticed a familiar car in the drive. *Cohen?* I picked up the pace, hurrying around the house to the front porch, where Cohen sat on the steps, illuminated by the light above the front door. His hands folded together, his gaze toward the woods.

He's back.

No. He's not, I reminded myself, because he could have come for any number of reasons. But if that were the case, why stop by here rather than the Mitchell house?

"Cohen," I said as I neared him.

He pushed to his feet, turning to me. "Brody, hey…"

"Brody's here!" I heard Dwain's voice coming from inside, as though they'd been awaiting my return.

"Welcome to the O'Ralley home," I said.

"Yeah, I was impressed I didn't get shot straight away."

Confused and upset as I still was, how could I not laugh? His beautiful smile returned, which just seemed so much worse if he'd dropped by only so he could take it away from me again.

He started to say something when I heard the creak of the screen door, and Big Daddy came barging out.

I practically threw myself between him and Cohen. "Big Daddy, now is not the time. Can you just give it a minute?"

"I need a minute first," he said as my siblings start-ed filing out of the house behind him.

Suddenly my heartbreak was becoming a family affair.

"No, I know how you feel," I said, more than a little agitated. "Clearly, Cohen came over here to talk to me, so can you give us—"

"It was my fault he went away," Big Daddy blurted out, and I could read the guilt in his expression.

"No," Cohen said behind me.

"Yes, it is. I overheard you talking to Dwain about being at his place one night. Rage overtook me, the feud mixed with my own past with his mother. I felt like he was using you to hurt our family. I was thinking I'd just be giving him an earful, but then he told me that, apparently, he found out his great-grandpa really did steal our family's secret recipe, and that really set me off. I thought he was trying to make me even more upset, or confuse the hell out of me. I really couldn't figure out why he'd said that, so I snapped."

"You chased him away? How could you—"

"No, it's not—" Cohen started, but Dwain shushed him.

"Brody," Lee said, stepping beside Big Daddy. He towered over all of us, looking impressive as ever, not just because of his stature, but because of the serious expression on his face. If anyone could shut me the hell up, it was Lee, since he'd never been the sort to speak unless he had something to say.

"Let him explain himself," Lee added in such a calm manner that I bit my bottom lip. "And if you're still raw about it after, then give him hell. But, Big Daddy, you need to be out with whatever it is, because we don't need no more secrets in this house."

He was right, but I knew if the next words that came out of Big Daddy's mouth had to do with this Mitchell getting off our property, I was going to lose my shit.

"Okay, Big Daddy," I said, giving him his chance.

"I know I shoulda come to you with this sooner. Truth is, Big Momma was the love of my life, but Pam White was my first heartbreak. Tore my heart to pieces when she left me, and it only made it all the worse that she started seeing a goddamn Mitchell. The rumors were humiliatin' enough as it was, but the feud added to it because suddenly it was like I was a disgrace to the family. Hell, you might have thought I'd lost the duel between our families, the way this town acted. Only thing that made it all bearable was that I was lucky enough to meet the woman I was really meant to be with. Still, people talk all the same, so when the walking reminder of all that embarrassment and shame carted back into town, I have to admit, it was a real blow to my pride.

"When I heard you and Dwain talkin' that night, found out what you'd been up to, I just... I didn't want some Mitchell to break your heart and leave you the talk of the town. Whether or not I can ever get it into any of my kids' thick skulls, you're my pride and joy, and I only ever want the best for ya. So I thought I was doin' right when I went over to confront him. Then he threw the other curveball by admitting his family stole our family's secrets, and...it was a lot to take in. Part of me believed he was trying to boast, and so I just blew up even more. But the fact that he told me that secret kept playin' on my mind, and how he'd acted, especially knowin' he left...because I sure as hell knew it wasn't because I threw a tantrum. Even worse was when I saw you at breakfast after. If nothing else could have shaken my confidence in my own suspicions, that sure as hell really got me to thinking...what if I'd been wrong? What if Cohen had really been sincere, and you two really cared about each other, and I'd gone and ruined it all?"

"Yeah, that sounds about right," I spit out. Still, it was a lot to think about. They really had stolen the recipe and Cohen had known?

"I'm gettin' to it," he said bitterly, like he was struggling enough with copping to his faults. "Even after breakfast, I tried to lie to myself and make myself believe he'd just done a number on my kid and that I'd done the right thing. But between the way he acted when I was making such a fuss, then telling me that secret and leaving after, I kept thinking...if he was hell-bent on hurting you or this family, he never would have done any of that. He would have stuck around just to piss me the hell off and really do a number on your heart. Made me second-guess all my ridiculous ideas about the whole thing. It was eating away at me, and then he had the balls to step on our property, and if that didn't tell me everything I needed to know, I really would have been some kind of ass. I was wrong. And I, well, I'm..." He growled a little before finally managing, "I'm sorry, son."

I froze. An apology from Big Daddy was about as rare as a word from Lee.

And it wasn't just his words; it was the damned expression on his face. All that guardedness and anger and frustration I was used to had dissolved. He was hurt from hurting me. It reminded me of how he'd looked as Big Momma was slipping away from us.

Cohen stepped up beside me, and I turned to him.

"I imagine you two have your own talk you need to have," Big Daddy said, glancing between us. "Then we can have our own father/son duel."

"Okay. I'll let you know where I stand on the duel after."

He certainly knew I wasn't going to ask for an actual duel, but I could tell by the look on his face he was concerned about how angry I was going to be with him.

"Come on, guys," Lee told everyone, guiding the O'Ralley crew back inside, leaving Cohen and me in silence, and my thoughts went back to the night when he had been packing up.

He took a breath as the front door closed. "I know Big Daddy thinks it was his fault, but it wasn't," Cohen said. "Ultimately, I made the choice to go."

"I know that, which is why I'm reluctant to be too hopeful about the reason for your visit. But on the plus side, I think that's the first *I'm sorry* Big Daddy has ever uttered."

I was trying to crack a joke to lighten the mood, maybe in case it was about to turn as serious as it had the night he left. But I couldn't let go of a burning question. "Why didn't you tell me he'd talked to you?"

"I would have if it had just been about that, but I'd been feeling bad all day anyway. I was out at the distillery looking around. I found an old box under the floorboards. It had a letter from…from my great-grandpa to yours. He was in love with him, and he admitted to stealing the recipe. As soon as I finished reading it, Big Daddy showed up, and all I could think was that he was right about us Mitchells. We were no good. He deserved to be angry with me. Mitchell Creek shouldn't even be ours. How could I come between you and your family after that?"

"I—"

"I need to get this out," Cohen cut me off, then said, "It was more than that. I just… I don't know if I deserve you. Even though I've started to fall in love with Buckridge, I had this feeling that I just didn't belong here. That I'd come between you and your family and that you deserved better than that, than me. I know it sounds crazy, but I'm still all twisted up about losing my biological mom, and my dad never coming for me. As much as I love the parents who raised me, I never felt like I belonged, until I was with you. I was scared you would walk away from that, or

I'd drive you away, or you'd resent me for losing your family. I think a part of me thought it would hurt less if I did it now."

"You do belong here. I've seen how you've taken to this. I never thought someone could pick up something so fast." And wait, had he said he felt like he belonged with me? My heart raced at the thought.

"It's more than the Mitchell legacy." He hesitated. "It seems like I got close to that exit and then...got nervous...backed up on the interstate."

That made me laugh. Leave it to us to have this conversation with silly metaphors. "That's a shit idea if I ever heard one."

"It's all right. Now that I'm a country boy, I drive a tractor."

He winked, and I laughed again.

It was nice—not only settling back into the way we usually talked with one another, letting our guards down, but to hear him say I wasn't the only one who felt like we had something special.

"I've had boyfriends in the past," he went on.

"This seems like a strange confession to make now," I joked.

"Shut the hell up, O'Ralley." He couldn't keep

from chuckling, though, as he continued, "What I'm trying to say is, I thought I knew what it felt like to be with someone...the only way it could feel. Then you came along, and it was like waking up one day and finding out magic's real. Oh God, now I'm just sounding ridiculous."

"Well, you can say a lot more ridiculous things to butter me up to make me feel better about your having left," I teased.

He moved closer, his body pushing against mine, his nose grazing mine as he took my hand. "I didn't know touching someone could feel like this...or that looking into someone's eyes could feel like this. It's just like walking into the Mitchell distillery for the first time. It was different and scary, but even when I thought I might be having a nervous breakdown, there was this deep feeling that it was right."

"God, this is such a mess," I said, which clearly confused him. As his brows tugged closer, I added, "I warned you you'd go and fall in love with me."

A tear escaped my eye as he threw his head back for a laugh.

"It's about time, though. Because I love you, and I love that I can say it without feeling like some lovestruck kid who got in over his head too soon."

"Well, we did that, but we did it pretty damn well. I love you too, Brody O'Ralley."

We leaned into each other, kissing—a kiss that reminded me of what he'd nearly taken from me. I allowed myself to really breathe him all in. It was as good as ever, but so much more now that I knew I hadn't been totally wrong about how he felt and where we were heading.

I growled softly as we pulled away from one another. "God, we're gonna have to sort out some details to make this work."

"Isaac will be here, so he can sort that stuff out."

"Isaac will be here?"

"Yeah, I think we have some things to catch up on."

"More interested in the future," I confessed.

"Like talking about how maybe I can start putting some babies in you," he joked, his eyes sparkling in the porch light, so full of life again, the way I'd come to know him best.

"Certainly worth a couple thousand tries."

"Thousands? I thought you knew better than to underestimate me."

We laughed together, moving closer, our expressions turning serious as we both seemed to accept that things were right again.

I heard a gagging sound coming from the downstairs window, followed by a giggle from Mel, and Cohen and I shared a laugh.

"I think I should move into your place...immediately," I added.

He snickered, and we kissed again.

Yes, there was still plenty we had to figure out. But we could figure it out together.

EPILOGUE

Cohen

One Year Later

"I NOW PRONOUNCE you husband and husband," Mel said. She'd gotten ordained just for this.

I locked eyes with Brody and smiled, my chest swelling the way it always did when I looked at him. He returned it, and I could read his expression, knew he was feeling exactly what I was—love, surprise at how we'd ended up here, and happiness.

"Time to kiss, gorgeous," Isaac said from beside me. Walker stood in front of him, Brody beside Walker.

"I know." Walker wrapped a hand around the back of Isaac's neck and tugged him closer. Their lips met, and the crowd cheered. Brody's eyes glistened as Walker and Isaac sealed their ceremony, each of us watching them from our perches as their best men. I mean, I couldn't deny they had great taste. We *were* the best.

"I'm married!" Isaac flung himself at me, and I caught him. "I'm going to be barefoot and pregnant in no time."

There was laughter from around us as we all hugged and congratulated them.

We were on Mitchell/O'Ralley property, with the new, much larger distillery behind us. Brody had moved into my house with me right after I'd come home, and Walker and Isaac lived with us for now, but they were having their own place built on the property. It had been an eventful year, to say the least.

As we all worked our way back down the aisle, through the white chairs on either side, I smiled at Mom and Dad, who'd come out for the ceremony and to see what we'd done with O'Ralley & Mitchell. We'd had a long talk, the three of us, and Dad was trying to get better about spending time with me, but it wasn't just him. I was working on getting better at connecting with him as well.

The property was decorated beautifully—Lauren had helped put it all together—and per Isaac's request, in all whites and pale pinks. There were bows in the trees, fairy lights, and flowers strung all around the gazebo Isaac got built just for this. I'd tried to tell Isaac white was for virgins, but he'd shushed me and joked about Walker being his first. Walker just rolled his eyes like he often did with Isaac, but it was done with love. There wasn't a doubt in my mind about that.

Big Daddy had grumbled through the whole planning process, but I knew it was because he thought he was supposed to. He loved this shit, the whole big-happy-family thing. I wasn't sure I'd ever seen him smile so much.

Things hadn't changed between him and me overnight. There was a lot of history for him to work through, but we had, and I respected the hell out of him. He was a good man who wanted nothing more than for his family to be happy and his business to stay afloat. I couldn't fault him for that. It had to be hard, knowing my family had stolen from him, that what we had should have been theirs, but he'd gotten over it and accepted me. Took a big man to do that.

It had been hell trying to get him to accept money from me, but I'd been determined to do the right thing. After weeks of back-and-forth, we ended up finally deciding to bring the two distilleries together, which I'd always hoped to do. The fence had come down, and plans for a new distillery had been in the works. There were times through the process where I thought I was going to kill Big Daddy, Dwain, or hell, even Brody, and I was sure they felt the same about me, but it was done now. O'Ralley & Mitchell hadn't been open but a month, yet it had been a hell of a month, everyone from Buckridge and maybe half of Georgia wanting a first glimpse and a first taste of what our families could do if we worked together.

Most problems in life would be solved easier if people were willing to do that—just work together.

I supposed the sexy photos we posted on social media of the brothers, me, and Isaac didn't hurt either.

Strong arms wrapped around me from behind, the familiar feel of Brody's lips on the back of my neck. "You're spacing off."

I looked up to find that everyone had moved toward the building while I was standing alone on the lawn like a crazy person. "Was thinking about sneaking away with you somewhere you could blow me."

"Oh, well, that's funny because I was thinking

you'd be the one to blow me," Brody countered.

"Get your asses over here!" Dwain called from the doorway. "We know better than to leave the two of you alone. We won't find you for an hour."

"Hey!" I called back. "I can go much longer than that."

Dwain rolled his eyes but chuckled.

"Let's go inside, handsome." Brody laced his fingers through mine, and we walked together toward our distillery.

For the decor inside the building, we'd gone with a rugged style, a mixture of all dark wood and log pillars, now lightened by Isaac's wedding touches of white lace and pink flowers.

Lauren looked over at us, shared a smile with her date, then walked over and nudged my hip with hers. "Look at what you did…bringing the Mitchells and O'Ralleys together like this. I knew you were special from that first night."

"Well…I am."

Brody rolled his eyes just as Big Daddy approached.

Lauren said, "I'll let you get back to your family. Ice cream tomorrow?"

"Sounds like a date," I replied, and she went to sit down.

"Hell, it looks like a unicorn threw up in here," Big Daddy grumbled.

"You be nice," Brody told him.

"I'm old and in charge. I don't have to be nice if I don't want to." But then he gave me a half grin and winked before stomping away.

I said, "You know he has to pretend to hate everything because that's how he is, but he's really loving this shit."

"You're an expert on him now. All that wedding planning, work meetings and fishing trips just the two of you did their job."

Big Daddy and I did spend quite a bit of time together now, which was strange as fuck. And Lauren had become even more of a staple in my life, Isaac's too. The two of them were a damn handful together.

"I can't help it if he's realized how fucking awesome I am. Are you jealous?" I teased.

"Always up to no good, aren't you? Trying to make Big Daddy like you more than me."

Before I could reply, Isaac interrupted. "It sounds like the two of you are talking about yourselves, and this is my day, so I was thinking it should all be about me, okay? Good. Okay."

"Wait. What about me?" Walker said. "It's my day too."

"Yes, of course it is." Isaac patted Walker's chest as if placating him.

"Christ, I love you. Come dance with me." He picked Isaac up, threw him over his shoulder, and made his way to the dance floor. Everything was all out of order with this day, but Isaac and Walker had said they didn't care. They were doing this their way.

"Your mama would have loved him." Amelia stepped up beside me. She and I met for coffee or lunch once a month. She shared a ton of stories about Mom, crazy things they used to do together, and more about my parents as a couple. I was lucky to have her in my life. Being close to her made me feel close to my biological mom, and I knew that no matter how much I loved my bio-mom, that didn't take away from the mom who was there with us today.

"I wish she could have known Isaac. Also, don't tell him how much she would have loved him. It would go straight to his head."

Amelia laughed. "God, she would have gotten a

kick out of you two."

My chest felt full. "Thank you."

She kissed me on the cheek and sneaked away.

It was all a whirlwind from there—dancing, laughter, food, speeches, cake, conversation. Mom and Dad talked about the trip Brody and I had made to San Francisco to see them a few months back, before asking, "When do you leave for Peru?"

Brody and I had plans to eventually travel all over the world together. We were starting with Machu Picchu. I wanted him to see everything. I wanted to see everything with him.

"Not for like four months," Brody answered. "With O'Ralley & Mitchell just opening up, we didn't feel right leaving yet."

"That makes sense," Dad replied. Then he and Big Daddy got into a conversation about business, and I knew we'd lost them for a while.

When the band played a slow song, the first one since Isaac and Walker's dance, Brody stood up and held his hand out for me. "Dance with me?"

My chest squeezed, and I smiled. Christ, I loved him. "I thought you'd never ask."

For the second time that day, Brody took my hand

in his, this time leading me to the dance floor. Our arms wrapped around each other, my face in his neck, taking in his scent.

"You know," Brody said, "sometimes I sit back and think that I can't believe all this happened, but then I figure...our families were always supposed to be intertwined some way, ya know? Like it was laying the groundwork for this, for us." Brody's hand traveled up and down my back.

"That was awful sweet. You trying to get in my pants?"

"Don't really have to try, do I? You're always begging me to get up in there—*Brody, I've never had anyone as good as you. Brody, you're such a god. How did I get so lucky to have you?*"

I laughed, deep and hearty. "Fuck you, and you wish. Pretty sure it's the other way around."

We sobered again, just dancing and holding each other, and I said, "I like that...something good coming out of the feud. It was all making the way for this moment to happen. This is our new legacy, ya know? Not that fucking feud. The O'Ralleys and Mitchells together, the way it's supposed to be."

We danced half the night. When everyone was

drunk and exhausted, Isaac said, "I think it's time for us to go. Thanks for giving us the house tonight. I have a feeling we're going to be loud. I don't want you to be jelly."

Walker's cheeks flushed. He still wasn't as outspoken as Isaac.

I rolled my eyes. "You wish." We were staying at the O'Ralley house tonight, and they were going home. Then tomorrow they'd be leaving for their honeymoon.

I pulled Isaac into my arms and hugged him. "I love you."

"Love you too."

When we parted, he took a few steps away, then said, "Oh, Cohen." I looked at him, and he tossed something my way. "Catch."

The bouquet fell into my arms.

"Looks like you're next." He winked at me, then walked away with his husband.

"Ah, hell. Does that mean we're doing this again?"

"Be nice, Big Daddy," Dwain intervened.

I looked at the flowers, then Brody. "You willing to marry a no-good Mitchell one day?"

Brody smiled. "If he's you and he asks me real

nice." He pulled me to him and took my mouth, the flowers crushed between us.

I didn't know what the future held, only that I intended to live it out with Brody by my side.

The End

To hear about new releases from Riley and Devon, make sure to sign up for their newsletters:

http://eepurl.com/cc_DQb

ABOUT THE AUTHORS

Riley Hart has always been known as the girl who wears her heart on her sleeve. She won her first writing contest in elementary school, and although she primarily focuses on male/male romance, under her various pen names, she's written a little bit of everything. Regardless of the sub-genre, there's always one common theme and that's…romance! No surprise seeing as she's a hopeless romantic herself. Riley's a lover of character-driven plots, flawed characters, and always tries to write stories and characters people can relate to. She believes everyone deserves to see themselves in the books they read. When she's not writing, you'll find her reading or enjoying time with her awesome family in their home in North Carolina.

Riley Hart is represented by Jane Dystel at Dystel, Goderich & Bourret Literary Management. She's a 2019 Lambda Literary Award Finalist for *Of Sunlight and Stardust*. Under her pen name, her young adult novel, *The History of Us* is an ALA Rainbow Booklist Recommended Read and *Turn the World Upside Down* is a Florida Authors and Publishers President's Book Award Winner.

Find Riley:
Reader's Group: facebook.com/groups/RileysRebels2.0
Facebook: rileyhartwrites
Twitter: @RileyHart5
Goodreads:
goodreads.com/author/show/7013384.Riley_Hart

A good ole Southern boy, Devon McCormack grew up in the Georgia suburbs with his two younger brothers and an older sister. At a very young age, he spun tales the old-fashioned way, lying to anyone and everyone he encountered. He claimed he was an orphan. He claimed to be a king from another planet. He claimed to have supernatural powers. He has since harnessed this penchant for tall tales by crafting worlds and characters that allow him to live out whatever fantasy he chooses. Devon is an out and proud gay man living in Atlanta, Georgia.

Find Devon:
Facebook: facebook.com/groups/devonsreadingroom
Twitter: @devon_mccormack
Instagram: devonmccormack
Bookbub: bookbub.com/profile/devon-mccormack

CPSIA information can be obtained
at www.ICGtesting.com
Printed in the USA
LVHW020403270121
677550LV00016BA/2851

9 781950 261079